AGAINST

REGULATIONS

BEX JALISE

This book is a work of fiction. Any references to real people or real places are used fictitiously. Other names, characters, places, and events are products of the author's imagination, and any resemblance to actual events or places or people, living or dead, is entirely coincidental.

To my lieutenant

CHAPTER ONE

Tori Keller dropped to her knees and focused on controlling the flow of her breath the way she'd been taught. Inhale through the nose; exhale through the mouth. Repeat. She swung her head from side to side. A thick blanket of smoke smothered both life and light out of the world making it almost impossible to see past her grimy mask.

It wasn't real.

Inhale. Exhale.

She just had to make it out of the room.

Reaching in front of her, she groped in the darkness until her hand grazed her prize for all this effort—the dummy's arm. Tori gripped it as tight as her bulky—and not completely broken in—gloves allowed and dragged the life-sized doll forward until they were face to plastic face. Then, hooking her arms under its armpits, she raised herself to a low crouch and backed toward the door, one painful inch at a time.

The clock on the drill had already expired, but if they were waiting for her to radio in a mayday, signaling she quit, then she hoped the crew had made themselves nice and comfortable out there. Kellers didn't quit. Her father had made sure she understood that since the day she'd learned to walk. Kellers didn't give up. And Kellers didn't leave anyone behind. Tori's father lived by that code. *Had* lived by that code. She could still hear the rumble in his voice, as though he dragged each word up from his core. She heard it now, steamrolling through her head, as she edged closer to the exit. She wished she could turn it off.

"Kellers don't quit, Tori. Tighten your grip. Use your legs, not your back. Firefighters use all their senses. Come on, Tori."

The heel of her boot hit the door. She gently laid the dummy on the ground, sure to keep its airways open as though it had been a real person and reached up to turn the knob. She threw open the metal door with a bang and dragged the dummy across the threshold, staggering in the daylight.

Truck 19's crew waited outside, and when she tore her helmet and mask off, gasping for fresh air, cheers erupted. Marco Ramos, the second of the three candidates training on Truck 19, rushed to her side and clapped her on her back.

"Man, Keller, you don't know when to quit, do you?"

Tori coughed and bent over, bracing her hands on her knees. Without looking up, she shook her head and said, "How mad is he?"

"Lieutenant Nichols?" Ramos asked, glancing at their officer. "Nah, he's fine."

Tori chuckled and lifted her gaze to find Nichols with his arms crossed over his chest. His jaw clenched in that really intense way she always found more sexy than intimidating, though she was reasonably certain he'd intended it to be the latter. "You're a horrible liar, Ramos.

But I appreciate the effort."

"Keller," Nichols bellowed over the congratulations from the crew. "Do you, or do you not, know the meaning of evacuation?"

Tori's chest tightened as the voices quieted around her. She deserved what she had coming. She knew it. The crew knew it. And Nichols was going to make sure she didn't forget it. She'd disobeyed a direct order, and while there were no serious consequences for her actions in the controlled environment of a drill site, in a real-world incident, disobeying a direct evacuation order was the difference between life and death. Just ask her father.

"Yes, Lieutenant, I know the meaning," Tori said, standing tall and straightening her shoulders. Kellers also took responsibility for their actions.

"Why did you decide to ignore a direct order?"

"I had the body in sight, and knew I could reach it," she said.

Nichols stood directly in front of her, but she kept her gaze steady over his shoulder on Ramos, who nodded with encouragement and support. She'd met Ramos her first day at the academy, and they'd quickly become friends, bonding over body-breaking exercises and hours of lectures. But Jon Nichols was a different story. Looking directly at the lieutenant in a no-pressure situation without losing her concentration was difficult enough. But intense Jon Nichols—the one in front of her now with the flashing hazel eyes and hardened jaw—wiped all sense and logic clean from her mind.

"And when I ordered you to issue a mayday?"

Tori swallowed the lump in her throat, her father's voice becoming insistent in her head, anchoring her thoughts to this moment, instead of letting her get lost in thoughts about Lieutenant Nichols. "Kellers don't give up, Lieutenant. And we don't leave anyone behind."

The lieutenant's eyes darkened before he turned away from her with a smirk to address the rest of the crew. "Did you hear that, boys? Kellers don't leave anyone behind. So, I guess the score stands at candidates with two bodies and the crew with one. It looks like the candidates win today's wager. Which means—half you fools are on latrine duty while the other half scrubs out the kitchen. You can figure out who is who. Candidates are kicking back this shift." A round of moans went up. "Don't forget to pony up for the pizzas. Newbies' choice tonight."

"Risky move, Keller," Ryan Davies, the third candidate, said as they stowed their gear back at the firehouse. "If that had been a real fire, you could have died in there."

Tori shrugged. It exhausted her some days how much it took out of her not to think about that part. Most days, she failed. "You worried about me, Davies?" Not likely. The only thing Davies cared about was his own skin.

Davies snorted. "More like worried about the rest of us. You think Nichols is going to let Chief Keller's kid go up in flames? If you pull that stunt on a call, he'd be sending us back in to pull you out by your pretty hair. Then who knows how many of us would call in maydays?"

Chief Keller's kid. Tori flushed at the label. She could hardly remember a day when that hadn't been her nickname. Tori, Chief Keller's kid, Keller. It was bad enough ignoring the near-daily comments from the crusty old-school crowd about female firefighters and how women didn't belong on the job, but she also had to live down her father's reputation. A highly decorated officer, her father's name instilled both fear and respect in lower-ranking personnel. A hard act to follow.

It would have been easy to hide behind Chief Michael Keller's name and rank. It wasn't as though her father hadn't offered to pave the way for her. But along with all the other family mottoes burned into Tori was her personal favorite: Kellers earn what they get.

Growing up a firefighter's kid hadn't been a life of luxury by any definition, but Tori had always been proud of what she had and the work it took to have it. She had been proud of her father, though she'd never told him that, and often wondered if a harder working man had ever existed. She'd always hoped to make him just as proud—but on her terms, not his.

"Don't listen to him," Ramos said, nudging her with his elbow. "He never would have gone in after you."

Tori laughed as they stepped out of the equipment room and took in the satisfying sight of the seasoned crew hard at work cleaning while they relaxed for the first time since they'd arrived at the firehouse early that morning for their twenty-four-hour shift. "What should we get on the pizza tonight?"

Ramos grinned, mischief lighting his eyes. "I hear Owens and Fitz hate onions."

Tori waggled her eyebrows. "Perfect."

"Keller. My office."

The prickly edge in Nichols's voice sent shivers down her spine. She knew she'd gotten off too easy at the drill site. A public reprimand was one thing—most firefighters got put in their place at one point or another—but being called to the lieutenant's office didn't bode well for her. It meant he wanted to be able to say things he couldn't say in front of everyone else. It was how officers told candidates to pack their bags and not come back.

Lieutenant Nichols waited for her in his office, which was nothing more than a dorm room with a desk. Officers had the perk of having their own sleeping space instead of sharing the common bunk room with the rest of the crew. As a woman, Tori also had a separate bunk room. It slept five, but as the only woman on this shift, she had it all to herself. Nichols had left his door open, but she felt obliged to knock and wait for permission to enter anyway.

"Come in and have a seat," Nichols said as his eyes scanned over a document in his hands. Tori perched on the edge of the only chair in the small room, waiting for him to finish. Finally, he looked up from his reading and handed her the paper. "Read this."

Tori skimmed the page. It was a set of fire department orders from more than a decade earlier with her father's name on top. The order detailed the circumstances in which a company was to evacuate a fire. Tori glanced at the neat row of binders above the desk and wondered if all the papers in there held her father's signature.

"I was a candidate under your father in this house. Did you know that?" Nichols asked.

"No, I didn't." She lied.

The summer she'd graduated high school, her parents had thrown a party in her honor. Her father had invited every member of his crew—including candidate Jon Nichols. She'd practically been a kid then, so he hadn't spared her a second glance. He probably didn't even remember being there. Tori, on the other hand, had been very aware of him and still remembered the fresh-faced firefighter who had stared at her father with open admiration.

"I remember your father saying the same thing you said earlier. Only then, it was 'Truck 19 doesn't give up. Truck 19 doesn't leave anyone behind.' But there's a second part of that statement you left out. And that is: *unless your own life is in danger.* I know you want to be a good firefighter, but right now, you're running the risk of being the worst kind—a dead one. If you get lost in the fire, who's going to be there to answer the next alarm? We save who we can, Keller, and we get out alive. That's the job."

Tori's head spun, and her vision clouded as though she was still crawling her way out of a smoke-filled room. "How do you walk away?" she asked, keeping what she really wanted to know to herself: *Why didn't he walk away?*

Nichols crouched in front of her and searched out her eyes. "You listen to your officer," he said, his tone softening to something resembling sympathy. It was the same tone everyone used when her father's memory shadowed a conversation. "We make the calls, so you don't have to. Your job is to listen."

Her father had made the call. He had no one to listen to but himself.

Tori stood and handed him back his copy of her father's order. She didn't need it. There was probably an identical copy somewhere in the boxes of binders her father had given her when she'd told she'd been accepted into the fire academy. Tori couldn't say for sure, though, since she'd never opened them. They were still gathering dust in the corner of her apartment where he'd left them.

"Sorry about today," she said, turning to leave. "It won't happen again."

"Hey, Keller," Nichols said after her. "Tell Ramos to call in the pizza order. And between you and me—Delaware and Beast can't stand mushrooms."

Tori grinned and looked over her shoulder. "Got it, Lieutenant. Extra mushrooms."

An hour later, Ramos plunked himself beside Tori at the dining table with a paper plate piled high with pizza. "Onions and extra mushrooms. My favorite."

Tori chuckled and took a large bite of her slice as she watched the other crew members pick toppings off with their fingertips. "Something the matter with your pizza, Delaware? We ordered from the place you recommended."

"Laugh it up, newbies," Delaware said. "You got lucky today. We'll get ya next time."

"Lucky?" Davies chimed in. "Nothing but skill out there, baby."

Fitz snorted from across the table. "What are you talking about— skill? By my count, Ramos got one, and Keller got one. You came up with a big goose egg. If you had any skill, it was managing to get yourself paired up with these two."

"Keller ignored not one, but two, direct orders that could have gotten her or someone else killed in an actual call," Davies fired back.

Tori's face burned. Davies was determined never to let her forget her mistake. He was always keeping score, which was why no one ever wanted to partner with him at the academy. Delaware and Fitz watched her carefully, most likely gauging her sensitivity level. Would she shoot back an insult? Deny it? Burst into tears? Only a month into her probation period, they hadn't gotten a chance to really know her yet. If they had, they would have known that Tori didn't cry. Ever. Kellers didn't cry. That rule had come from her mother.

Dad missed her dance recital? Kellers didn't cry. Dad had to work on her birthday? Kellers didn't cry. No father/daughter dance for them. No Christmas morning this year. Sorry, Dad couldn't make it to your graduation—but Kellers didn't cry.

And she wouldn't now, either.

"Back off, Davies," Ramos said next to her. [illegible] on Ramos to have her back. Not like Davies. Being [illegible] academy somehow meant he didn't have to act like part of [illegible]

"I'm not saying anything that's not true," Davies said. "Even the lieutenant said—"

"What, exactly, did the lieutenant say?" Nichols asked, setting his plate down in the empty spot on the other side of Tori. He lowered himself to the bench and swung his legs over, casting her a glance before pinning his stare on Davies. "Can I offer you some advice, Davies?"

"Sure, Lieutenant."

"If you're lucky, you're going to have a long career in the department. Hanging on to every mistake anyone makes will do you no service. It only invites others to do the same to you. Best to take your lumps, learn your lessons, and move on," Nichols said. He paused and lowered his gaze to his plate. "Keller," he said, keeping his head down. Even without him looking at her, Tori felt Nichols studying her. "Did you learn your lesson today?"

"Yes, Lieutenant," she said without missing a beat and taking note of Davies' glare.

"Then the matter is dropped," Nichols said before taking a large bite of pizza. "Mushrooms. My favorite."

Delaware groaned, and Beast threw a balled-up napkin at Nichols' head, and soon the rest of the crew relaxed and started joking around and enjoying their dinner, even with their least favorite pizza toppings. Tori's phone buzzed in the cargo pocket of her uniform pants. Her chest fluttered while digging it out when she saw the incoming call.

"What's going on there, Keller?" Owens asked. "You got all flushed. Your boyfriend calling you?"

.are table. Davies kept

. each time like a snake devouring a

.en quieter. Nichols remained still

.g a napkin balled into a fist, and the tiny

.. Realizing she was checking out her officer's jaw

.full of men staring at her, she ducked her head and

one noticed the heat deepening in her cheeks and neck.

"Um, no, nothing like that," Tori said to put everyone out of their misery, most of all, her. "No boyfriend. But I have to take this."

Ramos smiled up at her when she returned. "Well?"

Tori shook her head. "Another no go."

"You got a side hustle, Keller? What's your life like outside these fine walls?" Owens asked.

"I taught high school literature for five years." Another sore spot between her and her father. He'd offered to move her name up the academy list, so she didn't "waste time" doing something else before reaching her childhood dream of joining the Chicago Fire Department. But Tori had insisted on waiting out her acceptance along with the ten thousand other hopefuls, even if it did take five years to make it to the academy. "I've been looking for tutoring positions on my off days but haven't had much luck. So, right now, I've been taking any odd job I can find to make some extra cash. You sure your dad isn't hiring, Ramos?"

"I'll find out if you let me set you up with my friend," Ramos said with a full mouth of pizza. "He keeps asking."

Tori coughed, dislodging the mushroom she almost choked on. Able to breathe again, she shot Ramos a death glare. The skin on the back of her neck prickled as every nerve ending in her body became acutely aware of Jon's presence next to her. "Not the time, Ramos," she said out of the corner of her mouth. It shouldn't matter but discussing her love life at the firehouse wasn't on her list of things she wanted to accomplish during her training.

Delaware cleared his throat. "What does your old man do?" he asked. Tori smiled gratefully at Delaware before venturing a glance at Jon, who kept his gaze three inches in front of his plate. Delaware had also reported to her father for a time, and they'd remained friends even after her father had left Truck 19.

"Commercial painter. Houses. Office buildings. Stuff like that," Ramos said.

Delaware nodded thoughtfully before turning back to his more interesting meal.

"What else can you tell us, Keller?" Beast asked. He'd apparently gotten over his dislike of mushrooms since he'd inhaled half a pie already and was reaching for his next round.

Tori wiped the pizza grease off her hands and rose from her seat. "Slow down, boys," she said with a wink for Beast. "My probation just started. Let's pace ourselves. They say you gotta have some mystery to keep the relationship alive. Besides, I want to see how good of a job you guys did in the ladies' room today."

Tori tossed her garbage in the bin and strode down the hall to the designated women's bathroom and showers. When she pushed open the door, she stepped right into a pungent cloud of potpourri stink. After her eyes stopped watering, she noticed the rusty, metal AV cart the guys had pushed into the bathroom. It appeared they'd ransacked the feminine hygiene aisle at the drugstore. A variety of pastel deodorants lay at her disposal, as well as: a dozen shampoo bottles, body washes, and lotions of all different colors and scents. The bottom of the cart was stacked with every size tampon and pad on the market. Other women might have been offended by the enthusiastic display of feminine needs. Not Tori.

They liked her, or at least, they were willing to give her a chance. And that could make or break her training and future in the fire department. She opened the door and stuck her head out, finding relief from the dried fruits and perfumey flowers. The common room was silent, where no doubt, they all waited for her reaction.

"Nicely played, fellas," she called and was answered by cheers and deep belly laughs. "Next time, go easy on the potpourri, though."

CHAPTER TWO

Jon laughed along with the guys. As lieutenant, he wasn't supposed to participate in the ritual hazing of candidates. And while he didn't actively take part anymore, he also never stopped the guys from having a little fun at their expense—as long as it didn't get out of hand. To Keller's credit, she'd handled the crew's little joke better than he'd hoped. The whole situation had the potential of going very wrong, which he'd warned the guys when they'd asked permission to send Beast to the drugstore.

A month ago, Jon had been worried Tori Keller wouldn't meld well with his crew. During his own probation period, he'd spent many hours listening to Chief Keller extolling the virtues of his princess, Tori. Jon had chalked it up to the talk of a doting father about his one and only precious baby girl, but he couldn't be sure until she was under the firehouse's roof just how much of a princess she was. Tiaras didn't fit under the helmet.

Jon hadn't seen Tori since her graduation party, and he doubted she even remembered him. She'd been a kid more interested in hanging out with her friends than meeting anyone her father had worked with. Not that he'd blamed her. He hadn't been anyone worth knowing then, plus they had that five-year age difference that might as well have been fifty years. She'd been pretty then but had matured to be beautiful now, glowing with an inner grace that only came with age and grief.

Tori had surprised him. She worked harder than most candidates, harder than Davies for sure, and never complained about a drill or a chore. Often, she was the first to volunteer and pitch in when an extra pair of hands was needed. Chief Keller had raised a daughter with a strong work ethic, for sure. Though, after working under the man for several years himself, Jon shouldn't have expected anything less.

He enjoyed her intensity when she worked. He couldn't stop himself from noticing how she pinched her brow together in concentration, forming two little creases between her eyes. He'd caught himself staring at that spot a few times, wondering what it would take to make those lines disappear again.

Ryan Davies was a different story. According to his file, he'd graduated top of their class. He had a natural athletic ability and the makings of a world-class firefighter if he only possessed half the heart and motivation that Keller and Ramos had.

Jon's chest tightened as he spotted Ramos sitting down to play cards with Owens, Beast, and Fitz. Ramos was a good guy and a decent firefighter. Jon had no worries about his time as a candidate in Truck 19's crew, except for one: his closeness with Tori. It was none of his business, but still, the sight of the two of their heads bent together, sharing details of each other's lives, supporting each other, made him want to reassign Ramos as far away as he could. But that would leave Tori alone with Ryan Davies, and he wouldn't do that to her. Besides, what was she supposed to do for friends? When most of the firefighters—by far—were men, Tori might wait years before getting assigned to a house with another woman on her shift. Of course, she would make friends with the guys. That wasn't the problem.

The problem was: he wasn't one of them. No, that wasn't right. The problem was: he wanted to be.

He was the lieutenant. Her officer. Her boss. Her teacher. It was his responsibility to train her to save lives while protecting her own. How could he do that effectively when any time he was near her, he wanted to tuck her away where no one and nothing could hurt her? That wasn't the reality of the job. The reality was: she could get hurt. They all could. If he failed to prepare her the best he knew how, he could be setting her up for disaster, or worse. He'd never be able to live with himself then. He owed her more than that. He owed her father more than that.

It didn't matter that she smelled like lilacs on a spring breeze. Or that even though she pulled her hair back in a ponytail, there was still one rebel strand that fought its way loose. It really didn't matter that when she smiled, her whole face lit up and warmed him to the core. What mattered was that nothing could ever happen between him and Chief Keller's daughter, and he knew it.

"Seems your full of all sorts of luck today, kid," Owens said, slapping his cards down on the table. "Ramos just cleaned me out. You want in Nichols?"

"No, thanks," Jon said, the way he did every shift, though it never stopped them from asking. "I've got paperwork to finish up. Go easy on them, Ramos. It's been a while since they've played against someone who actually knows how."

Jon left the guys to relax and enjoy the few hours they had before lights out without their officer looking over their shoulders. It was a Tuesday night, and he hoped it would be a quiet one. It was usually the weekend shifts they went all night without sleep. Though, in the summer, it was anyone's game. Too many people out and about all hours of the night causing trouble, burning their midnight snacks, passing out drunk with a lit cigarette, getting in car accidents.

The door to the women's bunk room was open, and he heard the television playing as he approached. Tori sat cross-legged on the bed, staring at her laptop with the same pinched expression she wore when cleaning the equipment on the truck, not paying any attention to whatever was on the television. He hadn't realized he'd stopped outside the bunk room until she suddenly looked up from her computer and straight at him. Caught with nothing to say, he went with the first thing that popped in his head.

"Everything okay? I mean, after their joke and all?"

The creases between her eyes deepened for a moment as she made the mental switch from whatever she'd been concentrating on to his lame attempt at conversation. "Oh, that," she said, waving her hand in front of her face. "No, that's fine. I was kind of getting a little worried when they hadn't pulled something yet."

Of course, she would. She would have heard more than anyone the shenanigans that happened when a bunch of men were in close quarters for an extended period. "Well, they meant no harm."

One side of her mouth lifted in an impish grin. "And neither will I. They'll be repaid for their kindness in due time," she said.

He looked forward to seeing that. Something about her smile and the glint in her eye told him she knew how to make the most of an opportunity. It almost made him wish he hadn't decided to keep himself out of the house pranks. He'd used his officer status as an excuse to distance himself from the crew, but the truth was, he was sick and tired of the people he got attached to disappearing on him.

"You got something planned already?" Jon asked, leaning a shoulder on the door frame. There was no harm in knowing about the prank. It was only fair. He'd known what the guys were up to with the bathroom. "I can keep a secret."

"I'm sure you can, but I think I'm going to sit on this one for a while. If that's okay with you, Lieutenant," she said with a salute that made him want to laugh and hug her at the same time. He surprised himself with the thought, and with a terse nod, he hurried back to his bunk before he acted on his impulses.

Back in his room, he sat and stared at the row of binders on the shelf above the desk. Chief Keller had left Truck 19 to lead the crew on Squad 4 more than five years before, and yet his presence was still everywhere. His name was on the department orders they referenced. His image was in the pictures lining the walls. Even their truck had been acquired by Chief Keller during his tenure when he'd decided the old Truck 19 needed to be put to pasture. And now down the hall, slept the man's daughter. It was almost as though Chief Keller had orchestrated it himself.

Jon wondered if his mentor had, in fact, made a special arrangement for Tori to train at Truck 19. He couldn't imagine the chief doing so without talking to him first. The chief respected authority and would have spoken to any commanding officer before throwing his kid at them. When Jon had heard Tori was at the academy, he'd hoped to get the call, and when he hadn't, he'd figured the chief had other plans. But, somehow, Jon had won the draw and landed her in his house anyway.

It was a lot of pressure being responsible for Tori Keller. She wasn't just some candidate off the streets, a nameless face in the crowd. The whole department watched her, waiting to see how and if she would live up to the great Keller name. Much of her success or failure rested on his shoulders and how well he prepared her—especially since the chief could no longer navigate the waters for her.

He knew that feeling all too well. He'd been a junior in high school when his parents had been in that horrific car accident, ending his stint as a typical sixteen-year-old kid, and kicking off his run as an orphan with no idea what to do next. If it hadn't been for his older sister, Sara, he probably would have been another statistic. Twelve years Jon's senior, Sara took in her wayward baby brother without a second thought. "Family stays together," she'd told him time and again when he'd questioned her sanity at giving up her independence of much of her own life to monitor his delinquent ways.

Sara had been his only family until Jon had joined Truck 19. He had entered the academy right out of college. So there Jon was, twenty-two with a good job that required his presence only one out of every three days. With money to burn and time to kill, he'd done what every other twenty-two-year-old with no other responsibilities would do. He drank, and he gambled. It had been Chief Keller who'd sat him down for a long serious talk about life and his future and what Jon wanted out of it. If it hadn't been for Chief Keller navigating his turbulent waters, Jon would have drowned in depths far over his head.

He'd lost his chance to repay Chief Keller, but he could look after Tori for him. That much he could do

The next morning, Jon packed his duffel and waited for the next shift's officer to relieve him of his duty. It had been more of an eventful night than he had hoped, one that made coffee a morning requirement to fuel him long enough to get him home to crash in his bed. As he rounded the corner into the kitchen, he found someone had already beaten him to it. A fresh pot had been brewed and was warming in the maker. Tori sat at one of the tables wearing a baggy sweatshirt, her knees drawn up to her chin, and her face illuminated by the glow of her computer.

"Couldn't sleep?" Jon asked, helping himself to the steaming pot.

Tori rubbed her eyes and shook her head. "Not after that last call. Seriously, who leaves their three-year-old in the backseat of a car while they go clubbing until four in the morning? And then gets in an accident on top of that?" She shook her head, that loose piece of hair falling in her eyes. "That poor kid."

Jon rolled his shoulders, feeling the stretch in his shoulder blades. Those types of calls had always upset him in the beginning, too. Not that they didn't now, but it was a different type of upset. Wearier. Heavier. He thought of his niece and nephew and their little faces at that age. Those rosy, round cheeks and bright, innocent eyes. The kid they pulled from the wreck didn't have those eyes. He doubted that kid ever did.

"I filed a report with children and family services. Someone should be visiting the boy today," Jon said, sitting across from Tori at the empty table.

She bobbed her head, then rested her chin on her knee. "Good. That's good." Taking a deep breath, she blew the hair out of her eyes. "How's the coffee?"

Jon took a sip. It was delicious. More than delicious. It was liquid crack. "Is this our normal stuff?"

Tori lifted one tired side of her mouth into a grin. "It's my special blend from home," she said, leaning forward and lowering her voice. "Don't tell Davies. He's developed a complex, thinking there's something wrong with him that he can't make the coffee like this."

Jon matched her grin. "Better be careful. If word gets out that only you can make this, you'll forever be the one in charge of the coffee."

"Ahh," she said, tapping her forefinger to her temple. "Way ahead of you. Ramos knows where I keep it. And so does Beast and Delaware, so far. Fitz doesn't drink coffee, and I've never seen Owens make a pot."

"He doesn't know how to work it."

"That explains it. He certainly drinks enough of it, though." Tori chuckled. "And now you know the secret. So, really it is just Davies." The implication of what she'd said must have hit her. She straightened in her seat and dropped her feet to the ground. "You're not supposed to know that, though, right? As the officer?"

He took another sip of heaven. "I'll make you a deal. You make sure to save me a cup each time, and I won't let on to Davies. If I'm not the one making the pot, I can't be held responsible."

"Deal." Relaxing again, she stared at her computer screen but didn't make a move to touch it.

"Everything okay? What are you working on there?" he asked, recalling her concentration from the night before.

"It's a lesson plan a teacher friend asked me to help with. She took over my class when I left, but she had my plans to go off of. Now the principal is asking to see her plans for next year already, and this school year just ended. She's feeling a little overwhelmed, so I told her I'd offer some insight."

"Very thoughtful of you," Jon said. She'd probably been an excellent high school teacher. Smart, but not intimidating. Relaxed, but not a pushover. And best of all, a sense of humor, which went a long way with fifteen-year-olds.

Blushing, Tori opened her mouth to say something but was interrupted when Ramos and Owens walked into the kitchen. "Coffee. Nice," Owens said, grabbing the largest mug. "You make this, Keller?"

"You know it," she said. "Just for you."

"She's the best, isn't she?" Owens said with a cheeky grin, before settling down on the bench next to Jon and nudging him. "You try this yet?"

"Sure did," Jon said, watching Tori over the top of her computer screen. "Amazing."

She didn't move. But either something on her screen lit up her face with a pink glow, or she was blushing again. Twice in one morning. Not bad. Maybe next shift, he would go for three.

"You ready for later?" Ramos asked Tori as he took the seat next to her, their shoulders grazing. Jon tried not to focus on the distance, or lack of, between them and chastised himself for not claiming that seat when he'd had the chance.

"I am," Tori said. "Thanks again."

"What's later?" Owens asked.

Closing her laptop, Tori said, "Ramos got me a painting gig later today."

"What about you, Lieutenant? Going to work later?" Owens asked with a smirk.

"You got a hustle, too?" Ramos asked.

"Surprised?" Jon never mixed personal with professional, which meant he never talked about his side job, relationships, or family. The one person he'd let get that close had died and had taken all his secrets with him.

"A little, I guess," Ramos said, exchanging a look with Tori. Jon couldn't remember the last time he'd exchange a look like that with anyone, and the simple action caused his throat to go dry.

"What do you do?" Tori asked.

Owens snickered as the rest of the crew found their way into the kitchen. Had Tori asked him in private, he probably would have told her. But there was no way now that information was making its way out into the world.

"Nobody knows," Owens said, jabbing Jon in the ribs with his elbow.

"Nobody knows what?" Delaware asked.

"What Nichols does on the side," Owens said. "He must be a spy or something for how tight-lipped he is about it."

"How do you know there is a side job?" Tori asked, keeping her eyes steady on Jon as though trying to read him.

Jon nodded. "There is. I let that fact slip—once."

"I still say he's a stripper," Beast said, draining the last of the coffee. Jon glanced down at his half-full mug. He'd better sip it slowly to make it last. He doubted there was enough time to brew another pot and get another cup in him before the next shift arrived.

"I'm not a stripper. And it's nothing illegal, so don't bother guessing drug dealer," Jon said.

Tori peered at him closer. "We'll figure it out," she said as the door swung open, and several members of the next shift sauntered in.

Delaware laughed and patted her shoulder. "You can try. We all have. We got nothing. But I'll tell you what—you find out, and I'll do all your chores for a month."

"I'll add another month to it," Beast said.

"Three," Owens added.

"Three months, chore-free? I'll take it," Tori said, shaking each of their hands, then turning to Jon. "Get ready, Lieutenant."

This was going to be fun. This was going to be trouble. "Ready when you are."

CHAPTER THREE

Tori stifled a yawn and signaled the waiter for another cup of coffee. It was just like her mother to be late. One would think the fact that she had insisted on meeting for breakfast would guarantee at least a measure of promptness on her part. That one would be wrong. Tori would have preferred meeting for breakfast the next day after she'd been able to catch up on some sleep. She yawned again and checked the time, noting the missed call from Maggie: best friend and fire department paramedic. Another firefighter kid from the neighborhood. She'd also been on shift the day before, and Tori wondered if her night had fared any better for her.

Truck 19 had gone on two calls the night before: one false alarm and one drunk driver accident. She shivered, remembering the drowsy little boy in the backseat who had been roused dramatically from his sleep when his mother's car collided with a light pole.

Anna Keller burst through the restaurant doors in a flurry of movement, catching Tori halfway through her second cup of coffee, fourth for the day. Her mother had always been vivacious, filling her days and her wardrobe with a kaleidoscope of color, and this early morning did not disappoint. Her skirt resembled a collection of scarves someone had found stuffed in the back of a closet and then sewn together with the exact purpose of swooshing and swaying around her mother's knees. Her cherry tank top rivaled the red of the fire truck, drawing the attention of several other patrons as she floated to their table.

"Tori, honey, you didn't change?" her mother asked as she slid into the booth opposite her.

Tori glanced down at her navy-blue uniform shirt and matching cargo pants and shrugged. "I came straight from the firehouse. You said it was important and not to be late." She paused and tapped her wrist where a watch should have been. "Speaking of . . ."

"I know. I know. I'm sorry. But I'm here now, so let's gab. How was your shift yesterday? The crew behaving themselves? Delaware?"

Tori tucked a wayward piece of hair behind her ear for the hundredth time that morning. No matter what she did, it refused to stay and play nice in the elastic band. "Yeah. Nice guys. They know their stuff. I'll learn a lot from them."

"And your officer. . ."

"Jon Nichols?"

"Yes, Nichols."

Her mother paused to smile at the waiter bringing her cup of tea without her ordering it. How often did her mother eat at this diner? It was a well-known fact her mother didn't like to cook for one, and guilt stabbed at Tori for not being around more lately. But between the long hours at the academy, and now her schedule at the firehouse while taking extra work where she could find it, she hadn't had much time for social calls. At least that was what she told herself when another day went by, and she hadn't visited her mother.

"Do you like him?" her mother asked.

Tori swallowed the boulder that had lodged in her throat. If her fluttery butterfly of a mother—her father's words, not hers—picked up on her attraction to him just by saying his name, what did the guys at the firehouse notice? Forget them. What about Jon? She thought about earlier that morning when it had just been the two of them in the kitchen talking over their morning coffee like it was the most natural thing in the world. Two people starting their day together. That was what she'd been pretending before they'd been interrupted by the rest of the crew.

For twenty-three hours and forty-five minutes, she had fought and sometimes lost, to suppress any thoughts about Jon Nichols that strayed from officer and firefighter. But for fifteen minutes—fifteen sleep-deprived minutes—she'd let herself think of him as something other than her officer. What that something was, she couldn't say, but it had been warm and comforting, and she wished she could have stayed there a little longer.

"He's a good officer. Firm, but fair," she said, pushing an empty sugar packet around on the table with her spoon. "I mean, he knows what he's doing. Obviously. He isn't an officer for no reason. I . . .I just hope I do well, you know? Like, I really want to impress him—with my firefighting skills, not anything else. Not like personally. Professionally. Impress him professionally."

"Tori," her mother said, placing a hand on top of hers with a knowing smile. "I only wanted to know if he was a nice guy."

"Oh," Tori said, ducking her head and sinking back into the booth. "Yeah. He's a nice guy. Decent, upstanding type." Tori squirmed in her seat while her mother studied her for another beat, then said, "Let's talk about something else. Like, why it was so important I meet you today and not tomorrow."

"Because I miss my baby," her mother said with a pout.

"Mom," Tori said, a warning creeping into her voice. She needed a nap more than she needed her mother's sentimental teasing. Her body still hadn't adjusted to the semi-insomniac lifestyle firefighters adopted, and her patience bordered on non-existent.

"Okay, okay," her mother said. "I do miss you. That part is still true. But there's something I wanted to talk to you about that's a little time-sensitive."

That perked Tori up. "What's going on, Mom?"

"Your Aunt Karen invited me to go on a cruise with her, and I have to let her know if I'll go by this afternoon or she loses her reservation. Seven nights in the Greek islands. Can you imagine?"

No, Tori couldn't. Growing up, they'd done their fair share of vacations and travel when her father had been on furlough, but they'd never left the country unless she counted the day trip to Toronto when they'd visited the Niagara Falls. Aunt Karen, however, worked for an airline and had been everywhere.

"It sounds amazing, Mom," Tori said. "But why do you need to talk to me about it?" Her mother's mouth pulled down at the corners, an expression so rarely seen on Anna Keller, that Tori momentarily feared the worst. "Are you alright? Is Aunt Karen? This isn't a bucket list trip, is it?"

"What? Of course not. Don't be ridiculous," she said, fiddling with the stack of bangles she wore on her arm. "It's an over-fifty singles cruise."

The term "singles cruise" was a roundhouse kick to Tori's gut. Singles cruise. Why wouldn't it be? Aunt Karen had divorced her husband in her thirties and had been living her life free and single since. She didn't feel the need to settle down again after having done it once already. Been there, done that. Fool her once, she said when people asked if she would ever marry again.

And though, technically speaking, Tori's mother was single, it had only been seven months since they'd lost her father in that warehouse blaze. Was seven months enough time to pass before going on a singles cruise? Not that there was an expiration date on grief like it was a package of ground beef, but still. Aunt Karen was only trying to help, and maybe if Tori had been around more, her mother wouldn't feel the need to cruise around Greece with tanned cabana boys serving cocktails for breakfast.

"It's not like I'm going because I want to meet anyone, but it's a free cruise with your aunt. I'm not ready for the dating scene. I may never be. But the Greek islands, Tori." Her mother sighed and took on a far-off dreamy look. "But I won't go if you don't want me to. If you're not comfortable with the idea," her mother added, leaning forward and taking Tori's hand in hers.

Tori's heart ached for her mother. How could she say no? Her mother sounded so hopeful, and didn't she deserve to move on with her life? Find some joy? A joy that didn't involve Dad. Tori fought back the bile that threatened to rise and met her mother's glistening eyes. *Kellers don't cry.*

"Mom, you should go," Tori forced herself to say. "It will be good for you. It sounds amazing. I'm almost jealous I can't go, too."

Her mother breathed a sigh of relief, releasing Tori's hand in favor of the menu. Tori closed her fingers, trapping in the warmth her mother's hand had left behind.

"You don't want to be stuck on a boat with us old bitties," her mother said, her signature smile returning. "You know, it's been months since you've been out on a date, honey. I may not be ready to move on, but you should be. You haven't been on a date since Dad died. What about that *nice* officer?"

Tori almost spit out the mouthful of coffee she was about to swallow. "I'm not getting involved with my boss, Mom. What would Dad say if I started dating my training officer?"

Besides the fact that she'd taken a solemn vow never to date a firefighter. Ever. Too many times, she'd witnessed her mother pacing the kitchen, waiting for her father to come home while assuring Tori everything was fine. Too many years, watching her mother pretend not to worry when the news reported a particularly unruly blaze while her father had been on duty, wondering if that was the day a call would come, or there would be a knock on the door.

And then there was that one time.

Tori didn't mind walking into a burning building herself, but there was no way she would be on the other end, waiting and worrying. Tori wasn't built for waiting. She was a fighter. That was what her father had called her, though sometimes he'd said it while they were actually fighting, the exasperated tone of voice clashing with the flash of pride in his eyes.

Her mother pressed her lips together, assessing her daughter, then said, "He would have wanted you to be happy."

"He would have told me not to mix business with pleasure. And that ranks are there for a reason."

"True," Mom said. "Your father did love compartmentalizing. But at the end of the day, he wouldn't want you using his passing as an excuse to not move on from that Tyler."

It always amused Tori the way her mother said her ex-boyfriend's name. Always with a scrunched-up face and a shudder as if she had a mouth full of lemon.

It wasn't that Tyler was a bad guy. He was perfectly fine by all standards. Steady, boring job. Decent looking. Polite to her parents. There was nothing wrong with him, but he hadn't been entirely right, either—something her father had picked up on very early in their relationship, which had been enough of a reason for Tori to keep the charade going for much longer than she should have. Immature as it had been, those small acts of rebellion had thrilled Tori. And though her father had never admitted it, she had the feeling he'd also enjoyed their battles of wills.

She'd broken up with him the day before her father's funeral. She hadn't been able to stomach one more minute of his attempts at consoling her. And since the break-up, she'd hadn't had the energy to even think about a new relationship. She didn't see the point without her father rolling his eyes and making snarky comments at the expense of her dates.

"Speaking of moving on," Tori said, "Let's talk about something else."

"Like what?" her mother asked.

"I got another side job today. House painting."

"How many is that now? Your tenth side job? I don't know why you work so hard when you should be enjoying yourself."

Of course, she didn't know why. Her father had designed it that way, and Tori didn't have the heart to tell her mother differently. Her father had enlisted her help years earlier to set up automatic bill payments through their bank for everything. Her mother hadn't physically paid a bill in ten years and had no idea the pension she received from the department barely covered the mortgage and utilities. Tori had been making monthly deposits into her mother's account since her father had died to keep her afloat.

Tori smiled. "Something like that. I wish I could find something steady, but it's not easy with this schedule."

Her mother patted her hand. "You'll figure it out. You always do."

While Tori still hadn't jumped on board with both feet regarding the singles cruise idea, by the time they'd left breakfast, she could admit she enjoyed seeing her mother looking forward to something again. All the brightly colored skirts in the world couldn't hide the fact that her mother was still mourning her husband's loss. They both were.

As Chief Keller's daughter, it wouldn't have been unheard of for her to request a certain house to be assigned to for training. It was known to happen, and most times, no one batted an eye. But Tori hadn't wanted to do things that way. She hadn't wanted to use her father's name—though everyone already knew it—and she didn't want to ask for special favors. Truck 19 was a coveted training spot. All one hundred and fifty candidates in her class had been vying for her position, and she'd been one of the lucky ones to get it. Stationed just outside the downtown Chicago limits, Truck 19 received calls for anything from high-rise to warehouse to garbage can fires. When her probationary period ended, she'd be ready for any house in the city.

Tori wasn't a stranger to hard work, her father had insisted on her developing a strong work ethic at a young age, something she'd hated as a child, but was grateful for as an adult. She welcomed the work, especially now, as the long shifts made her feel closer to her father and kept her mind busy at the same time. She'd prepared herself as much as she could for the sore muscles and fatigue that went along with it. But what she hadn't expected was the giddy schoolgirl rush of emotions flooding her every time she was near Lieutenant Nichols. At first, she'd chalked it up to good old-fashioned nerves resulting from her career change. But she'd been on Truck 19 for a month now, and the nerves weren't getting better.

The day she walked into the firehouse to begin training, she felt like she already knew him. There had hardly been a conversation about work with her father that hadn't included something about Jon Nichols. Nichols had been the best firefighter to come through the academy in years. Future candidates would be lucky to have him as an officer. No one in her father's eyes worked harder or was more deserving of praise than Jon Nichols. She was practically his groupie.

But thinking about Jon Nichols as anything other than her lieutenant was pure fantasy. A fantasy she needed to put an end to before it started becoming a distraction in the field. That was the last thing she, or anyone else at Truck 19, needed. A firefighter's head had to be clear and focused when pulling up to a scene. Not admiring the way the officer filled his turnout gear. It didn't help that inter-firehouse romances were against regulation. If anything were to happen between them, she would have to be reassigned to a different house, different shift. And she loved being on Truck 19 and working with one of her best friends.

Shaking her head free of her fangirl feelings for Lieutenant Nichols, she attempted to tame that wayward strand back into a ponytail one last time before giving up and letting it fall in her face. Who needed to think about Nichols when she had so much more going on in her life? But maybe, just in case, she should give some consideration to Ramos's offer to set her up with his friend. It had been way too long since she'd been on a date, even a bad one.

"Hey, girl, what are you up to?" Maggie Jennis, Tori's best friend, asked when she answered the phone later that morning.

"Getting ready for my new side job," Tori said. She had just enough time to catch up with her friend before meeting Ramos at the address he'd texted her.

"You and your side jobs," Maggie laughed. Maggie also worked for the fire department as a paramedic at a firehouse not too far from Truck 19. While Tori had been developing lesson plans waiting in line for her turn at the fire academy, Maggie had been going to paramedic school. "You just got off work and have two days off before the next shift. Don't you need to sleep or something?"

"I can sleep later."

"No, you can't," Maggie said. "We've got plans, remember?"

No, Tori didn't. "That's tonight?"

Maggie had grown up down the street from Tori. Every year on the last day of school, since they'd been kids in pigtails, they started the evening at the local school carnival and ended it with a trip to the old-fashioned ice cream shoppe, until they got old enough to skip the ice cream and head to the bar. The whole neighborhood turned out for the carnival, and once the girls had moved on to high school, then college, the annual tradition had become a way to stay in touch with friends who had gone their separate ways.

"Heck, yes, that's tonight. You're not bailing on me, are you?"

Tori would need quite a few more coffees to get through the day. "Nope. Never. I'll meet you at the tilt-a-whirl."

CHAPTER FOUR

Jon hadn't meant for his second job to take on urban legend status at the firehouse, but it had, thanks to the one day he'd been too overwhelmed and in too foul a mood to discuss it. The guys had misinterpreted his silence to mean that Jon had wanted to keep it a secret, and from that day on, they'd teased him about the mysterious double life he led and wiled away too many hours imagining the most outlandish possibilities. Jon had been everything from a pirate to a male escort, according to his crew. At first, he'd kept quiet because it had been fun to listen to their ludicrous stories. Later, he kept quiet because the truth of the situation would be a monumental letdown after all their fantastical theories.

If anyone could find out easily enough what he did in his free time, it would be Tori. It had been her father who had helped him get the ball rolling when he'd started. Chief Keller had been thorough, and a bit of a packrat, which meant, he'd kept everything. If Tori dug deep enough, she'd find a trail of paperwork leading her directly to the answer she was looking for.

Jon pulled his car into his reserved parking space behind the low building. It had taken him five years, but he'd finally saved up enough to put a decent down payment on a property that checked off all the boxes on his list of must-haves: a ground level entry, multiple office spaces, common area, and a high-ceilinged area large enough to fit a training course.

His sister was already there, her car in the space next to his. Five years ago, when he'd floated his idea to her for feedback, he hadn't expected her to love it as much as he had. Sara had jumped in, headfirst, helping him with plans and loans, fielding phone calls when he'd been at the firehouse, filing permits, and anything else needing to be done that he couldn't handle while on the truck all day or working for a local practice, building his patient base.

He stood outside the building, *his* building, and smiled. In just six short weeks, Nichols Pediatric Therapy Center would be open for business. And he owed it all to Chief Keller, who had seen something in Jon when Jon hadn't. He'd helped him find the right school that allowed him to earn his physical therapy degree while working for the department and had even written him a letter of recommendation. But, more than that, on quiet nights when everyone else had been asleep in the bunk room, the chief had allowed Jon to use the training dummies to practice for class. The chief had even turned up at Jon's graduation, cheering and taking pictures alongside Sara, as though he'd been his own son.

Jon swallowed the lump forming in his throat, wishing Chief Keller could be there to see everything they'd talked about in those late hours and early mornings come to fruition.

"There you are," Sara called from the entry. "Get in here. Let me show you what we've done."

"Sorry," he said, wiping his eyes before she saw evidence of his sentimentality. "How's it going in there?"

Sara ushered him inside and locked the door behind them. "The painting will happen later this week, and the flooring guy is coming next week, so it's a little quiet in here now. I've been taking measurements to order the filing cabinets and storage units. The offices and exam rooms are all built out, and I can show you the paint and floor samples."

Jon nodded and inspected the work. He knew it would be flawless. Sara wouldn't allow it to be otherwise. "It looks great. You picked great colors." Jon's only stipulation when it came to paint choice was that she stayed away from the standard bland medical office look. His practice catered to kids, after all, and he wanted the space to be bright and fun. She'd picked a cheery yellow for the reception area, but the individual office spaces and exam rooms ranged in color from a playful green to bright purple. He followed Sara to the gymnasium floor, his favorite part.

Jon planned on installing a physical therapy obstacle course he'd designed himself. He created each station to be used on its own or as part of the more extensive course. His goal was to make therapy fun for kids and not another dreaded doctor visit, building his theory on mind over matter. If kids saw therapy as play, they would work harder, and make more significant strides at healing both mind and body. Kids who needed physical therapy had generally been through enough and didn't need a constant reminder there was something wrong with them.

"How are we going to install the course?" Sara asked. What she was really asking was, "Are you finally going to tell people what you're doing?"

Jon grimaced. Sara was right. Installing the different therapy stations was more than a one-person operation. Even with her husband Mitch's help, it wouldn't hurt to have a few more hands on deck. The smart thing would be to come clean with the guys at the firehouse. He was confident he could rope at least two of them into volunteering an afternoon. But that would mean giving up his man of mystery facade, and a part of him hoped Tori would figure it out first.

"Let's get the floor in first, and then we'll talk about the course," Jon said. "How are we in renting out the office spaces?"

To make sure he could afford the mortgage on the place, he'd decided to rent out extra office spaces to other pediatric care providers. He hoped to pick up another physical therapist or two, maybe a speech pathologist. He'd like to see the place turn into a whole pediatric wellness center.

"I've got a few appointments set up today, and another few tomorrow. A nutritionist, couple physical therapists, and a counselor," Sara said, ticking off her fingers.

Jon nodded. "Good. It would be great to have a few of those spaces taken by the time we open the doors."

"Speaking of which," Sara said, raising her eyebrows. "Have you decided on a party yet?"

Sara had been pushing for a grand-opening party. She wanted the whole event: catered food, a tour of the facility, live entertainment. It was a good idea. Great idea, even. Announce themselves to the neighborhood, stir up some promotion. She planned to invite the local pediatricians and staff from the area hospitals. They would make it a family event and encourage kids to test out the course.

His hang-up was having to talk to people. Guests would expect him to talk about the facility, maybe explain why he decided to open it in the first place. How was he supposed to stand there and talk about the first child he had pulled from a burning house? How he'd looked into that little face and had seen his niece and nephew? How he'd questioned whether he was cut out for the department? How Chief Keller had pulled him aside and told him the fact that he doubted it proved he was meant for it? You couldn't do the job with a hardened heart. The trick was to protect it. Never to harden it.

Jon sighed. "You know what? Go ahead. Let's have a party."

Sara squealed and threw her arms around his waist. "I love parties. Just wait—this one will be spectacular."

He arched an eyebrow at his overzealous sister, remembering the time she'd hired an entire petting zoo to set up in her backyard for his nephew's first birthday party. "Not too spectacular. We're on a budget, you know."

"You worry too much," she said, checking the time. "I gotta go. I have to pick up AJ and Nicki."

"Already?" It was barely lunchtime.

"Not all of us just woke up, you know," Sara said with a laugh.

Jon grinned. Guilty. He hadn't meant to fall asleep after returning home that morning, but he'd made the mistake of laying down to watch the morning news, and next thing he knew, it had been going on noon, and he'd been late to meet Sara.

"Alright, you got me," he said. "Thanks for taking care of everything here. It all looks great. Really."

"What have you got going on the rest of the day?"

"I'm going to head into the office. I've got a few patients this afternoon."

"Still haven't quit?"

"I've got a few weeks," Jon said. "I gave them my notice, but I've got to pay the bills somehow. Especially now that we're going to have such a spectacular party."

They walked back to where the front desk would be after the floors were installed. Sara scooped up her bag and hugged Jon. "Okay. You lock up. I'll be back later to meet with the prospective renters. You coming over for dinner tonight?"

"What are you having?"

The truth was—it didn't matter. Sara was one of the best cooks he knew, and since they'd started this little venture together, Jon had taken to eating at her house at least twice a week so they could review plans and determine the next steps. Plus, he liked spending time with AJ and Nicki. They were two of his biggest inspirations.

"I've got a pot roast in the slow cooker as we speak."

"Yeah, I'll be there," he said, patting his stomach. "I'll bring some rolls."

"Oh, get the ones from the bakery by your office. Those are the best." She stepped one foot out the door before turning around. "And Jon? It would be nice if you brought a date to the party." He narrowed his eyes as a warning. She threw up her hands, surrendering. "Just a suggestion. It's been over a year since she left."

Just a suggestion. Sara had been just suggesting he date for the last couple of months. Who had time for that? Relationships were too much work, something he had an overload of as it was. The simple fact was that at the end of the day, what he had left to offer someone else wasn't enough. It certainly hadn't been enough for Jackie, who had taken off across the country while he was at the firehouse—with his mother's ring still on her finger. Sure, she'd left him a note, which amounted to a whole bunch of excuses, the biggest one being he'd left her alone too much.

Jackie couldn't handle the amount of time he spent at the firehouse or the fact that he couldn't just call in sick or take a day off when he wanted to. It hadn't been as though he enjoyed missing holidays and birthdays with her. But it happened sometimes. His shift was his shift. It wasn't as though fires and emergencies took time off, and neither did first responders.

He'd never told Sara, but Jon had been relieved to find Jackie gone one day. He'd known something was wrong between them when he'd spent more time dreaming up a future practice than dreaming up a future with her. The part that had really angered him, and still did, was the fact that she'd kept the ring. His mother's ring. Something else he'd never told Sara. He was afraid of what Sara would do. Track Jackie down and cut it off her finger, maybe.

Jon meandered around the building one more time, finding his way back to the obstacle course arena. There were fifteen stations in total, all custom designed by him, each to help develop a different muscle group. If done correctly, a complete circuit would amount to a full-body pediatric workout. He'd been teasing the idea to his current patients, and the response had been more positive than he'd hoped for.

Technically speaking, he wasn't supposed to solicit his current patients. But that hadn't stopped his most loyal ones from pledging to follow him to his new practice. Due to his rotating schedule at the firehouse, working one out of every three days, he'd had to get creative with his patient scheduling to ensure no one got lost in the shuffle. He'd developed a pattern of visits, rotating his patients through the week. Most of the parents didn't mind as it allowed them a little more wiggle room with their schedules and other kids if they had them. For a few, he knew it had been a sore spot. Those were the ones he didn't anticipate moving with him. He'd find out soon enough, though.

He tried to imagine the space filled with people at the grand-opening party. He would have to come clean to the crew by then. Hopefully, a few of them would be able to make it. Delaware and Owens would probably come with their wives and broods of children if he asked them to. If Chief Keller had taken on a fatherly role with him, those two had been his wacky uncles over the years, at least before he'd been promoted over them and had distanced himself.

Had it been wrong for Jon to think of Tori when Sara had mentioned a date? He stretched his fingers and cracked his knuckles. The mere thought of her had his hands aching to reach for her. If he invited the crew to the party, it wouldn't be out of line to invite her, as well. But date? No, he couldn't do that.

It was against regulation for one thing, unless they went down to headquarters and signed an official document declaring, yes, they were both adults, and yes, they agreed they were in a relationship. It was an awkward and slightly demeaning process in his opinion, but he saw the necessity of it, especially when talking about an officer and a candidate. But the other more important thing was, he couldn't stand the idea of disappointing her in the end, which he was bound to do.

But he also couldn't think of anyone else he wanted to ask. He ran his hands through his hair. It was safer to disappoint Sara—she had to love him. That's what big sisters did. He turned out the lights and locked up the building. He wouldn't worry about any of that now. He had patients to see and bills to pay. Sara's grand dreams of seeing him settled down could wait.

Jon had to hurry if he was going to make it to the bakery before it closed to get the rolls Sara loved so much. Little buttery clouds of dough, he'd heard her say on more than one occasion. Open later than most bakeries, they still served customers up until seven in the evening, making them a neighborhood favorite of those needing last-minute dinner or dessert items. But if he wasn't in the door by seven on the dot, he was out of luck. With twenty minutes to spare, he pushed through the bakery door, almost running right into the person on the other side.

"Whoa, slow down there, cowboy. There's still time," someone laughed.

Flustered by the near run-in, Jon took a moment for the person in front of him to sink in. "Jennis, right? Ambulance at Truck 46's house?"

Maggie smiled. "That's right. You're Tori Keller's lieutenant, right?"

A warmth washed over Jon at the unexpected sound of Tori's name, though maybe it had more to do with the implication that he was Tori's anything. "Jon Nichols," he said, extending his hand before noticing two large cups of coffee currently occupied both of hers. "Late night planned?"

"These aren't both for me," she said with a smile. "I'm meeting Tori, actually, and I promised to bring her some caffeine. But, yeah, it will be a late night. It's kind of an annual tradition we have. We hit up the neighborhood carnival then head out for some drinks with friends. Hey, you should come. It will be a good time. I'm sure Tori will be happy to see you. She says all you guys on 19 are great. There will be a lot of other department families there, too."

Which was exactly why he tended to avoid those types of things. Off-duty was their family time. Their social time. For him, it was work time, and there was still more of it left at Sara's house after dinner. Pushing aside the growing curiosity to see what off-shift Tori Keller was like, he shook his head. "Sorry, I'm going to have to miss this one. I have plans already."

Maggie hesitated, then shrugged. "Maybe next time."

Jon held the door open for Maggie. "You ladies have a good night."

She smiled and headed toward a black Kawasaki cruiser. Maggie carefully nestled the coffees in the saddlebag, then mounted the bike. She flashed one last smile in his direction before pulling on a helmet and revving the engine to life. Jon chuckled to himself. He knew of Maggie's father, though he'd hadn't met the man yet. Vic Jennis was a founding member of the Chicago Fire Department Motorcycle Club. The man was rough around the edges, so he'd heard, being both a biker and a firefighter, but had a heart of gold. It looked like his daughter had picked up some of his habits.

A flash of doubt crept in his mind as he watched her cruise down the street to meet Tori. Should he have said yes and ditched his sister's house to hang out with a bunch of neighborhood families—and Tori? Would she have been happy to see him as Maggie had said, or would she think it was weird and obtrusive? Maggie probably was being polite. But, still. There was a chance that maybe she wasn't.

"Next," the man behind the counter yelled in Jon's direction.

Jon blinked and erased the thoughts racing in his head. Too late now, anyway. Maggie was gone, and people were waiting on him.

"I'll take a dozen of the dinner rolls, please," he said.

CHAPTER FIVE

Still recovering from her late night with Maggie, and knowing she had to set her alarm for an ungodly hour in the morning for her shift, Tori decided to forgo any unnecessary social outings. Ramos, however, had other plans and had given her a five-minute notice before he picked her up to go to a bar in a trendy north shore neighborhood.

She so desperately wanted to tell him to forget it—no way, not happening, you lose—but her mother's words came back to scold her. Maybe it was time she got back out there. Not by dating Ramos. She shuddered. It would be like dating her brother. But it would be nice to get out of the house for something other than work. Again. After the last two days, her mother could rest easy in the knowledge that her daughter was, at the very least, making herself available to possibilities—a step in the right direction.

"I'm glad you made me come out," she said to Ramos, who nursed his beer next to her. "Even though I'm exhausted, I needed this."

Ramos nodded and took another swig. He'd been uncharacteristically quiet on the drive to the bar, but Tori had thought he'd loosen up once they got there. "What did you do last night? Why are you so tired?"

"Well, first, my boss on my side job is a real pain in the butt."

"Hilarious, Keller. Maybe if you listened better, it wouldn't have taken us an extra two hours."

"Hey, I told you I'm a beginner painter," Tori said, smacking his arm playfully. "I'll get better and faster. You'll see."

"You'd better. I'm not paying you by the hour."

"Now who's the funny one? Anyway, after I left you, I met up with Maggie for our annual carnival and drinks night."

"Ahh, Maggie," Ramos said with an odd little smile. "And how is the biker babe?"

"Still single, if you're asking."

"I wasn't asking," he said, ducking his head away. "Just being polite." He glanced over his shoulder and started picking at the label on his bottle.

"Everything okay with you?" Tori asked. The longer they sat at the bar, the twitchier Ramos grew. Red flags started to wave all over the place. The muscles in her legs clenched as they decided between running away and sticking it out.

"Yeah. Sorry," he said. "There's something I have to tell you."

Run, run.

"There you guys are," Davies said, clapping a hand on Ramos's shoulder and leaning against the bar. "Glad you could make it out."

Tori's eyes nearly fell out of her head as she stared at Ramos, silently demanding an explanation. What had he been thinking? Ramos had to have been drunk already when he'd called her. There was no other way he would think she wanted to spend her free evening with Ryan Davies.

Tori leaned toward Ramos while Davies occupied himself with

ordering a drink. "What is going on here? Why is Davies here?"

"He called and told me he wanted to make amends. So, here we are. Making amends."

"You should have told me."

"Would you have come?"

Tori rolled her eyes and sat back in her chair. "No, probably not."

Ramos tipped his bottle in her direction. "And there you go. Just hear him out. We've got a long road of training ahead of us still."

Tori lifted a shoulder in response without actually agreeing, but Ramos was her ride, so she was stuck, at least until she got desperate enough to pay for a long cab ride home. She sat quietly, sipping her drink and watching the reflection of the other patrons in the mirror behind the bar. She wasn't going to make the first move, not after being tricked into being there. If Davies wanted to make amends, he'd better put on his big boy pants and get to work, because it wasn't her job to make it easier on him.

"Hey, Tori," Davies said, popping up on her other side as if by magic. "I'm glad you could make it tonight. Us candidates have to stick together."

"In the spirit of honesty," Tori said, dragging her gaze from the reflection of the couple behind them to Davies, "I should tell you I was brought here under false pretenses. Ramos failed to mention we were meeting anyone else."

From the corner of her eye, she saw Ramos rake a hand over his face before lowering his head to his chest. Nope, she wasn't going to make this easy at all. Davies nodded as though he'd expected that reaction from her, and maybe he had. They'd known each other for almost a year now, most of it while butting heads.

"I don't blame you," Davies said. "I know I can come off as pretty abrasive sometimes. I'm going to work on it."

She hadn't been expecting that response. Maybe Ramos was right, and Davies was trying to make up for being such a jerk most of the time. It would be nice to get along for the remainder of their training period. Chances were, they would all be reassigned to different houses when they finished, so if she were very lucky, she wouldn't have to deal with Davies again.

"I appreciate it, Davies. I will try and do my part, as well," she said, raising her glass to toast their new truce. Ramos lifted his head with a sigh of relief, and she could see him relax back into his usual demeanor. Just this once, she'd forgive him for tricking her.

An hour later, they sat talking and laughing at Davies's failed attempts at picking up different women at the bar. "Davies, can I offer you my professional opinion as a woman?" Tori asked, cringing over his last attempt.

"Shoot."

"You're trying too hard. Relax and breathe. Don't laugh like everything she said was the funniest thing you ever heard. Don't be too eager to please by overdoing it on the compliments. Just chill. Women can sense the intensity, and it's scaring them off."

Davies nodded and took it all in stride, to Tori's relief, because it could have gone either way with him. Davies usually had two settings. Cool-headed firefighter or overly sensitive man-child.

"Now, who wants to help me find out what the lieutenant's side hustle is?" Tori asked.

Davies groaned and set his beer on the bar with a heavy thud. "And I thought we were doing good here."

They had been doing good, and Tori didn't know what had set Davies off now. She turned to Ramos, who had grown quiet and was much too fascinated by the inside of his bottle.

"What am I missing?" Tori asked, swinging her head from one side to the other. "I was only joking around. I don't expect you to help."

"It's not that," Davies said. "It's your whole . . . thing with the lieutenant."

"What thing?"

"You know what thing," he said, leaning around her to nudge Ramos. "Tell her what I'm talking about."

Tori swung around in her seat. "Ramos? You're a part of this? You have something to say to me?"

"Come on, Davies," Ramos said, hanging his head. "I thought you came here to call a truce. This isn't helping."

"Why are you taking her side?" Davies demanded, turning on Ramos. "Oh, the dynamic duo still, huh? Just like at the academy."

"Is somebody going to tell me what is going on here?" Tori asked, raising her voice to be heard over the two bulls locking horns.

Ramos sighed. "He's talking about whatever is going on between you and Nichols."

"Nothing is going on between Nichols and me." Tori's heart sped up, beating against her ribs in a frenzy to be released. "You guys are crazy."

"I don't think we are," Davies said. "It's pretty obvious to anyone in the room with you two longer than three minutes that there's *something* going on. I'm all for having a little fun, but not when it starts affecting things at the firehouse."

"Okay, Davies, let's not get carried away," Ramos said. "Nothing's been affected. We're just saying it's no secret you two are . . . drawn to each other."

"Don't be blind, man," Davies said, his volume rising higher. "You saw what happened last shift at the drill. You know if either of us had defied the lieutenant's order, he would have reacted in a hugely different way."

"Tread lightly, Davies," Tori said with a clenched jaw. Her hands fisted on the bar in front of her.

It was the same story she'd heard all through the academy: Chief Keller's daughter and her special treatment. There was no special treatment. There could have been, and it would have been so easy. She could have easily coasted on her father's name and memory, but she'd made the choice not to. She'd busted her butt at the academy right along with them, studying and training, and still, it hadn't been enough for some of them. A few classmates, like Ramos, had been able to disregard her family name and take her on her merits. But others, like Davies, thrived on hanging on to any excuse why she might have done well. Any reason they could find other than she'd earned it.

"You're going too far," Ramos said. "You saw her at the academy. She stood toe to toe with most of the men. The instructors didn't go easy on the women, and the women never asked them to, especially Tori."

"I'm not talking about the academy. I'm talking about Truck 19." Davies pushed off his seat and squared off in front of Tori, who also stood and planted her feet. She'd taken Judo classes as a child, and three different throwing techniques came to mind. "We have ranks for a reason," Davies continued. "Orders given are not a suggestion. They save lives, and not just yours. If you've got a death wish, keep it to yourself. Nichols was soft on you, and you know it." He shook his head. "You two are a dangerous mix."

Tori bit the inside of her cheek. *Kellers didn't cry. Kellers didn't cry.* "It's time for me to go." Her voice came out like a jagged knife, ripping the space between them, leaving behind frayed edges of what could have been a shiny, new friendship.

Who was he to lecture her on ranks and orders? Yes, she was Tori Keller. And if anyone knew about orders and the consequence of defying them, it was Chief Keller's daughter. It had only been two weeks before her first day at the academy when she'd received the call from her father's oldest friend in the department, a man she'd respected and thought fondly of as an uncle. Chief Mulrone had told her there had been an accident. They'd already sent a car and driver for her mother. Another was on the way to take her to the hospital.

Her father had pulled everyone out of a warehouse fire. He told them to wait until the engineers subdued the growing blaze and brought it under control. But someone didn't listen and sneaked around back, broke a window, and jumped inside. Her father hadn't known until the mayday signal blared over the communication units. Chief Keller wouldn't allow anyone else in the building—it hadn't been safe—but Kellers didn't leave anyone behind.

It had been just like her father to rush into a building he'd already ordered everyone else out of. He could never turn down an opportunity to help someone, even if they didn't want it. Tori squeezed her eyes shut, blocking out the memories of that night.

She had called her father earlier that day. He had insisted on discussing her department training and had told her he'd wanted to select her training officer, that he would make sure to have her assigned to one of the best. Tori had fought against the idea. She wanted no special treatment, then or now. That wasn't how she wanted to live her life.

"Just stay out of it, Dad," Tori had shouted at him over the phone. "I can do this on my own."

"It's not a question of whether you can do it," he'd shouted back. "I know you can."

"Then, why can't you leave it alone?"

"There's nothing wrong with me wanting to make sure you get the best training out there." He'd always had to have his way. He'd never been able to leave well-enough alone where Tori had been concerned.

"Don't do it, Dad. I mean it," Tori had said, gritting her teeth. "That will be the end of things between you and me."

Hours later, Chief Mulrone had been on the phone, and Tori had found out first-hand the feeling of a heartbeat skidding to a stop.

What happened during her drill had been different. Tori hadn't run into an evacuated building; she'd already been in it. The body had been in sight. It hadn't been like she'd groped around blindly with no idea where to find the last dummy. She'd been only seconds behind Ramos and Davies.

It wasn't the same.

Was it?

"Are you okay?" Ramos asked, gripping her arm as she tried to push past the pair of them.

Tori opened her eyes and shook herself out of the haze of the worse night of her life. "I'm fine. I'll be fine." She didn't even sound convincing to herself. "I have to go home."

"Don't listen to that jerk," Ramos said, walking with her toward the door. "We all know how hard you work. I'll take you home."

"Ramos," she said, stepping out into the crisp night air.

He didn't look at her; he just kept walking toward the car. "Hmm?"

"Ramos, look at me."

He paused, and very slowly, dragged his gaze to hers.

"Do you think Davies is right? I'm not talking about the academy. At Truck 19, do you think he's right? Was Nichols too easy on me?"

Ramos took a deep breath and shoved his hands in his pockets. "He's not wrong."

Tori cringed. Though she'd been expecting that answer, she still hadn't been prepared to hear it. Definitely not from Ramos, who had stood by her side through every snide comment and sideways glance.

"It's not your fault," he quickly added. "I know you didn't ask for it and would prefer not to get special treatment. But you can't control how other people see you. And I'm not even talking about the woman thing."

"Woman thing?"

"You know what I'm saying, don't get all political on me right now. You asked a question, so I'm giving it to you straight because that's what friends do." Ramos stood in front of her, placing his hands on her shoulders. "There are going to be some people, officers in particular, who might treat you differently just because you're Chief Keller's kid. And it would be that way if you were a man, too. Your dad just died."

"Seven months ago."

"Yeah, but to people who live their lives one-third at a time, seven months is not that long. And there will be some people who feel they owe it to your father to take care of you, protect you."

"And that's what you think Nichols did?"

Ramos shrugged and lowered his hands. "I don't think he meant to. But, yeah, maybe. And you can deny it all you want, but I know you well enough to know there's something between the two of you."

Tori started to protest, but he stopped her.

"All I'm saying is the vibe between you and Nichols is not the same between you and Fitz, or Owens, or even me."

"Nothing is going on between us. Not like that. And it won't. He's my officer. *Our* officer," Tori said. "Besides, I'm not looking to date anyone now, especially not Jon Nichols. But does that mean we can't be friends? We work in pretty close quarters. It's not like I can avoid seeing him."

"I don't know what to tell you," Ramos shrugged. "Just don't mess anything up. Please? I like working with my best friend. Promise?"

"Promise."

Tori backed away and raised her hand to hail a cab. They were on a busy street lined with bars and clubs as taxis idled on the curb waiting for their turn at a fare. She didn't feel like being around anyone. Especially not Ramos or Davies. "You can go back to Davies. I'll take a cab."

"Tori."

"Really, I'm fine. I'll see you tomorrow," she said as one of the waiting cabs pulled up next to her.

She sank into the back of the car, her arms crossed over her chest, fuming. Who did they think they were, dictating who she was allowed to have feelings for? It was none of their business. Not that she had feelings for Jon Nichols. Why did everyone think she did? So, he was a good-looking man. Okay, a very good-looking man, with his dirty-blonde hair, hazel eyes, and healthy build. So, what? There were plenty of good-looking men out in the world, weren't there? The only reason they thought there was something between her and the lieutenant was that she was the lone woman in the house with seven men.

Tori snorted to herself. She was like Snow White. Did Snow White date one of the dwarves? No, she did not. She went out and got herself a prince. Granted, she had to die first. Tori hoped it wouldn't come to that. Grabbing her phone, she jabbed the screen with her thumb until the other end rang.

Maggie's sleepy face filled the screen. "Tor? This better be good."

"Do you think there's something going on between Nichols and me?"

"Tori? Where are you? Why are you in a cab?"

"Ramos and Davies ambushed me. I'm on my way home. Now, answer my question."

Maggie rubbed her eyes, then flipped on a light. "What do you want to know?"

"Do you think there's something going on between me and Nichols?"

"I think," Maggie said slowly and deliberately, "that both of you like to entertain the idea of something happening, but neither of you is willing to act on it."

Tori was too tired and had one too many drinks over the last two days to make sense of Maggie's diplomacy. "I'm not going to pretend to understand you right now."

"I love you, Tor, but sometimes you are very stubbornly dense."

"Go back to sleep. Maybe you'll make more sense in the morning," Tori said. "And I love you, too."

Maggie laughed, blew her a kiss, then hung up. Tori leaned her head back on the seat. Everyone was crazy, looking for drama everywhere. The bottom line was Tori didn't date firefighters. She never had, and she wasn't going to start now.

But maybe it *was* time for her to start dating *someone* again if only to get everyone off her case.

CHAPTER SIX

S omething was different. Something had happened since their last
shift, and now the dynamic between the three candidates was off
balance. Normally, Keller and Ramos would be busy chatting over a cup
of coffee, while Davies tried to break into the inner circle of Truck 19.
Not that Keller and Ramos weren't friendly, but they tended to step back
and defer to the crew, instead of forcing their presence on them.

Jon's crew had been together for years now, establishing their rhythm,
both on and off the truck. Keller and Ramos waited to learn the steps
before joining the dance. Davies, on the other hand, was break dancing to
a waltz. But maybe the most disturbing part was that none of them would
make eye contact with him. Not even Davies, who was usually the first to
suck up to him.

Keller and Ramos were on opposite ends of the kitchen while Davies
sulked in the corner by the television. Something definitely happened. He
shouldn't care. What went on outside of the firehouse was out of his
jurisdiction. He held no claim to their personal lives and what they chose
to do with them once they were off duty, but when their outside lives

carried into the firehouse, something had to be said.

"You seeing this?" Delaware asked, joining Jon in the doorway of the common room.

"Yep."

"Any ideas?"

Jon checked the time. "It's still an hour before roll call. Let's see what happens then. Could be we got some cranky babies here. If it's something more, I'll deal with it."

Delaware clapped him on the shoulder. "Got it, Lieutenant."

A sudden need for a cup of coffee gripped Jon, and it had nothing to do with the fact that Tori was the closest to the coffee maker. Maybe nothing was an exaggeration. It certainly didn't hurt the situation.

"Keller," he said, reaching for a mug. "How's the coffee this morning?"

"Morning, Lieutenant," she said without looking at him, disturbing him more than it should. "Ramos made it, so it's strong."

"Sounds good to me. It's nice having someone in the house who knows how to make a good pot of coffee," he said loud enough for Ramos to hear from where he sat, pretending not to watch them. He poured his cup, then saluted Ramos with it before taking a sip. Leaning against the counter, he tried to think of something to say. Something personal, but not too personal. Friendly, but not flirty. "How did the painting go?"

Her eyes darted to Davies as she took a tiny step backward. A sickening feeling settled into the pit of his stomach. Had something happened between Tori and Davies? The sickening worsened, and he had to take another sip of coffee to try to burn away the rising resentment. No way a woman like Tori Keller would start up anything with a meathead like Davies. She was a hundred times too good for him. And if that thought wasn't bad enough, the next one was worse. What if Davies had tried to start something up against her will?

Jon shoved one hand in his pocket, while the other gripped the ceramic mug so hard he thought it would crack. His chest burned as he studied Tori's expression. She was annoyed, that was certain, but not afraid by any means, and unless she told him otherwise, Jon had no reason to request Davies to be transferred away from her.

"Good," Tori said, keeping her eyes away from him. "I never knew painting could be so tiring, though. Back muscles I never knew I had are still screaming at me."

She twisted her torso, drawing his attention to the small of her back, where he'd had the urge on more than one occasion to rest his hand.

"Lieutenant?" Tori asked, her voice barely above a whisper. "Can I talk to you a minute before roll call?"

Jon followed her gaze to the other two candidates who seemed to have lost interest, and tilted his head, motioning toward the doors. She nodded and followed him out of the kitchen, allowing for enough space between them, so it didn't appear they walked together.

"What can I do for you, Keller?" Jon asked as they rounded the corner, heading toward the bunk rooms.

"Before you hand out the assignments," she whispered, causing Jon to strain to hear her next words. "I would like to volunteer for latrine and kitchen duty."

Not what he'd expected, but it piqued his curiosity. No one had ever volunteered for latrine duty before. "And why would you do that?" He stepped inside his office and set his coffee—Tori's secret blend—on the corner of his desk.

Tori hovered in the doorway, casting glances over her shoulder. "Honestly?"

He nodded.

She took a deep breath and braced herself on the door frame as though she was afraid to divulge a secret buried deep in her soul. "I think you may have gone easy on my last shift, and I don't want the rest of the crew to think I received any special treatment."

"Because you're a woman?"

"No, Lieutenant," she said, meeting his eyes for the first time. "Because I'm a Keller."

Everything clicked into place. Jon knew his guys well enough to know that if Delaware, or Fitz, or any of the others had a problem, they would have gone to him directly and called him out. No. This was between her and Ramos and Davies. And if he were still a betting man, he would put his money on Davies running his mouth again.

"Do *you* think I was too easy on you?"

"I disobeyed an order."

"That wasn't an answer."

"I think," she hesitated and chose her words, "I think I'm here to learn. And following the officer's orders is part of that. Otherwise, people get hurt."

Her eyes clouded over as she said it, and Jon could tell her thoughts had turned to her father. He'd warned his guys not to mention the accident when Tori came into the house. He hadn't wanted to put his candidate under more stress than she was going to endure in training. He needed his candidates clear-headed, which she obviously was not. A few hours of cleaning toilets might be just the thing she needed.

"Fine," he said, turning to his desk and picking up a status report left by the previous shift's captain. "You want it; you got it."

He heard her walk away, and when her footsteps faded down the hall, only then did he release his breath and sink into the chair with a groan. Had he gone easier on her than he would have if it had been Ramos or Davies who'd disobeyed the order? He hated to think it was true, but he couldn't exactly deny the charge either. He'd been set to read her the riot act when she'd emerged from the drill room, two full minutes after he'd issued the order to evacuate, but then he'd heard the words coming from her mouth that he'd heard so many times in his training days. Perhaps he had gone easier on her because he saw at that moment what he'd been missing.

The crew lined up on the apparatus floor a minute before eight, ready for roll call and the inter-department announcement that came over the loudspeaker at the onset of every shift. Jon joined them on the apparatus floor just as the bells sounded on the intercom. All the usual stuff. Four house fires in the prior twenty-four hours. No injuries or worse reported. Everyone went home. Jon waited until the last crackle of the speaker died down, then continued with the morning routine of roll call.

Some officers made a big show of it, demanding their crew stand at attention while they rattled off names and placed little checkmarks next to each one as they responded, "Here." But Jon didn't believe in treating his men and woman, like children. There were eight of them. He knew who was there and who wasn't, and therefore, had checked them all off during the announcements. Skipping ahead, he went straight to the assignments. His crew knew their roles, each performing their duties like a well-oiled machine, and on a typical day, he would have skipped this part, too. But there were candidates present, and part of their training was learning to sit through the boring stuff.

"Owens, you're driving today," Jon said. "Delaware, outside-vent. Beast, forcible entry. Fitz, you're the can-man. Candidates: Ramos, you're with Beast, first watch. Davies, you stick with Fitz, second watch. And Keller is with Delaware, third watch."

Davies pouted over his assignment. It was no secret Davies thought of himself as a forcible-entry guy, someone who got to swing the ax and break down doors. He'd heard Davies compare himself to Beast on more than one occasion, causing Beast to erupt in good-natured laughter over being so openly idolized. Too bad for Davies, though. It wasn't his call to make. The thought of keeping him far away from Beast to torment him for giving Tori a hard time tempted Jon.

"Keller is on kitchen and latrine duties today," Jon continued. "Ramos and Davies take truck inventory. Everyone else knows what to do. Get to work."

Delaware caught up to him as Jon marched off the apparatus floor, leaving them to start their daily chores before the first alarm sounded. "Hey, Nichols," Delaware panted. He was older than Jon by fifteen years, and a life with a happy marriage and kids had made him softer. Lucky guy. "Kitchen, latrine, and third watch for Keller?"

"You worried about her, Delaware?"

"Just seems a little much, even for a candidate."

Jon halted and pivoted on his heels to face Delaware, his longtime friend, but subordinate. "You want me to play favorites? Who would that benefit? She disobeyed an order last shift. She makes up for it on this one."

Delaware narrowed his eyes, assessing his officer. The downside to working with the same people for so long was that they learned to read between the lines at the most inopportune times. "She asked for it, didn't she?"

Jon smirked. He was never able to keep up the stern lieutenant facade with Delaware. The man had watched him grow up in the department. "She's got some spunk, doesn't she?"

Delaware laughed and rubbed his chin. "Like her old man," he said, shaking his head. "Carry on, Lieutenant. Carry on."

Retreating to his office to work on the never-ending paperwork, Jon allowed his mind to wander to the what-ifs. What if Chief Keller had never gone into that warehouse fire after that stupid candidate? What if Jon had trained under someone else and had never formed such an attachment to the chief? What if Tori wasn't a Keller? What if she hadn't joined the department? What if the first time they'd met had been under different but normal circumstances? At the grocery store? At a bar? Through mutual friends?

It didn't take much for his mind to burrow deeper into dangerous territory for him. What if his parents hadn't died so young? What if he hadn't called them to pick him up that night? What if Sara hadn't been saddled with raising him when she had enough growing of her own left to do?

The fire department had saved him. It had given him order and purpose. There was a right way and a wrong way to do things, and Chief Keller had demanded he'd learned all the right ways. In the few years following his parents' death, Jon had often gotten lost for days at a time in the tangled web of what-ifs. The department, with its chains of command and procedures, had laid a straight path out of the messiness of his mind. If he stayed on that road and followed the orders, everything became a crisp black and white. There was no gray area.

Until Tori Keller walked into his firehouse, blurring all the straight lines with every step she took.

It was clear she wanted to succeed on her own terms, not on her father's name and legacy, and he respected that. He'd seen too many candidates coast through training, confident their father's or grandfather's reputation was all they needed to make a career out of the job. Not Tori.

The lights in the corner of every room flashed a moment before the blaring alarm went off. "Truck 19. House fire. 3520 Lexington." The message repeated three times over the loudspeaker as the lights continued to flash in a strobe-like manner. No more what-ifs for now. It was time to get to work.

Jon hurried to the apparatus floor and surveyed the crew pulling on their turnout gear and jumping in the back of the truck. "Where's Keller?" he barked over the alarm to Delaware, her designated mentor for the shift.

Delaware shrugged on his coat as Tori burst through the door separating the kitchen from the garage area. She was still wearing yellow rubber gloves that stretched halfway up her arm. She must have been elbow-deep in one of the bathrooms. She ripped them off as she ran, flinging them to the side for later. "Sorry," she said, hurrying to her gear.

"Let's move," Jon shouted harsher than he intended.

Tori nodded and stepped into her boots while pulling up her suspenders. She shoved one arm in her coat as she hopped aboard the truck, settling into her seat next to Delaware. He had to hand it to her— she had one of the fastest ready times he'd ever seen. He'd read her stats from the academy. She'd consistently won best time marks for turnout gear. Owens hadn't even started up the truck yet. As Jon climbed into the passenger seat, he made a note to run a dressing competition later. It would be good for his crew to be bested by a candidate. He had to keep them on their toes.

Jon received updates on the scene over the radio as Owens raced through the congested city streets as best he could. "Truck 19," he called to the back, "we are the second truck." A round of groans went up behind him. The first truck on the scene controlled the operations. As second truck, they were relegated to assisting, which meant handling the boring jobs no one wanted but were necessary to perform.

"Cool it," Jon added. "Truck 32 was on their way back to their house and was only a block away. We'll get it next time."

Jon jumped from the truck before Owens came to a complete stop and found the officer on the scene. "Captain," he said, with a nod of respect for the higher rank. "Truck 19. Where do you want us?"

Captain Domenico watched the flames on the house in front of them pour out the second-story window. "Nichols, good to see you. No one was home. Daycare and work, thank God. But it's spreading faster than we like. Engine 28 is a minute out. Can you get a couple of guys to crack that hydrant down there and help hose off the neighbors? We want to keep this thing from jumping."

"We're on it," Jon said, leaving to find his crew waiting for their orders outside their truck. "Engine 28 is on its way. Captain wants us to hose down the neighbors. Beast, Ramos, get ready to crack that hydrant."

"Got it, Lieutenant," Beast said, nudging Ramos's shoulder. "You heard the man."

"Hoses? That's the engine's job," Davies complained. "We're search and rescue."

Jon looked to Fitz, Davies' babysitter for the day, to handle the situation. Fitz aimed to take the lieutenant's test the next time it came around. He might as well get some of that leadership practice now.

"We do what we need to do, Davies," Fitz said. "Are you just going to stand here and watch that fire jump because of the type of rig you rode in on?"

"No, but—"

"Did you learn anything from Keller's stunt last week?" Fitz said, standing toe to toe with the larger Davies. "You follow orders. You do your job, and everyone goes home. Got it?"

"Got it."

Jon turned to hide his smirk. If Davies knew Fitz better, he would recognize that Fitz was as harmless as they come. The man was all bark, no bite. But even the yappiest dog bared his teeth once in a while.

"Nichols," Captain Domenico called out. "You got someone to vent on top?"

Jon scanned the faces of his crew until he landed on the one he'd been looking for, and he wasn't disappointed in what he saw. Pure anticipation and determination. No fear. "Keller!" he shouted. "Delaware, you're up! Owens, bring the ladder around!"

CHAPTER SEVEN

This was it—Tori's chance to prove she belonged in the department on her own merits. It was her chance to prove she could follow orders and be a part of the team, in a real, contributing way, not because of her father, not because she was a woman, but because she knew the job just as well as the other candidates. Shoving her helmet in place, she caught the lieutenant's eye as she turned to follow Delaware. Nothing. He was a stone. He was probably one heck of a poker player, which would explain why he declined to play with the rest of the guys. They'd might as well hand their money over before dealing the cards.

"Keller." Delaware stood by the open equipment compartment doors. "What do we need?"

Tori jogged to his side and surveyed the assortment of tools. "Ax and hook." She glanced up at the slanted roof of the bungalow. It didn't look stable with all the flames trying to consume it from the inside. "Do we need a roof stabilizer platform?"

Delaware raised his head. "We'll be okay. Take this." He handed Tori the ax, as she hoped he would. "Ready?"

Tori nodded and fell into step beside him as Owens swung the ladder on the back of the truck into position. She climbed up the side of the truck and one rung at a time, ascended the ladder behind Delaware until she stood on top of a burning house. In her month as a Truck 9 candidate, she'd never stood on top of the flames like she did now. She'd thought it would be more worrisome to her than it was, and that thought scared her more than the actual fire.

She balanced on the edge of the roof with Delaware, waiting for him to make the call. She was his shadow this shift. As far as she was concerned, he was a firefighting god, and she was his willing disciple. Delaware surveyed the damage. He pointed to several spots where the surface was darker than the rest and uneven.

"See that?" he asked.

She nodded. The heat from inside the house had already started compromising the state of the roof. Buckling wasn't a good sign. Avoiding those areas was crucial to survival. "Heat damage."

"Good," he said, nodding his approval. "Start over there." He pointed to a section of the roof that looked untouched. "I'll be on this side."

Using the blunt end of her ax to poke along the roof, Tori tested the support before securing her footing on the slanted shingles and settling into a spot that felt stable. The purpose of venting was to release the built-up heat and smoke inside the building. Like in life, sometimes you just had to let out some steam before the whole thing exploded.

She chuckled to herself as she swung the ax, burying the blade into the shingles. Her father would have liked that analogy. He had been fond of stereotypical dad jokes, bad puns, and obscure analogies. He definitely would have gotten a kick out of that one.

She swung the ax again and again, chipping away at the roof, first through the shingles, then the plywood underneath until she broke through, and a plume of smoke rose. Satisfied with the job, she turned as Delaware released his own billowy smoke into the sky and noticed the discoloration of the roof behind him. During the minute it took for them to break through, the heat from inside had continued to rage and cause damage, weakening the support under him. She scanned the rooftop surface between her and Delaware. The flames were hard at work, determined to eat away at the previously safe area, leaving them stranded on little islands until, eventually, those would give way, too.

"Delaware," she yelled. "Don't back up!"

Delaware froze as Jon's voice came over the intercom. "How's it going up there?"

"Vents are in," Delaware said. "But it looks as though we painted ourselves into a corner."

"How bad?" Nichols asked.

"You might want to swing the ladder around to us," Delaware said, turning around carefully to face Tori. He prodded the roof and cringed when it buckled beneath the pressure. "Make it quick. Get Keller first."

The crew swung into action, with Owens taking control of the mechanized ladder. It was positioned between them, but Owens would have to get it moving and direct it to one, then swing over to pick up the other. Tori inspected the heat spots as they grew darker and more ominous. Then something caught her eye. There was a distinct pattern to the buckling. The darkest spots seemed to be separated by a six-inch space of semi-sound structure. There had to be a support beam under the roof. Thicker than a standard construction two-by-four, the beams would take longer to turn to ash. The rest of the roof was going to start crumbling, but those six inches would hold out a little longer. And she was closer to it than Delaware.

"No," Keller shouted into her radio. "Get Delaware first. There's a beam there I can wait on while you get scooped up."

"Keller," Delaware said with what Tori imagined to be his dad voice.

"I got this. I'm closer to the beam and can get there easier. We don't have time to argue." Owens already had the ladder in motion; it was just a matter of left or right.

"Your call, Delaware. I can't see the roof," Nichols said in their ears.

Tori could see the internal struggle playing itself out. Delaware was old-school, hold the door open, ladies first. But up here on this roof, with her gear on, she was no lady. She was a firefighter.

"Come get me," Delaware said into the intercom. "You'd better be right, Keller."

"Please," she said. "Schoolyard hopscotch." That's all it was. A hop and a skip. She could probably make it in one jump. Delaware would have needed at least two, plus his added weight—deadly combination. She watched Owens steer the ladder toward Delaware before she made her move. Quick like a cat. One smooth motion. On the count of three. One, two . . .

Tori gripped her ax in one hand and bent her knees. Just like ballet class, all she had to do was leap lightly in the air and land on soft feet. That was the plan. Easy enough. Except she'd never been particularly good at ballet.

"Keller," shouted Nichols through the intercom. "Move."

It wasn't just smoke coming through the hole she'd opened, but now flames shot straight up, licking the air as though tasting freedom for the first time. No time like the present. Tori jumped, and to her surprise, made it to the beam without it cracking in half beneath her. Delaware was already on the ladder, and it was coming back in her direction. She inched closer to the edge, keeping her hands outstretched like a tightrope walker, as the ladder came to rest in front of her. Swinging her leg over the side, she climbed on and moved down to meet a grinning Delaware as Owens retracted the apparatus away from the burning house.

"Not bad, Keller. Not bad at all," Delaware said, clapping her on the back.

"Now, that's how you start a morning," Fitz said seated in the truck, while Delaware and Beast chuckled their agreement.

Ramos sat across from Tori. He'd shed his coat before climbing in the truck, throwing it in the equipment bin along with Beast's. They'd gotten soaked handling the hoses, but at least they'd gotten to do something. By the time Tori and Delaware had returned to the ground, two engines had arrived and had taken over the duties of fire extinguishing. And with no victims to rescue, Truck 32 had everything else under control, leaving Truck 19 free to return to the firehouse without the pouting Davies having seen any real action.

"That was some fancy footwork you had up there, Keller," Ramos said. They were the first words he'd said to her all day. Not that she'd been in the mood to discuss anything either after he'd waylaid her at the bar the night before. "Good thing you spotted that support beam, huh?" He extended his fist, and she bumped his knuckles with a smile, relieved to find steady ground with him again.

"Yeah, Keller," Nichols said from the front passenger seat. "Good catch."

"Delaware's a good teacher," Tori said, uncomfortable with the praise. She didn't want Davies to start in on her again about whatever he thought was going on between her and Nichols. Better to deflect and keep her distance.

Delaware furrowed his brow but didn't say anything, accepting his unwarranted compliments on the subject. Even if he suspected something, which Tori wasn't ruling out, at least he had the sense to let it go in front of the rest of the guys. If Davies was right about perceived treatment, Tori had to be careful with her interactions with Nichols from now on. Teasing, which could easily slip into the realm of flirting, would have to be kept to a bare minimum, if at all. Joking around with the crew was one thing, but all her interactions with the officer going forward had to remain strictly professional.

"Keller," Ramos said, finding her as she pushed the cleaning cart out of the men's bathroom an hour later.

"I'm all done in there if you need it," she said, counting the steps it would take to get to her shower to scrub off the experience of cleaning the men's room. That would be the last time she volunteered for that duty. Halfway through the job, she'd stopped disinfecting, went to her bathroom and retrieved a package of the drugstore potpourri the guys had used to play a joke on her and had set it out on their counter. It was evident that cleaning alone wouldn't get rid of that smell.

"I'm good," he said, eying her rubber gloves. "I wanted to talk to you about earlier."

"What about?" She appreciated the fact that he was talking to her again, but all she wanted at that moment was a hot shower. "Can it wait until after I wash up?"

"Yeah, that's probably not a bad idea," he said, backing away while scrunching his nose.

"Funny, Ramos. Just remember that's *your* bathroom I smell like."

Tori had just turned the water on in the shower stall when the alarms blared again, alerting them to another run. Car accident this time. Shutting the water off, she ditched her plans of washing off the chores and ran to the apparatus floor. She wasn't last this time. Her chest swelled with pride when both Davies and Owens shuffled in after her, and she wasn't the only one who noticed. He tried to hide it, but Tori caught the amusement in Jon's eyes as he climbed into the truck.

"Seems to me," Jon said once the truck was en route, "this crew has gotten a little slow to load. I think after this run, we're going to have ourselves a little competition."

Fitz clapped his hands together and ran them back and forth as though trying to spark something. "I love a good competition."

"What are we playing for?" Beast asked.

"What happened to good, old-fashioned pride?" Nichols asked.

Delaware and Owens rolled their eyes and groaned. "We're too old for pride. Pick something better."

"Okay," Nichols said, his tone taking on an edge. "How about because I say so?" He paused, letting his words sink in. "And twenty bucks?"

"Done," Fitz said, while Delaware and Beast nodded.

"Candidates too?" Davies asked, never wanting to miss a moment when he thought he could shine.

Tori could see him sizing up the competition already. Delaware and Owens were the oldest on the truck, and therefore, he must have assumed, the slowest. Beast wasn't called Beast for no reason, and it wasn't an ironic nickname either. The man was huge. Almost as wide as he was tall. If the contest required strength, Beast would be the odds-on favorite by a mile. But Nichols had mentioned speed, and size didn't always work in your favor when agility was called for. Fitz, however, was closer to Jon's age. Not much taller than Tori, she didn't consider Fitz a large man, but he was athletic and sinewy. Davies' eyes narrowed as he looked Fitz over.

Tori also noticed how he skipped over her and Ramos. Graduating number one at the academy had given him tunnel vision. Somehow, he'd convinced himself that number one overall was the same as number one in every category. And while, yes, he did top the charts in most of the areas, there was one where he did not. And it happened to be the one drill she did rank at the top.

"Of course, candidates, too." Nichols looked over his shoulder to the back of the cab. "Unless Ramos and Keller have a problem with it."

He'd addressed both of them, but his eyes were on her. As the officer in charge of her training, he had received her file and seen her rankings. He would have known she held the best time for dressing and boarding unless he'd forgotten. But she didn't think so. He didn't seem the type of officer to skim over the stats or not take note of their strengths and weaknesses. Was he setting her up for a win? Why? In the end, it wouldn't matter. She planned on walking away with an easy twenty extra bucks in her pocket and her bragging rights intact.

After dinner, her pocket heavier with the addition of the crisp twenty-dollar bill nestled in it, Tori scrubbed out the pots and pans from dinner. Davies had been in charge of cooking, and she swore he'd purposely forgotten to grease every pan and let things burn a little longer to make her job harder. Hadn't he ever heard of lining a pan with foil? He was a pouting man-child because she smoked him and all the others in the timed competition.

Tori smiled to herself, for once not minding being elbow deep in a greasy pot. They guys had all been so sure of themselves, patting each other on the back, egging each other on. Only Ramos had regarded her as actual competition because he'd lost to her so many times before. So had Davies, but apparently, he had a short memory.

"Still relishing your victory?" Nichols asked, appearing next to her with more dirty dishes while the others either watched television or gathered to play cards. He set them next to the sink, then lingered, resting against the counter and crossing his legs at the ankle. Cool and casual. Nothing to see. Just a couple of colleagues hanging out.

"I have to admit, it was kind of nice to shut Davies up for once," Tori said, all too aware of how close the lieutenant stood next to her. He must have showered before. There was only a faint hint of smoke clinging to him behind a layer of soap. Tori breathed him in. She loved that smell. It was the smell of home.

"I bet," he said, making no move to back away. Did he lean closer? Or was that her?

She kept her head down. No one could accuse her of flirting if she didn't look at him, right? Flirting involved looking at the person, and she wasn't doing that. Just because they were close enough that every time she scrubbed the side of the pot, her arm grazed against his, didn't mean she was flirting. She was there first. If he didn't want her arm touching him, he could move. The skin on the back of her neck prickled with every brush of the arm.

"I didn't mind that part at all, either," he said. "It might have been a part of my whole diabolical plan."

Tori stopped her scouring and glanced up into his smiling face. She thought she liked intense Jon Nichols. Mischievous Jon Nichols, however, was a whole different level of gut-clenching anxiety. "So, you did know about my academy scores?"

"Of course, I did. Having a bit of fun at a candidate's expense is one of the perks of being the officer on duty. I figure, coming in fourth behind you and two old men ought to shut Davies up for a few days, at least," he said with a wink. Oh, good lord, he winked.

Heat rose in Tori's face, but she covered it up by wiping her arm across her forehead and making a show of turning down the temperature of the water. Clamping her mouth shut, she returned to her feverish cleaning. If she dared open her mouth now, she'd say something that fell squarely in the flirting camp. Something along the lines of, "Is that a crowbar in your pants, or are you happy to see me?" Hopefully, something not that corny. Who was she kidding? Or course it would be something lame. But how could anyone look into those gleaming eyes and not match the tone? He was practically begging her to play along.

"So," he said, rapping his knuckles on the counter, "you got any guesses for me?"

Guesses. Right. Jon's side job and the bet she had going with the other guys. "I have a few theories," she lied. She had nothing. She'd been doing her best to try and not think about Jon Nichols. She'd been failing, but at least she could say she was trying.

"Can't wait to hear them." He started to back away but stopped and leaned toward her. "You want any hints?"

That heat in her face spread down her neck and back. "That would be cheating, Lieutenant," she whispered, feigning shock as a metal spatula slipped out of her hands and landed in the sink, spraying her with soapy suds. Just what she needed. If anything could break the tension she felt mounting, it would be the sound of his laughter as she stood there covered in bubbles.

"Back to work, Keller," Nichols said with a feigned stern expression. As much as he tried sounding like the task-master officer, he couldn't stop his smile from breaking through, and she didn't really want him to.

CHAPTER EIGHT

Jon was on a break in between patients when Sara ran into the practice with AJ and Nicki in tow. "I need a favor," she panted, smiling at the receptionist at the desk and pushing the kids into Jon's exam room.

"What's going on?" Jon asked, running his eyes over the kids to make sure all their limbs were still attached and that no one was seriously hurt.

"I've got to get Nicki to her soccer game, but AJ has baseball practice, and Mitch is stuck on a job site overseeing something electrical," Sara said. "I already let the painters into the building. Can you run over there when you're done and lock up?"

"Sure," Jon laughed. "I think I can handle that."

"Thank you so much," Sara said, blowing him a kiss, ruffling AJ's hair, and pushing Nicki toward the door. "Oh, here." She pulled a slip of paper from her purse and handed it over. "It's the check for the painters."

Jon saluted her, then winked at his waiting niece and nephew. "Does she always get this wound up?" he asked, knowing the answer, but he liked to get a rise out of his sister, maybe a little too much sometimes.

"You know she does," AJ said the same time his sister rolled her eyes and said, "Only around you."

Jon laughed and kissed them each on the top of their heads before Sara herded them out for their day of activities. Thirty-two years old and Sara still fretted over him as though he were AJ's age. Making sure he could lock a door to his own building, as though he would say no. Once a big sister, always a big sister. Strangely, he enjoyed the fuss. It was comforting to know she still had his back after all these years, and he hoped AJ and Nicki would turn out the same.

Jon only had two more appointments for the day, and he made sure to finish them on time. No small talk, not that he was big on that, and no hanging around when he finished, though he wasn't known to do that either. Sara had given him an assignment, and he wasn't going to let her down. Besides, if he were going to hang out at work, he'd much rather do it at his place.

He parked his car in his usual spot in the back of the building and let himself in. Right away, the smell of fresh paint hit him. Not a bad smell, in his opinion, but there was a lot of it. Which was a good thing because it meant things were getting done. The sound of music coming from the other side of the building pulled him in that direction. He walked down the hall, peeking into offices and exam rooms. A few of them looked done, but the majority still had a way to go, so why couldn't he find anyone?

The music came from the gymnasium, which was where he would probably find the painters. It sounded like they were having a party on his dime. It was a good thing Sara had sent him to take care of things. He wouldn't want her to have to deal with lazy crews, something he had practice with. Then again, knowing Sara, she'd have them whipped into shape a lot faster than he could.

The double doors leading into the gym had been propped open with a paint can, so Jon was able to slide in unnoticed, and he was glad he did. He leaned against the door frame and folded his arms while a slow smile began to creep across his face. There, in the middle of his gymnasium floor was Tori Keller in a ratty pair of denim shorts and a paint-stained T-shirt, dancing along to whatever Taylor Swift or Katy Perry song blasted on the radio. She had her back to the door and was using the paint sprayer as a karaoke microphone.

The song ended, and Tori finished with a flourish, taking a deep bow for her adoring fans. Jon couldn't help himself. He applauded and hollered as though he'd been sitting front row at the concert of the century. Startled, Tori dropped the sprayer and spun around on her heels, getting her foot caught in a fold of the canvas drop cloth, blanketing the gymnasium floor.

Recovering her balance, she took another deep bow, her face burning a healthy shade of pink. "Thank you. Thank you. I'm here all week," Tori said, a broad smile stretching across her features. "No, really, I am. That's how long it will take us to finish this job." She turned the volume down on the radio, then met Jon at the doorway. "What are you doing here?"

Jon stood dumbfounded, staring down into her bright eyes. With neither of them in their navy uniforms, it was almost easy to forget how they knew each other. His hand itched at his side, yearning to reach out and tuck her hair behind her ear, to see if it was as silky soft as it looked.

"Everything okay?" she asked, her cheeks deepening in color as she caught him staring.

"Yeah, yes," he stammered, then cleared his throat to start again. "Sorry. I wasn't expecting you. You're the painter?"

"Yeah, sort of, I guess. Technically, Ramos and his dad are the painters. I'm just . . .here. But you still haven't told me what you're doing here."

"Don't you know? This is my building," Jon said, watching those little creases form between her eyes.

"Your building? The woman who let us in said this was a pediatric therapy practice."

Jon nodded. "That was Sara, my sister. She's the office manager. Didn't you notice the name of the place when you got here?"

Tori shook her head and pointed toward the front of the building. "There's no sign out there. Didn't *you* notice there was no sign when you got here?"

Jon lifted one side of his mouth into a grin and ran a hand through his hair. "I came in through the back. I guess I'll have to ask Sara about that later." He stared at the smudge of paint she had under her right eye, tempted to swipe at it with the pad of his thumb. She returned his gaze, though her cheeks remained flushed, and her feet started to shift beneath her. But she wasn't going to give in or back down, and he liked that about her. Respected it even. "So, where is everyone else?"

"Ramos and his dad went to get more supplies. I'm priming the walls."

"Is that what you call it?"

Tori gasped and pressed a hand over her heart. "What is it you're suggesting, sir? That I am not a professional-grade primer? I'm shocked."

"Let's leave it at: it's a good thing you've got another career to fall back on. Painting may not be your calling. Headliner at Caesar's palace, on the other hand . . ."

Tori scrunched her nose up and laughed, playfully smacking his arm.

"Alright. You caught me. I'm totally a Vegas showgirl wanna-be," she said, popping her hip out and making a show of fixing her hair. He was slightly disappointed when she got that rebel strand to stay put. "The whole fire department thing is just until I can perfect my act."

"Your secret's safe with me," he said just as her hair fell forward again. He'd like to tell himself it did that just for him, as improbable as it was, but they were in his building so he could pretend all he wanted.

"Speaking of secrets," Tori said, taking an exaggerated look around the gymnasium. "Lieutenant Nichols, the physical therapist?"

"Pediatric physical therapist, to be exact," he said. "Looks like you've got a couple of months of no chores coming your way."

"Certainly, was easier than I thought it was going to be," she said with a smirk. "Too bad, too. I was looking forward to going full-fledged stalker on you."

"I sort of was, too," he said.

What would it be like to be stalked by Tori Keller? He would know. His senses had become so attuned to her, he could feel her presence before seeing her. Not that he minded. He looked forward to that first tingle when she set foot in the firehouse every shift, and wondered how he could have missed it when he'd walked in. It must have been the shock of her being there, completely out of context of the firehouse. His throat tightened as her eyes held steady on him. She seemed to be trying to merge his two lives in her mind as well.

"Well," Jon said, clapping his hands together, trying to wake himself from the spell her smile cast on him, "We should get this room primed before Ramos gets back. I wouldn't want you to lose your potential future as a grade-A wall primer."

"What do you mean, 'we'? You can't help. You're the client."

"My building, my rules," he said, checking the paint sprayer to make sure it didn't need a refill. He picked the nozzle up from where she'd dropped it on the floor and pointed it directly at her. "Got a problem with that?"

Tori's eyes widened as she backed away. "You wouldn't dare."

"I would totally dare. Building owner, remember?"

Biting the corner of her lip, she tilted her head, considering his proposal. What would he do if she called his bluff? The thought of actually spraying her with primer held a certain appeal, in a juvenile playground crush sort of way, and he had a feeling she was the type of girl who would find it funny, but he wasn't sure he was ready to test that theory.

"Deal," she said, with one decisive head bob. "But if Mr. Ramos asks, you made me. I'm not losing this job because of your stubbornness."

Jon's laughter erupted from his chest. "My stubbornness? You're one to talk." He pointed the sprayer at the wall and picked up where Tori had left off before her impromptu concert. Tori grabbed a brush and pan with a smile and worked on edging the walls along the baseboards. "Can I ask? Why are you so concerned with an extra job? I know being a firefighter won't make you a millionaire, but it's enough to live on. Unless you got a secret family stashed away somewhere? A gambling debt?"

"No, nothing like that," Tori said. Sadness swept across her face in a way that made his chest squeeze. He tried not to look at her, difficult as that was becoming, but he didn't want her feeling like he demanded any more of an explanation. It was none of his business what she did or why. "It's no secret my dad died a lot earlier than he should have." She sighed and wiped the back of her hand across her forehead. "Let's just say, his pension checks aren't quite enough to keep my mother in the lifestyle she's grown accustomed to."

The sprayer fell to his side as he faced her for a breath before focusing back on the painting. With a goal like hers in mind, he couldn't afford to let her down, or worse, give Ramos's father a reason not to keep her on the payroll.

Tori reminded him a lot of Sara back in the day. His sister had also tried to hide the gruesome details of their financial situation from him, but he'd been a stupid, selfish kid. He'd been struggling just to breathe in his grief's suffocating grasp to see what Sara had been going through. A sudden urge to wrap his arms around his sister and maybe pay off her mortgage for her overcame him.

Tori continued edging, and he filled the gaps with the sprayer. When they finished the longest wall, Tori hopped off the ladder she'd been using to reach the top and dropped her brush in her paint tray.

"Listen," she said as Jon turned off the air pump. "I didn't mean to bring you down about my mom or anything. I didn't want you thinking I had some drug habit to support, or whatever."

"You didn't bring me down at all," he said. "I'm . . .I'm a little in awe of you right now."

She jerked her head back and furrowed her brow, and Jon began to think maybe he'd offended her or came on too strong, and it scared her. But then, her face lit up with that smile of hers. "I do have a certain flair for edging a wall, don't I?"

Jon laughed and agreed. "I lost both my parents when I was in high school."

The smile vanished from her face. Jon wasn't trying to dampen the mood she fought hard to keep light and comfortable. He only wanted to be able to convey how much respect he had for her trying to take care of her mom.

"I'm so sorry," she whispered.

Jon shook his head. "No. No. This isn't about that but thank you. I only brought it up because you remind me of my sister. She took me in and put me through high school, then college. She took care of everything, and never once made it seem like it was a strain on her, which it had to be. She was a nurse at the time—another millionaire's job."

"I only met her briefly this morning, but she sounds amazing."

"She is," Jon said. He took a small step closer. He had to. "And so are you."

Her mouth fell open. Whether it was in shock or to say something, he'd never know.

"Keller," Ramos shouted from the front of the building. "We got your coffee. Oh, Lieutenant."

"Ramos," Jon said, turning to face his candidate. "And this must be your dad? Mr. Ramos, pleasure to meet you, sir." He extended his hand to the older version of Marco Ramos. Mr. Ramos's handshake was a firm one pump then release. He was a man who knew what hard work was and didn't spare any time on the fluffy pleasantries. Jon liked him already. "My apologies. My sister, Sara, hired the painters, and she never actually gave me a name. Everything looks great so far."

"This place is yours, Lieutenant?" Ramos asked, his eyes shooting from Jon to Tori. "Sara just said it was a therapy practice."

"Yep. I'm busted," Jon said. "Jon Nichols, Pediatric Physical Therapist, at your service. Looks like Keller will get three months chore-free."

"Looks like," Ramos said to Jon, but his eyes didn't leave Tori. Tori ducked her head and looked away.

Jon reminded himself to breathe and relax. They'd done nothing wrong, but the accusatory expression on Ramos's face was unmistakable. "Well, I have some work to do in my office, so I'll leave you all to it. Let me know when you're calling it a day."

Two long hours later, Jon closed up shop, and waved both junior and senior Ramos off, with Tori following close behind them. He made one last walk-through of the building, locking doors and making sure windows had been closed, before leaving through the back door and almost running right into someone waiting there.

"Excuse me," he said, stumbling back to keep from knocking Tori over. It was her smile he saw first. "I thought you were gone."

"I was," she said. "But I left my phone. I was about to knock, but—"

"Come on. I'll walk you back inside," Jon said, opening the door again.

"Thanks," Tori said. "I don't mean to keep you. I'm sure you have better things to do, but I do appreciate it."

"I'm in no hurry. I was going to grab something to eat. I haven't had anything since Davies's cuisine last night."

Tori scrunched up her nose. "Now, I'm really sorry. That's just not right."

He should ask her to join him. That's what friends did, right? They could be friends. There was nothing wrong with that. A guy could do a lot worse than being friends with Tori Keller. Look at how happy Ramos was all the time.

"Do you have any plans right now?" Jon asked. His voice sounded strained to his ears, and he wondered if he'd said it out loud.

Tori lowered her head, but not before he saw her grin. "No. I was going to head home. Maybe do some laundry."

"There's a good Italian place up the street."

"Cannata's," Tori said, nodding. "Yeah, I've been there. They have phenomenal calamari."

"I was thinking of stopping there to grab a bite to eat." Spit it out, Nichols, you're losing her. "You want to go . . .with me?"

Tori tilted her head down and away. Never a good sign. She was too polite to flat out turn him down, especially when she had to report to him in two days. What had he been thinking? They could never be real friends. Not when his desire for more than her friendship kept growing, and not when he was her officer. But the question was out there now, and he would have to accept whatever answer she gave.

"Sure," she said finally.

He almost asked her if she was serious but didn't want to push his luck. "After you," he said, holding the door open for her.

"Physical therapy, huh?" Tori asked after they'd placed their orders. "How'd you get into that?"

"Your father." Jon played with the edge of his napkin on the table. "One of my first calls resulted in a kid getting hurt pretty bad. It hit me hard. And the chief mentioned the kid needing therapy after getting out of the hospital. Next thing I know, we're researching therapy schools, and he's writing me letters of recommendation."

"Sounds like Dad," she said. "He always thought he knew what was best for everyone."

"He was usually right."

"You think?" Tori asked.

Jon searched the depth of her gaze. Her eyes had gone soft and hazy as though a fog had rolled in behind them. Maybe he should have lied and not told her about the role her father had played in his life, but that didn't feel right. He didn't want to lie to her. Especially not about her father.

"He was with me," Jon said. "He always told it how it was, no holding back. What was it that he said? The truth hurts . . ."

"Only once," Tori finished for him. "But a lie hurts every time you hear it."

"That's right," Jon said, smiling at the memory of his mentor. He could almost hear the chief whispering it in his ear now, urging him to be open with Tori. Or was it a warning not to hurt his little girl? "He had a lot of those sayings, didn't he?"

Tori chuckled. "Sure did. He was the worst when he got all sentimental. I swear that man was a walking Hallmark card sometimes." Tori gazed down at the food the waitress delivered and poked at her pasta with her fork. "He was stubborn, though, wasn't he?"

Jon agreed. "He definitely knew his own mind. Yes."

Her eyes met his, and they knocked the breath from him. Gone were the clouds that had been there moments ago. Her eyes were clear and sharp and focused like a laser on him. "You remind me of him sometimes."

CHAPTER NINE

What was she doing?

This was Jon Nichols. *Lieutenant* Jon Nichols. Her officer. Tori couldn't date her officer. Not that this was a date. They'd just happened to be hungry at the same time. No big deal, right?

Except that it felt like a monstrous deal.

She kept one hand tucked under her leg, and one gripping her fork to keep them from shaking. She kept trying to think of something witty to say but came up painfully short. All she could talk about was her dead father—his fallen mentor and friend. Not quite the clever and enticing banter she was going for. At this point, even her crowbar line sounded better. She ate dinner with Ramos all the time, and even managed to string together words to form coherent, and not depressing, sentences. This could be the same. Friends. Just friends.

Except that sitting across from Jon didn't feel like it did when she sat across from Ramos. And that scared her.

"How's your mom doing?" Jon asked, changing the subject from one parent to the other.

"My mom? She's good." She didn't know why his question surprised her. It seemed like almost everyone asked how her mother was handling things, even seven months later. "She's getting ready to go on a cruise."

"A cruise? Where to?"

"The Greek islands, with my Aunt Karen," Tori grinned, remembering how nervous her mother was to tell her. "It's a singles cruise."

Jon's eyebrows shot up, making Tori snort with laughter. "A singles cruise? Really?"

Tori controlled her laughter and waved her hand. "That part is more for my aunt. She's the love them and leave them type. My mom just wants to get away and go to Greece. It will be good for her, though, a change of scenery."

"You don't sound too convinced."

Tori shrugged. "I guess the singles cruise part doesn't sit well with me. She says she's not interested in meeting anyone, but on a trip like that, she'd be the only one. I'm concerned what men on that boat will be thinking."

"I can see that," Jon said. "But, knowing your mom, I bet she'll be able to handle things just fine."

Tori leaned back in her chair and studied Jon's expression. What did he mean by "knowing your mom?"

"You know my mother? I didn't realize you two had met." Of course, they'd met at her party all those years ago, but did that constitute knowing her mother?

"We've met on a few occasions. Fundraisers and department events," he paused and locked his eyes on his dinner. "The funeral."

Of course. The funeral. Half the department had turned out to pay their respects to the chief and his family. Tori had been in such a fog that one face had melded into another, none of them standing out in her memory. Other than family, like Aunt Karen, and a few close friends, she couldn't name anyone who had come.

"Those few days were such a blur," she said, pushing her pasta around on her plate. "I can hardly remember any of it."

"I remember your eulogy. Well, I remember one part of it. You said, 'Anyone who knew my father knew he was always right. He always had the answer. He always knew the best way to do things. And because of that, I used to think he was a superhero. So, when Chief Mulrone told me what happened, my first thought was, well, of course, he did.'"

Tori pinched the bridge of her nose, trying to stop the tears that threatened to spill over into her marinara, which was salty enough. Kellers didn't cry. Tori sucked in a bracing breath but didn't move her hand away from his. His fingertips were rough from years of labor, but warm—the way her father's had been. "Do you think it's weird our paths didn't cross more?"

"We did meet once," he said. "Your graduation party. You wore that blue dress."

Jon pulled his hand back, and Tori's eyes fell to the space on the table where it had been a moment ago. Her pulse quickened as though it was trying to catch up to his retreating hand and pull it back. "Besides, if I had a daughter, I wouldn't want her around the dirtbags at the firehouse, either," he said with half a grin.

"Present company excluded, obviously," Tori said.

"Obviously."

Jon was probably right. Just another way her father had tried to protect her. It hadn't prevented the department from being in her blood, though. Memories of her father and their complicated relationship swirled together until they were a jumbled mess like the pasta on her plate.

She'd loved visiting her father at the firehouse when she'd been a child, sitting in the truck, trying on his helmet and boots. A ripple of excitement had shot through her every time she'd heard her father tell the crew that she would be the next great Keller firefighter, following his and her grandfather's footsteps.

She remembered how she couldn't wait for him to come home after shift so she could ask him about the calls he went on. What had he gotten to do? How big had the fires been? They'd sit huddled on the couch together for hours while he told her stories, sparing no detail, she wouldn't allow it.

After her mother had given up trying to convince him that he'd give Tori nightmares, she'd shake her head at the two of them, instead. "Two peas in a pod, you two," she'd said. "We should have named her Michael Junior."

But then Tori had hit her teen years, and the attention she'd craved so much as a child no longer seemed doting to her, but suffocating. She'd told herself she was trying to be her own person. She was independent.

Her father had deserved a better daughter than the one he'd been stuck with. He'd deserved someone like Jon who'd appreciated him while he'd been alive, instead of taking him for granted the way she had, fighting with him almost any chance she'd gotten.

"Are you okay?" Jon asked, the corners of his mouth turning down. There was a tiny drop of sauce on his bottom lip, begging Tori to reach across the table to wipe it off.

"I guess I'm more tired than I thought I was," she said, her eyes lingering on his lips longer than they should have.

"I swear you'll get used to the hours. It always takes a few months."

Jon's napkin had slipped to the floor while they were talking, and as he leaned to the side to reach it, she couldn't help noticing the muscular line from his neck and down his arm. She forced her eyes away just as he sat up again before he could catch her leering at him like a lovestruck schoolgirl. This whole thing was crazy. She had to get out more. That was what her problem was. And it didn't help that he'd remembered what she'd been wearing the night they'd first met a decade ago.

"When are you going to tell the guys?" Jon asked.

Tell the guys? She was in no way going to tell the guys she'd been checking out their lieutenant. "Tell them what?"

"About finding out about my side hustle? The practice?"

She should have been more excited about having no chores for three months, especially after her last bathroom duty stint, but the idea of claiming her prize had slipped her mind. She shrugged. "I don't know. You've kept it a secret this long for a reason. It's not my place to out you now, is it?"

"Three months without scrubbing pots, toilets, or the truck is a pretty sweet deal."

"It's not that bad." The idea of sharing a secret with Jon made her feel closer to him like they were the only two members of an exclusive club. If she couldn't have anything else where Jon Nichols was concerned, then she was going to hold on tight to whatever she could get her hands on for as long as possible.

When Tori ignored her buzzing phone on the end table the next morning, it quieted for only three seconds before starting up again. This time, Tori dragged her head off her pillow and checked her screen before answering. "Mom? Is everything okay?"

"No. No, it's not," her mother said, sounding like she was practically in tears.

Tori had been afraid of this ever since her mother had told her about the cruise with Aunt Karen. It must have finally hit her mother what it meant to be on a singles cruise. That it meant *she* was single. For the first time in thirty years, her mother was a single woman again, and the enormity of the implications must have shaken her.

"Tell me what's wrong, Mom," Tori said, stumbling out of bed and rubbing her eyes. "You know we can talk about everything." She used her best "everything will be okay" voice. The same one her mother had used when Tori had been a teenager, and her world had ended every other week.

"I have nothing to wear on this cruise," her mother said.

"Excuse me. What?" Was she serious? This was what she called about at the stupidly early hour of—Tori checked the time—okay, nine in the morning wasn't that early, but still. "What are you talking about? You have a closet full of clothes." She staggered toward the kitchen; her one open eye set on the coffee maker.

"Nothing good enough to wear in Greece. I need to go shopping. What are you doing today? Can you come with me?"

Sure, if Tori had gotten up three hours earlier like she'd planned. She had too many errands to run before meeting Ramos back at Jon's building for another round of priming and painting. "I have a lot of work to do today, Mom."

"Come on, hon. I leave in a few days, and I've got nothing. I swear it will only take a few hours. I'll buy you lunch, then the rest of the day is yours."

Tori groaned and closed her one good eye a moment too soon. "Crap," she yelled when her little toe collided with the box of her father's binders sitting on the floor outside her kitchen. It had been almost a year since her father had personally delivered them with a smile and a greasy bag of tacos. Both the tacos and her father were long gone, but those boxes remained.

"Victory Celeste Keller. Language," Anna chastised her. "Don't be so dramatic. I will be on an entirely different continent for a whole seven days, and you can't spare me a few measly hours to make sure I don't embarrass either one of us while I'm there?"

"Now who's being dramatic? And I'm not too worried about my reputation in Greece," Tori said, feeling herself give in as she leaned against the wall, rubbing her toe. "But if it means that much to you . . . two hours, plus lunch. A fast one. Like hotdogs on the street corner fast."

"Deal. Meet me outside Macy's in twenty minutes."

Thirty minutes later, Anna Keller hurried to greet Tori outside the main entrance to Macy's. Skipping the observation of her mother's lateness, Tori returned her mother's hug before looping their arms together and guiding her toward the door. "Where are we starting? Loungewear, swimwear, or dinner wear?"

"Let's get the worst part over with first. Swimwear."

Tori led the way, then loaded her mother's arms with options before stuffing her into a dressing room. "How's your week been, hon?" her mother asked through the changing room stall.

"Busy," Tori said. "Been working with Ramos and his dad all week." She checked the time on her phone, and if she wanted to keep that job, which she did for more than one reason, they had to get a move on.

"Do you ever regret giving up teaching? Ugh. Not this one."

"Sometimes I miss working with the kids and seeing their eyes light up when things click into place," Tori said, catching the swimsuit her mother had tossed over the partition. "But I've always known I belong in the department."

Her mother laughed softly. "That's for sure. How many years in a row did you dress up as a firefighter on Halloween? Four?"

"Five. And then maybe once more at for a college party."

"And now look at you. A firefighter and a painter."

"You make the painting thing sound way more glamorous than it is. Funny thing, though, the building we're painting now belongs to Jon Nichols."

"Jon Nichols—your lieutenant?"

"That's right. It turns out he's a physical therapist, too. He said dad helped him out with school and stuff."

"Well, that's interesting." Another suit came flying out of the dressing room.

Tori picked it up off the floor where it had landed and set it on top of the other. This was her mother's routine. Before she finished, Tori would have amassed a nice little pile of discarded options.

"Hey, Mom?" She wasn't sure if this was the right time to ask or not, but like her mother had pointed out, in a few days, she would be an entire continent away. "Why didn't you tell me you knew Nichols the other day when we were talking?"

"What? Oh, I don't know. I didn't think it was that big of a deal." Two more Lycra concoctions landed on the floor with a slap.

Maybe not, but Tori hadn't stopped thinking about it since Jon had mentioned it the day before. It was like an itchy scab. She knew she shouldn't pick at it and leave well enough alone, but she couldn't help herself. She had to keep scratching until she either felt relief or it started bleeding. "Mom, did Dad pull any strings with the department without me knowing?"

"I don't know what you're talking about."

Anna Keller was many things. A good liar was not one of them. "Yes, you do. He told me he wanted to pick my training assignment. I told him not to, but. . ."

"But you think he did anyway?" her mother asked, pulling open the dressing room door and pinning Tori with a stare. "You think he would go behind your back like that?"

Tori tilted her head and returned her mother's narrowed gaze. "You think he wouldn't? You know what he was like when he thought he was right."

Her mother sighed, then closed the door again. "Does it matter if he did?"

Yes. It did. It meant her father had gone behind Tori's back, orchestrating her career to his liking, the way he'd tried to do with all aspects of her life. It meant she was guilty of everything she'd denied since the day she'd walked into the academy. It made her a liar. But Tori couldn't tell her mother that. Her mother wanted to remember all the things her husband had done right in his life—and there were a lot. That was all Tori wanted to remember, too, no matter how many times they'd butted heads over the years.

"Did you pick one yet?" Tori called out.

"Yes," her mother said, emerging from the dressing room victorious and waving a green suit the air. "I will look like floating asparagus, but that's okay. Asparagus is a good vegetable."

Tori laughed, ready to move on from both the swimwear section and the conversation. "Next stop: loungewear."

Two hours later, Tori sat on a bench, a hot dog in one hand, a soda in the other. "You didn't have to be so literal about lunch."

"You said fast, and the guy was right there. I'm just trying to help."

"Yeah, yeah. Thanks for lunch."

"Oh, shoot. We should have gotten you a dress for the ball while we were in there."

Tori froze, hot dog hanging in midair, a glob of mustard dangerously close to splattering her lap. "What ball?" The annual fundraiser ball Tori had been pretending didn't exist. The same ball she'd helped her mother prepare for since she'd been old enough to name her colors.

"The fire department ball. It's only a month away. You should start looking for a dress now. It always takes me weeks to find the right dress. Then the shoes and the bag. And the accessories. We should go back in."

"Mom," Tori said, setting her drink down and pulling her mother back to her seat. "We have plenty of time. And that's *if* I decide to go."

"What do you mean if you decide? Of course, you're going. They're going to honor your father at the dinner. They've asked me to say a few words. Didn't they ask you, too? They said they would."

Tori shrugged. "I guess they figured there wasn't enough time for a second speaker." She hoped she was a better liar than her mother. The planning committee had called with their request, and she'd turned them down. She'd already given her eulogy. Chief Keller may have been a hero to some, okay most, but he'd hated being lauded as one. He would roll over in his grave if he knew people were still singing his praises. "I love my job, which is more than most people can say," he'd said. "Expecting to be thanked for it is selfish."

"You have to be there," her mother pleaded. "You know how I am about speaking in front of crowds. Promise me you'll be there."

Tori sighed. "Okay. I'll think about it. But we don't have to look for a dress now. I need to go. I have a job to get to." She finished her lunch in four bites, then stood and wiped the mustard from the corner of her mouth. "Will you be okay getting home by yourself with these bags?"

"What, this?" her mother asked, pointing to the five bags of new clothes at her feet. "This is nothing. You go handle your business now that you've helped me with mine. Oh, and Tori," her mother called as Tori hailed a cab. "Think about getting a date for the ball, too. It would be nice to have someone to dance with."

Tori rolled her eyes, then quickly chastised herself for allowing Jon's face to come to mind as soon as her mother suggested a date. This whole fantasy she'd been building in her head had to come to an end. If she was going to get Jon Nichols out of her mind for good, she needed to get serious about this whole getting back into the dating game thing. And fast. Before her little crush turned into something more dangerous.

CHAPTER TEN

Jon hovered in his office doorway as the crew filtered into the firehouse early the next morning to relieve the prior shift of their duties. He nodded in greeting to Beast and Fitz as they lugged their shift bags past him to the locker room. Davies arrived next, looking like he'd had a rough night. The day wasn't about to get any better for him. Chief Mulrone had scheduled another drill for them later that morning, and it wasn't going to be a walk in the park.

Jon didn't usually camp out in the hallway at the beginning of the shift, but he was waiting for Tori. He'd been happier to see her at his building than he'd like to admit. He was in too deep, and he knew it. She was Chief Keller's daughter. He owed everything to that man.

It had been dumb luck that she'd landed at his house for training. But Jon had welcomed the chance to do right by his mentor, and he aimed to see it through. Even if it meant keeping his distance from the woman he was falling hard for.

"Keller," Beast yelled from the common room. "You're cooking today. You up for it?"

The sound of Tori's laugh drifted down the hall and washed over Jon. "I've got a few tricks up my sleeve. You won't be disappointed."

"Confidence. I like that in a cook," Beast said, followed by his loud bark of laughter.

Tori rounded the corner, her smile slipping when she saw him standing there. "Good morning, Lieutenant," she said, adjusting the bag on her shoulder. Anywhere else, he would have offered to take the load from her. But he wouldn't do her that injustice here. Not with the men watching. He knew how much it meant to her to be taken seriously and seen as an equal. Any outward show of chivalry would undermine everything she'd worked hard for.

"Keller," he said. "Can I see you a minute after you stow your gear?"

She nodded, continuing past him, without even half of the smile she'd walked into the firehouse with. Firefighter Keller was back on duty. She was right, of course, to be that way, but he wished they could go back to the restaurant and be Jon and Tori again.

"Lieutenant? You wanted to see me?" she asked, appearing before him, her hair pulled back in a tight ponytail the way she did for every shift. Her pants had been cleaned and pressed, and her uniform shirt was tucked in neatly at the waist. She was the picture-perfect candidate ready for her shift.

"You should tell the guys," Jon said, motioning to the kitchen where they were all gathering for either a cup of coffee or something to eat before muster. "You won the bet. It's only right." And it would make things so much easier on him if she outed him before he had to do it himself.

Tori narrowed her eyes. There was a hint of humor in her expression, but then like flipping a switch, it was gone and replaced with something colder and distant. "You want me to tell them," she said. There was no use denying it. She'd already seen through his charade once.

Jon nodded. "It would make things easier for me if they found out, yes."

"Why not just tell them?"

Jon let out a heavy breath. There was no good reason, but she'd earned the bragging rights, and those go a long way with this crew.

"I'll think about it," Tori said. "I'm going to get some coffee. Rumor has it, Davies made it and tried something new in the mix."

Jon scrunched up his nose. That didn't sound the least bit appealing. "What do you think he did?"

Tori chuckled and shrugged. "I have no idea, but I want to find out. Coming?"

Would he like to join her in a morning cup of coffee? Absolutely. Would he like the entire crew of Truck 19 present at the time? That would be a firm no.

"I'll be there in a minute. I've got some stuff to do before roll."

Jon waited until after the crew had their breakfast, and they'd settled in for the morning before rounding them up for the day. It was no fun for him if they had a warning. The officer or not, he still liked to get his kicks while on duty.

"Load up," he yelled, walking through the common room. "Everyone on the truck in ten seconds."

The sound of scrambling feet behind him brought a smile to his face.

"Drill time," Beast called out, rushing past Jon to get to the truck. He knew what happened to the last man, and Beast had no intention of being that man.

Fitz and Owens were next, pushing each other out of the way as they raced to their positions. Davies and Ramos hurried from the workout room, leaving only Delaware and Keller to bring up the rear. Jon stood, with his arms folded facing the doors separating the garage from the living quarters waiting for the stragglers. Delaware jogged out with a sheepish grin and slipped into his boots.

"Am I the last man?" Delaware asked, shrugging on his coat.

"Nope," Jon said, checking the time. This wasn't like Keller. With only the one exception when she'd been deep into latrine duty, she was always one of the first on the truck, no matter what she'd been doing or where in the house she was. "Anyone know where Keller is?"

"Here." Her voice rang out from inside the truck cab.

Jon followed the voice and poked his head into the truck. There she was—nestled between Beast and Ramos. "Where did you come from?"

"I was doing inventory when you called everyone to the truck," she said with a shrug. "Right place, right time, I guess."

Jon turned and clapped a hand on Delaware's shoulder. "Sorry. Looks like you're the last man, after all."

The crew sent up a round of hoots and cheers at Delaware's expense, but he'd been around long enough to know sometimes you win, and sometimes you lose. They'd each have their turn as the last man eventually.

"What's wrong with the last man?" Ramos asked as Owens eased the truck out of the garage.

Fitz snickered. "It's like drawing the short straw. The last man has to make the house call."

"What house call?" Keller asked.

"You want to explain it to the candidates, Delaware?" Jon asked.

Delaware squirmed in his seat. "There's this woman, Margie Machaw, who calls the firehouse all the time. I'm talking five or six times a week. She's old and lonely, mostly. Harmless. The lieutenant and the other officers keep a logbook to track when she calls. If she goes more than five days without calling, whichever shift is on duty on day six, makes a house call."

"That sounds nice," Keller said, not understanding the whole story. "I'm sure she appreciates you checking on her."

This was the first house call they've had to go on since the candidates started. The shift before them had to make a stop by the old woman's house a few weeks prior. That lieutenant on duty had left a status update stating no changes to her domestic situation had occurred, which was exactly why no one wanted to be the last man.

Delaware sighed, and both Fitz and Beast laughed. Owens just shook his head. As the driver, last man or not, he was exempt from having to get out of the truck while making a stop.

"Really, it does," Ramos said. Jon noticed how he always took Keller's side, and a little part of him wished he could do that as well. Be the man Keller counted on to have her back. Be the one she turned to for support.

"What are we missing here?" Keller asked.

"You know what?" Jon called from the front seat. "Delaware, why don't you take all three candidates with you on the house call today?"

"How did I get dragged into this?" Davies griped.

Jon curled his lip but kept his head forward, so only Owens next to him was able to discern his disgust at Davies's display of selfish laziness. Jon had only seven and half months left with these candidates before they received their final house assignments, and he considered it a personal goal to break Davies of this particular trait. Either that, or he was going to owe some officer a year's worth of drinks to make up for it.

"You know what, Davies? Since you didn't volunteer, you get to make the house call every time from now on as well," Jon said. He counted to three. Then, right on time, Davies's next response followed, scripted the way his nine-year-old nephew would have said it.

"I didn't hear Ramos or Keller volunteer either," Davies whined.

Jon sighed and leaned his head against the seat. He didn't have the patience for this. If this had been the year before, he would have called Chief Keller, asking for advice on dealing with such a self-absorbed candidate. They would have met for a beer and swapped incident stories. The chief would have listened, then he would have told Jon to be the leader Davies needed, and not to expect Davies to be the follower Jon wanted.

"You also didn't hear them complain," Beast said, to Jon's relief. Beast's intercession gave him another second or two to put himself in the right mindset to deal with Davies. "Sometimes, it's best to keep your mouth shut and do what you're told."

"All I'm saying—" Davies started.

"We're here," Jon announced, swinging the door open and jumping from the truck before Davies could finish. He surveyed the outside of the cape cod style home. No one had mowed the lawn in a few weeks, and the gutters looked like they could use a good cleaning, but other than that, nothing appeared to be out of sorts. "Hey, Beast, check the cans in the alley." The next day was garbage day. The cans should be full. Delaware stepped up next to him, scanning over the exterior of the house as well.

"Windows are closed. Drapes are drawn," Delaware said as though ticking off a list of items. "Car is in the driveway."

Jon nodded. Margie didn't go too many places besides the grocery store anymore, not that they knew of, so the car was usually in the driveway, but she always pulled the curtains open. She liked natural light, she said, and it saved on her electric bill. Jon couldn't remember ever pulling up to the house and seeing the curtains closed. A pit sunk hard and deep into his stomach.

"Do we knock?" Keller asked, worry etching her forehead with creases.

Beast came back around the front from the alley. "Cans are empty."

Jon didn't wait. Taking the front stairs two at a time, he pounded on the front door. "Fire department, Mrs. Machaw. Are you in there?" he called through the door. Delaware tried to peer through the crack between the curtains in the front window. He turned to Jon and shook his head. "Mrs. Machaw! Are you in there?" Jon waited, straining to hear over his pounding heart. Why had they decided on five days before checking on her? Why not three? Why had they let any time go by? "Mrs. Machaw, we're coming in!"

Beast was already behind him, clutching a Halligan poised and ready to go. Jon nodded and stepped aside, giving him access to the entryway. Jon was the first one in when the door gave way and swung open. Blinking his eyes to adjust them to the darkness, he scanned the living room for signs of Mrs. Machaw's thin frame. "Spread out. Find her," he said, moving through the front room toward the kitchen in the back.

They'd waited too long. Jon felt it in his bones. Whatever they found was on him. He was the officer on duty; it was his call. No rule said they had to wait the five days, but Margie was a frequent flyer, often purposely not calling the house so that they would visit.

"Don't forget to take care of Margie," Chief Keller had told Jon on his last day on Truck 19 before taking over Squad 4. "She needs Truck 19."

She was a crazy old bird, but she was *their* crazy old bird. Jon had promised the chief he wouldn't forget, and that Truck 19 would continue to make good on the promise the chief had made to her years before Jon was ever in the department. The other shifts begrudgingly held up their end, but Jon had always made special efforts where Margie was concerned. He stayed on the phone with her longer than the other officers, listening to her complain about her arthritis, or recount for the hundredth time a baseball game she remembered her son playing fifty years ago.

Where was that son now? Halfway across the country, that was where. After everything his mother had done for him, he'd up and left her there to rot by herself. Jon wished his mother was still around. If she were, she wouldn't need to make up reasons to call a firehouse for attention, that was for sure. If Margie was alright, he swore to himself he would visit more, even by himself and off-shift if he had to.

"Got her," Keller yelled out, drawing Jon out of the kitchen and up the stairs to the main bathroom on the second floor.

Beast, Delaware, and Ramos were already clustered around the doorway, forcing Jon to push his way past them to find Margie lying on the dingy ceramic tile, her head cradled in Keller's lap. The room smelled like stale urine, and he had to keep himself from gagging. He wondered how Tori managed to keep herself so composed as she stroked the old woman's hair. Margie was disoriented, but awake and breathing, and that was the main thing.

"Mrs. Machaw," Jon said, kneeling beside Tori and taking the woman's wrist in his hand. Her pulse was slow but steady. "What happened?"

"Oh, Lieutenant Nichols. The darndest thing. My knees just gave out. The both of them," Margie said.

"How long have you been on the floor?"

"I don't know," she said, pinching her brow and deepening the crevices in her forehead. "But I knew you'd come. You always come."

Jon squeezed her hand and forced himself to smile at her. "Owens, get an ambulance over here," Jon ordered into his communication unit.

"Got it, Lieutenant," Owens replied.

"I don't need to go to the hospital," Mrs. Machaw argued.

"Mrs. Machaw, you've been lying here for days. When was the last time you ate something? We need to get you checked out."

"Don't be silly. I just need some help getting up. That's all." She tried to push herself up, but Tori's gentle hands kept her in place. Margie Machaw was as stubborn as Tori, and then some.

"That's not all," Jon said. His relief from finding her alive quickly dissipated into his usual annoyance at her antics. "You need to have a doctor look you over." And a bath, and some fluids, and a few decent meals. "You need to find out why your knees gave out and how to keep it from happening again."

"They gave out because I'm old. It happens. Just help me up."

"Mrs. Machaw," Tori said, compassion flowing from her tone, "it's fire department protocol to send for an ambulance. Lieutenant Nichols is just doing his job. You wouldn't want him to get in trouble, would you? Because, you see, Firefighter Davies," she tilted her head toward the door where Davies hovered behind everyone else, "he's kind of a stickler for the rules and a bit of a tattletale. He'd rat out the lieutenant in a heartbeat."

Jon chewed the inside of his cheek to keep from laughing as Mrs. Machaw narrowed her eyes to angry slits as she looked Davies over and pressed her lips together in a thin, pale line.

"You a snitch?" she asked Davies.

Davies flexed his jaw, fighting to keep his temper under control. "I just like to play by the rules, Ma'am," he said through gritted teeth.

Mrs. Machaw sniffed and raised her chin as much as she could. "Don't care much for snitches." She turned back to Jon. "Go ahead. Get the ambulance. I won't let you get into trouble on my account. Not after you came all the way over here to check on me."

"Thank you, Mrs. Machaw. I appreciate it," Jon said. He gave her hand another squeeze, then turned to give orders to the crew. "Davies, Ramos, get all the garbage outside for Mrs. Machaw. Delaware, check the kitchen—clear out old food, clean up the dishes."

He would come back the next day to handle the lawn and the gutters himself, and he made a mental note to remember to ask her who usually dealt with the landscaping and exterior of the house. He doubted Mrs. Machaw pushed a mower around herself. When he turned back to her, Tori's head was bent over her as she listened intently to something Mrs. Machaw whispered. He gave them a few more seconds as he watched them with curiosity. Tori nodded, her expression serious with a touch of humor.

"I promise," Tori said with a smile when Mrs. Machaw had finished. Then, Tori reached up to the towel rack and pulled the green towel down to the floor. She rolled it into a neat little bundle, then slid it under Mrs. Machaw's head as she pulled her legs free. "I'll be right back," she said, rising from the floor.

"Where are you going?" Jon asked.

Tori looked back at Mrs. Machaw and winked. "Woman stuff. Don't worry about it," she said, patting his arm as she brushed past him and down the hall to one of the bedrooms.

When Jon looked back at Mrs. Machaw on the floor, she was staring up at him with a sly smile. "You like her," she said, pointing a crooked finger at him. He shook his head to deny it, warmth spreading through him at the accusation, but Mrs. Machaw cut him off. "I like liars less than I like snitches. But I'll let it go this time."

CHAPTER ELEVEN

"You really sure about this cruise, Mom?" Tori asked as she adjusted her position on the over-sized pillow. Leave it to her mother to pick a never-heard-of Moroccan restaurant to meet at for lunch before her flight. The kicker was—they had chairs. Her mother had to special request the pillow seating. Tori's legs were still an aching mess from the last drill Nichols had them perform after seeing Mrs. Machaw off in the ambulance.

"I thought you were okay with me going. If the singles thing is bothering you—"

"It's not that," Tori said, which was true. But ever since finding Mrs. Machaw lying on her bathroom floor in her own filth, Tori had liked the idea of her mother traveling by herself so far from home less and less. Even though her mother wouldn't technically be alone, having Aunt Karen, who was older than her mother, as her companion didn't offer much comfort. "It's just—what if something happens? You'll be a long way from home, and your doctors."

"How decrepit do you think I am, missy?" her mother asked, ripping off a piece of flatbread and dipping it into an oil and herb concoction. "I'll have you know: I'm the picture of perfect health."

"I know, but—"

"What's all this about? Really?"

Tori shrugged, Mrs. Machaw's face swimming in front of her. Her clouded, worried eyes haunted Tori. The poor woman had no one. Sure, family photos lined her halls, bright shining faces looking out from behind dusty glass. She recognized the younger version of Mrs. Machaw right away in some of them, standing with her arm around a chubby little boy, laughing and squealing in her embrace, while someone Tori assumed to be Mr. Machaw looked on with pride. Another one where the boy had grown into a young man wearing a cap and gown flanked by his parents. Mrs. Machaw standing next to a full-grown man in a tuxedo and his glowing bride.

Where was that chubby boy now? He'd grown into that man and had left his mother. Delaware had told her he lived across the country now. No one knew how often he visited, if at all. Mrs. Machaw always seemed to talk about the next time her son would visit, and never when had been the last time. Tori couldn't help thinking of her mother growing older without her husband at her side, and how, even living in the same city, she'd been neglectful.

"Nothing, I guess," Tori said. "I just want you to be safe, that's all."

Her mother smiled and pushed the dish of oil in front of Tori. "Try this. You'll like this."

Tori did as she was asked, though she didn't have much of an appetite, while her mother continued talking about the cruise and her planned excursions, making sure to highlight the safety precautions the staff made for their fifty-five and older crowd. Years of living with the

Chief had prepared Anna Keller for conversations like this one. Tori knew her mother sensed a particular event had sparked her worry, and experience told her not to pry. Tori would discuss it when or if she felt the need to. So, instead of pressing it, Tori's mother did the next best thing.

Diversion.

Tori wondered how her mother was able to string along a monologue on almost any topic. She must fill her free time with hours of research and study in a wide array of subjects. Tori had grown up watching her mother distract her father with ramblings on everything from politics to movies, from spring gardening to Indy race car driving. Tori dared anyone to say her mother didn't work. She couldn't imagine the amount of work it took for her mother to be ready at a moment's notice to dispel any bad mood.

"Have you thought more about the ball coming up?" Anna asked, then took a much-needed deep breath.

Tori groaned and curled her lip. "I'll go," she said, then stuffed another piece of flatbread in her mouth.

Her mother brightened at the announcement as though Tori had just told her she'd won the lottery. "Who will you bring as a date?"

"Who are *you* bringing?" Tori fired back.

"I'm the widow. No one expects me to bring anyone. You, on the other hand, are a young woman with many more prospects than I ever had."

"Prospects?" Tori gasped, then swung her head around as though looking for a hidden treasure. "Where are they? Who are they? Do they expect a dowry?"

"Stop," her mother said, swatting at her. "You know what I mean."

"Yes, I do. And if it makes you feel any better, I have decided I need to start dating again." Her mother squealed. "If," Tori said, holding up her hand to stop the high-pitched sound coming from her mother, "I find someone suitable. I don't have a lot of free time to be hanging out somewhere, meeting new people. But I am open to the possibility."

"That's all I ask."

"And I make no guarantees about having a date in time for the ball. You might be stuck with me as your escort."

"A woman could do a lot worse than that," her mother said, clinking her glass against Tori's with a wink.

Later at home, Tori paced her living room floor, staring at the unsent text on her phone screen. She had meant it when she'd told her mother she was ready to start dating again if only to keep thoughts of Jon Nichols at bay. And the best way to not think about Jon Nichols was to spend time with someone who was not Jon Nichols. She took a steadying breath and hit send.

TELL YOUR FRIEND I'M AVAILABLE FRIDAY NIGHT FOR DRINKS IF HE'S INTERESTED.

She prayed she was doing the right thing. And if she wasn't? It was only one evening. Surely, she could get through one evening, making conversation with a stranger. Her thumbs flew over the phone screen.

YOU'RE COMING, TOO. I'LL BRING YOU A DATE.

Safety in numbers, after all. If worse comes to worst, Ramos can entertain his friend, and Tori could hang out with Maggie once she told her she was coming, too. Her phone pinged with a reply.

YOU WON'T BE SORRY.

She questioned that, but she had to give Ramos the benefit of the doubt. He would never knowingly set her up with a complete psychopath. She was putting way too much pressure on this one evening and needed to chill.

A picture of her with her father on their last big family vacation caught her eye. She'd been in high school and had just started venturing into the world of dating. Her father had made a special effort to have a heart to heart talk with her about growing up and entering the adult world.

"Don't expect to hit the jackpot with one lottery ticket. You have to play the game to win," he'd said. He'd always preferred to couch his life lessons deep in the cushions of pithy sayings.

She'd never thought having her father's approval on her dating life had been important. She knew what she wanted and had little patience for those that didn't fit the bill. She would have preferred her father had respected her judgment, instead of playing puppet master in one more area of her life. She gazed at her father's image frozen in time and wondered what he would think of her predicament now.

Resorting to blind dates because she'd filled her days with so much work, she didn't have the time even to pretend to play the game anymore. Prohibited from dating the one man she wanted to.

"Work hard, play hard," her father had been known to say on several occasions. She had the first part down. It was the second part that eluded her. But she was going to work on that. Starting now—or Friday.

WHO ARE YOU BRINGING? Ramos asked.

SURPRISE GUEST.

Tori was confident Maggie would agree to be the plus one that evening. More than once, Maggie had commented on how cute she thought Ramos was. But Tori didn't want to make promises she couldn't keep. And if Maggie, for some reason, refused, she'd have to scramble to fill the slot.

Her phone pinged again, and she thought it was Ramos confirming the date for Friday, but she couldn't have been more wrong. Jon Nichols.

BEEN THINKING ABOUT THE WAY YOU HANDLED MRS. MACHAW SINCE MONDAY. HOW'D YOU KNOW TO PLAY THE REGULATIONS GAME?

Tori smiled, her chest warming with the praise. SHE'S FROM A MILITARY FAMILY. FIGURED SHE'D UNDERSTAND.

JON: HOW DO YOU KNOW SHE'S FROM A MILITARY FAMILY?

TORI: SAW THE PICS ON THE WALL WITH HER HUSBAND IN UNIFORM.

JON: THERE ARE PICS ON THE WALL?

TORI: HOW MANY TIMES HAVE YOU BEEN THERE?

JON: TOO MANY. NEVER UPSTAIRS.

Tori stared at her phone, willing him to say something else. Anything else. She didn't want this little exchange to end on Mrs. Machaw. She pressed the phone to her chest, squeezing her eyes shut and using up every last birthday wish she would ever have to keep him talking. There wasn't a lot of time before he assumed they were done, but the only questions she could think to ask did not fall into proper rank and file standards. Things like: What are you doing now? What are you wearing? Do you want to come over? What's your favorite breakfast?

Why couldn't she be normal around him? If she wasn't talking about something completely depressing, then she was acting like that teenager with the crush, staring at him from the corner of her party, praying for him to look in her direction.

Her phone pinged.

JON: HOW'S YOUR TIME OFF BEEN?

And there it was. Tori's smile, the one that hadn't left her face since the first message had popped up, widened as she settled into the corner of her faded gray couch. She pulled a yellow pillow into her lap and pressed it into her abdomen, hoping it would smother the butterflies taking flight.

TORI: GOOD. HAD GOODBYE LUNCH WITH MY MOM BEFORE HER CRUISE. YOU?

JON: BUSY AT THE OFFICE. LOTS OF BASEBALL AND SOCCER INJURIES.

TORI: WHY DID YOU KEEP IT SUCH A SECRET?

JON: DIDN'T MEAN TO. YOU KNOW THE GUYS. DIDN'T TALK ABOUT IT ONE DAY, AND THEN IT BECAME A HOUSE-WIDE MYSTERY.

TORI: I DIDN'T TELL THEM.

JON: WHY NOT? IT'S YOUR PRIZE TO CLAIM.

TORI: FIGURED YOU WANTED IT SECRET FOR A REASON. NOT MY PLACE.

JON: I APPRECIATE IT. BUT I WASN'T LYING—YOU'D BE HELPING ME OUT.

TORI: ???

JON: MY SISTER IS ORGANIZING A PARTY, AND SHE EXPECTS ME TO INVITE ALL THE GUYS.

TORI: WHICH MEANS THEY'LL HAVE TO FIND OUT.

JON: RIGHT.

TORI: AND YOU FEEL WEIRD TELLING THEM YOURSELF?

JON: RIGHT AGAIN.

Tori bit her lower lip while considering. Giving her his permission took away any reason she had to keep her knowledge of his side job a secret other than her absurd little fantasy about it drawing them closer. But she couldn't exactly tell him that. And she definitely couldn't tell him that his urging her to broadcast their shared information filled her with an insane melancholy.

JON: SLEEP ON IT, OKAY? HAVE A GOOD NIGHT. SEE YOU BRIGHT AND EARLY.

Tori tossed her phone to the opposite corner. It wasn't as though they were going to stay up all night chatting, but a few more minutes wouldn't have been terrible. She hugged her pillow tighter to her chest. One good thing came out of their exchange. He'd shared with her another piece of information no one else knew about. Yet. That would all change as soon as she made good on her bet. But for the night, at least, it was something he trusted only her with. Her whole body warmed at the thought.

Her phone pinged again, sending Tori diving into the couch cushions to retrieve it from where it had wedged itself after she'd sent it flying from her hand. As she scooped it up, her heart thundered in her chest, only to have it crash when she saw it wasn't from Jon.

RAMOS: ALL SET FOR FRIDAY. TONY'S LOOKING FORWARD TO IT. SEE YOU TOMORROW.

Tony. Right. Tori had forgotten all about that. Tony and Tori. Tori and Tony.

She cringed, already regretting her decision. But it was too late to back out now that Ramos had gone and confirmed everything. The best thing to do was to grin and bear it. Tony and Tori. Tori and Tony. Nope. That wasn't going to work. Maybe he wouldn't mind being called Anthony.

Jon and Tori, on the other hand—now that had a ring to it.

Tori groaned and promised herself not to think about Lieutenant Nichols like that again, fully aware that this was now the fifth time, at least, she'd made that promise. And since she'd failed four times before, it was time to call in some reinforcements.

"Hey, Tor, what's shaking?" Maggie asked when she'd answered the phone.

"I need a favor."

"Is this like, you want to borrow my favorite sweater favor, or you need a kidney favor?"

"Somewhere in between, but closer to a sweater, I think."

"In that case, you got it. Whatever you need."

Tori smiled. That was Maggie for you—the best friend a girl could ask for, making promises without knowing any of the details simply because Tori asked for it. "All right, then. See you Friday night."

"Cool. What's Friday night?"

Tori inhaled a deep breath. "I told Ramos he could set me up on a blind date if I agreed to bring someone with me, and that someone is you. Cool? Cool," she said in one long exhale.

Maggie's laughter trickled over the phone. "Why didn't you just say so? I'll hang with Marco Ramos. He's cute."

"So you've mentioned."

"Who's he setting you up with?"

"A college friend. Tony something or other."

Maggie paused, then, "Huh."

Tori knew that "huh." It was layered with meaning and innuendo, and so many questions. "What, 'huh?'"

"Nothing. It's just . . .Well, I don't know. Are you really okay with being set up with a stranger when . . ."

"When, what?"

"When you have feelings for someone else."

Tori squeezed her eyes shut, grateful she chose not to video chat

Maggie so she could hide her flushing face. "Mags, I can't have feelings for anyone else."

"Why not?"

"You know why not. It's against regulation, for one."

"Just an excuse, Tor. There are ways around that."

Tori ran a hand over her face. "It's not just that," she said, her chest tightening. She'd never admitted this out loud, but if anyone understood, it would be Maggie, another firefighter kid. "I'm scared, alright?"

"Scared of what? You walk into burning buildings. You're like superwoman."

Tori scoffed. "Hardly. Besides, when I'm on a call, it's enough that I have to worry about myself. I couldn't handle worrying about someone else. I need to be with someone I know is safe."

Maggie didn't say anything, which worried Tori. It wasn't like her to hold back her opinions. If Maggie was quiet now, it was because she was either afraid of hurting Tori's feelings or making her angry.

"What, Mags? Say something."

"It's just . . .we never mentioned anyone specific this whole time, but—"

"But?"

"But, obviously, you're thinking of someone specific, and isn't that a sign? I know what happened with your dad sucked beyond all recognition, but you can't live your life afraid that will happen again. Statistically speaking, there's less than one-hundredth of a percent chance of dying on duty. Are you willing to walk away from something that could be great for less than one-hundredth of a percent?"

Tori ignored the nagging feeling in the back of her head that had started with Maggie's "huh." She wasn't ready to talk about statistics and the potential for greatness. She only wanted Maggie to be her wing-woman, the way she'd been since the third grade, and Tori had thought it would be a good idea to tell Bobby Murphy she'd had a crush on him. He'd laughed in her face, and Maggie had punched him in the arm for it.

"I'm not walking away from anything," Tori said. "I'm walking *toward* something. That's why I'm going on a blind date on Friday, and you're coming with me."

Maggie sighed the type of exaggerated exhale that meant she was tired of Tori's stubbornness. "Yes, I am. But you're paying for my drinks if Ramos ends up being a dud."

CHAPTER TWELVE

Jon propped his feet on his coffee table and leaned back, taking a long swallow of his bottled water, wishing it were a beer instead. But he was on duty the next day, and he wasn't about to jeopardize his career by chancing his name didn't get pulled for the random drug and alcohol testing. He always thought the guys who showed up for their shift visibly hungover—Davies—were tempting fate. One of these days, luck wouldn't be on their side.

He scrolled through his messages, rereading the conversation with Tori. He'd spent the last forty-eight hours filling his time with anything he could think of to keep from calling her. He'd done a relatively good job of staying busy, either with patients or with preparations for the new building. When he found himself idle for too long the day before, he'd borrowed a ladder from his brother-in-law and had spent a few hours cleaning out Mrs. Machaw's gutters, hoping the muck would keep his mind off Tori, but the sight of Mrs. Machaw's house, muck and all, only made the image of her in his mind more vivid.

Tori's patience and compassion during the house call had

overwhelmed him. She'd known exactly what to say and do, holding Mrs. Machaw's hand and muttering reassurances while the paramedics wheeled the woman out of her house and into the ambulance. The other firefighters, himself included most of the time, checked on the old lady out of habit. They stopped by, knocked on her door, and tolerated her long-winded explanations about her absence. They usually counted the seconds before they could move on with their day, patting themselves on the back for a job well done.

Tori was different. She'd showed genuine empathy and a warmth that most veterans on the job lost as time wore on. One emergency rolled into the next, one horrific scene after another, until one person became indistinguishable from the other. It wasn't that they stopped caring. They wouldn't be able to do the job if that was the case. There was simply too much to care about—that was the problem. A person could go crazy doing what they did if they didn't figure out a way to turn the volume down.

It saddened him to think it would happen to Tori one day as well. He was surprised it hadn't happened already after losing her father, then still showing up to carry on his legacy. Maybe she'd hold on to her glow longer than the rest of them. He wasn't sure if that was a good or bad thing.

When he'd felt he'd held out long enough, he'd given in and sent her an innocent text. He'd only wanted her to know that he'd appreciated the way she'd handled a tough situation and that she'd done well last shift with her quick thinking. If it hadn't been for her, getting Mrs. Machaw to the hospital would have been a much more dramatic ordeal. The rest of the conversation—well, that had been a mistake. Not a mistake, really. It had been a slight lapse in judgment. He'd cut it off when he'd felt himself slipping deeper into it than he should have.

What was it about her that made him want to tell her everything? It had to be her eyes. The way she looked at him when he spoke as though he was the only one that mattered. That what he said she meant more than the air she breathed. It was silly, he knew. She had to listen to him. He was her boss, but she looked at him like he was so much more. And it was addicting.

He scrubbed a hand over his face. How had he let a candidate get under his skin like this? Not just a candidate—Chief Keller's kid. He cringed. She hated being called that, and what it stood for. But there it was.

He took another swig of his beer.

He was hooked on Chief Keller's kid.

Morning came too soon and not fast enough at the same time. Jon had spent half the night running through his list of things he needed to do to open his own practice, and the other half thinking about Tori. At least part of his mind would soon be at ease. Jon was the first of his crew to arrive at the firehouse, which was eerily quiet. After stowing his gear, he headed for the communications control room to check the night's journal entries.

"Morning, Simmons," Jon said, greeting the firefighter who was stuck on third watch. Jon had always hated that shift the most—sitting in the control room from four in the morning until shift change. Depending on how many calls came in before then, third watch usually meant staying up all night.

"Morning, Lieutenant. Need the journal?"

"Please," Jon said, pulling an empty chair up to the desk. "Busy night?"

"Just a little fire," Simmons said, stifling a yawn.

Jon flipped open the logbook where they kept a record of every run Truck 19 went on. *Little fire*, Simmons had said. There had been a three-alarm restaurant fire that had tied up the truck for five hours overnight. No wonder it was so quiet. Jon closed the book and handed it back to Simmons, then swiped his department identification card into the computer system to clock in.

"Need any more coffee?" Jon asked as he stood to leave.

"No, thanks. I'm good."

Nodding, Jon left Simmons to finish out his shift while he went in search of a cup of coffee. He poured himself the last of the pot Simmons must have brewed overnight and grimaced as the bitter taste of burnt grounds hit his tongue. His morning coffee would never be the same after Tori Keller. He shook his head and dumped the rest of his cup down the drain.

"Wasn't that bad, was it?"

Speak of the devil.

"Keller," Jon said, without turning around. "You're earlier than usual." Couldn't it be Owens or Fitz? Or anyone else?

"My mom called to let me know she arrived in Athens—at four in the morning," Tori said, rolling her neck. "I wasn't able to fall back asleep."

Jon set his mug on the counter and faced her, leaning back against the sink. Dark circles she didn't bother trying to hide rimmed her eyes. It looked like she had gotten about as much sleep as he had. He hoped he hadn't been one of the causes of her restless night. Then again, maybe he did.

"You want me to make fresh coffee?" she asked, pointing to the now-empty pot.

"Please," Jon said, jumping out of her way. "Maybe show me where you keep your top-secret coffee grounds so I can pitch in, too?"

She glanced at him over her shoulder with half-closed eyes. "What happened to you not being able to take part in house pranks?"

"What prank?" Jon shrugged. "I just want to make coffee."

"Hmm," she said, appraising his level of sincerity. Then she reached into the cabinet and pulled out a large plastic canister of Beast's protein powder. She unscrewed the lid and breathed in the aroma of ground coffee beans and spices. "Here it is."

"That's where you've been keeping it?" Jon asked, amazed at the level of duplicity going on right beneath his nose.

"Who's going to mess with Beast?" she asked with a wink.

"Good point." Jon watched as Tori moved around the kitchen, making coffee, then scrounging in the fridge for something for breakfast. It was a scene so natural, so domestic, he almost forgot they stood in the middle of the firehouse. "We don't usually keep breakfast food here. There might be some cereal."

"Eggs," she announced, victoriously lifting a carton in the air. "Want some? I can scramble eggs like nobody's business. And there's some bread for toast."

"Sounds perfect," Jon said. The coffee started percolating, and the aroma alone was enough to wake him up from his dreamy stupor. "Better make a lot, though. The guys will be here soon, and I'm sure they'll want some, too."

"Got it." Tori cracked the first few eggs into a mixing bowl. "Can you pour me a cup when it's done brewing?"

Jon reached behind him to bring down another mug for her, and when the last drop of coffee fell into the decanter, he poured two cups, adding cream and sugar to both, then handed her a mug while she slid melting butter around a pan. "Have you given any more thought about telling the guys?"

"Have you?" she asked, watching him from the corner of her eye. "It's not like it's something to be ashamed of."

"No," Jon said, growing uncomfortable with the subject, though he was the one who had brought it up. Why couldn't she be like the others—eager to claim her winnings? She didn't always have to take the high road. Then again, this was Chief Keller's daughter he was talking about. And thinking about. He stepped away from her as though he'd been shoved. "It's gone too far and been too long. They've built up such a mystery around it. It would be anti-climactic now for me to just tell them."

"Tell who what?" Beast said, stomping into the kitchen. "And why is everyone still sleeping around here?"

Jon moved further away from Tori as she poured the beaten eggs into the pan. "Want some eggs?"

"Always," Beast said. "And tell who what?"

Jon looked to Tori, who kept her eyes on the eggs. Stubborn. So stubborn. "Fresh coffee, too." Jon took a sip of his, then set his cup down to start making the toast.

Beast looked from Jon to Tori, then back to Jon. He felt Beast's eyes boring into the back of his head. He was so busted. He had to change the subject.

"They had a three-alarm last night. Restaurant fire. They were on scene for over five hours," Jon said, waiting for the first batch of toast to pop. "They should be up soon. You want to relieve Simmons? He's in the control room."

"Already did," Beast said, pouring himself some coffee, then accepting a plate of eggs from Tori. "Keller, I don't know what we did to deserve you, but I hope you never leave."

Tori's eyes flitted to meet Jon's. A hopeful sadness Jon didn't know how to interpret darkened her gaze. Was she upset at the thought of being reassigned at the end of her probation period? He knew she'd grown fond of the house and the crew—most of them, anyway, probably not Davies—but was it wrong of him to want her to miss him as well?

"You're too kind, sir," Tori said with a fake southern accent and fanning herself with a potholder. "What's a girl to do?"

The sight of Beast blushing was a new one for Jon, and it caught Owens and Fitz off guard as well as they sauntered into the common room. "Beast, what's wrong with you?" Fitz asked, his voice a notch below bullhorn. "You're all flushed."

"Shut up and have some breakfast," Beast said, pointing to the eggs. "Lieutenant, where's the toast?"

"Right here," Jon said, setting a plate of toasted bread and butter on the table. "Help yourself."

Owens and Fitz didn't have to be asked twice and dug in as the rest of the crew arrived, and the previous shift's crew gathered their belongings to go off-duty. Jon stood at the counter, drinking his coffee and eating a piece of toast, watching his guys stuff their faces while laughing and teasing each other. As Ramos and Davies bickered over the last piece of toast, Jon caught Tori's eye from across the kitchen. A slow smile crept over her features as she surveyed the scene of rowdy overgrown children finishing their breakfast.

He couldn't help himself.

He sauntered to her side and lowered his head to her ear. "I don't know what we did to deserve you either," he whispered. "Roll call in fifteen," he announced louder for the crew. Then, before he could embarrass himself more, he turned and left them to finish eating.

He closed the door to his office and sank onto the bed, lowering his head to his hands. He shouldn't have said that. If he'd been a smart man, he would have kept his mouth shut. No. If he'd been a smart man, he would have locked himself in the office as soon as he'd seen her. Avoidance was the only sensible course of action. But it was close quarters at the firehouse. Avoidance might be the sensible thing, but it was also the nearly impossible thing. And on that note, he pulled out the list of things Sara wanted him to get done in whatever spare time he had.

It didn't look too bad. Most of it was phone calls and follow-ups. Things he could easily squeeze in between alarms if people left him alone. A knock sounded on the door. The outlook for a productive day didn't look good if they were starting already. Shoving the list in his pocket, he stood and called out, "What is it?"

"It's me, Lieutenant." Delaware.

Jon ran his hand through his hair, then opened the door. "What can I do for you, Delaware?"

Delaware held out a yellow trade form. "I need to switch shifts next week, so I can go to my youngest's kindergarten graduation."

Jon took the form from him and scanned it over. "Who's covering you?"

"I'm swapping shifts with Simmons."

Jon nodded. At least he got someone decent to take his place, unlike the last time he'd switched shifts and had stuck them with someone who barely knew how to tie his boots. Jon signed the form, remembering AJ and Nicki's kindergarten graduation ceremonies. He'd been off duty for both of them, and Sara had invited him to tag along while she sat in the school cafeteria listening to thirty five-year-olds sing off-key. At the time, he couldn't have imagined anything so ridiculous as a kindergarten graduation. But after he'd seen their little faces glow with pride, he couldn't imagine not being there to wrap them in a hug after they'd received their certificate of accomplishment. And they weren't even his kids.

"Here you go," Jon said, handing Delaware the form to turn into human resources. "You bringing flowers or candy?"

Delaware snorted with indignation. "This is my baby. She's getting both."

There were only a few minutes left before morning muster, so Jon walked with Delaware back to the apparatus floor. If he could get through this, he could steal a few minutes after to make a call or two, and he wouldn't feel like an idiot for trying to avoid Tori.

"So, there's a rumor going around the firehouse about you and Keller," Delaware said as they walked.

Jon's back stiffened. He didn't need rumors. Neither did Tori. People talked about her enough behind her back. "Rumors?"

"Ramos says she's figured out your side gig," Delaware said with a chuckle. "Been here six weeks, and she's dug up the answer to one of Truck 19's biggest mysteries? I don't know if I buy it. But Keller said he owes her a round of drinks on their double date tomorrow for spilling the beans."

The only thing Jon could think to compare his current state of breathless pain was when he'd been sucker-punched in the gut back in the tenth grade by the senior who didn't like Jon dating his sister. No, he was wrong. This was worse.

CHAPTER THIRTEEN

Tori tucked her hair behind her ears, then slid on her silver drop earrings, almost dropping them three times as her shaking fingers fumbled with them. Why had she thought this was a good idea? Blind dates were never good ideas. Ramos had been excited enough for them both, running his mouth about it throughout the entire shift the day before.

Tori had felt awkward about her personal life as the subject of firehouse debate for almost twenty-four hours, but it was sweet the amount of concern Delaware and Owens showed about who Ramos had set her up with. Even Beast had gotten in on the action, pushing for details regarding when and where they were meeting, then reassuring Tori he'd be only a phone call away. A bunch of big brothers. She'd rolled her eyes and teased them, but underneath her calm facade, she'd been bursting with affection for these men, with two notable exceptions: Davies, who'd sat through most of the day scowling, and Nichols, who'd been holed up in his office most of the day.

When Nichols had come out of hiding, he'd barely said more than three words to any of them. She didn't know what had snapped, but something had broken between breakfast and morning muster. Maybe he'd gotten word that something had gone wrong with his new building. She'd thought letting it leak to the guys that she knew about his side hustle would have been a mood booster since that had been what he'd wanted, but once the word got around the house, his mood had darkened, and he'd said even less.

She'd told herself all day it wasn't her concern. She'd done nothing wrong, so whatever had crawled up his bum was none of her business. He'd asked her to tell, and she'd planned to before Ramos ran his mouth. Knowing him, he'd tell Davies first, who he'd been chattier with since they'd ambushed her—something she wasn't entirely fond of. By next shift, if those two hadn't spread the word, she would. She doubted it would come to that. One thing she'd learned quickly in the department was that a group of men in close quarters for an extended time turned into a bunch of gossipy teenaged girls.

Except for Nichols—which was how the whole mystery about his personal life had begun in the first place.

She shook her head free of the web of thoughts about Jon Nichols. Tonight was date night. She had to get her head in the game.

Tori picked up Maggie and drove to the bar where she was supposed to meet Ramos and her date for the evening, Tony. Ramos had offered to pick them up, but Tori wanted her own transportation, an easy escape if she needed it. It wasn't difficult to spot Ramos in the dimly lit bar—there were only a handful of people scattered throughout the room.

"This place is a madhouse," Tori said with a smirk as she slid onto one of the many vacant barstools next to Ramos. "Thanks for making sure to save us a seat."

"Give it a chance," Ramos said. "This place gets packed after eleven."

Tori checked the time—just before eight. Eleven felt like a lifetime from then. "Marco, you remember my friend, Maggie, right?" It was a rhetorical question. Of course, he remembered. He'd spent the better part of the last year drooling every time anyone had brought up Maggie's name.

"Sure. Paramedic, right?" Ramos asked, shaking Maggie's hand as though it was the first time they'd met when, they'd probably met three of four times, each time his eyes bugging out of his head and his tongue wagging.

"Nice to see you again, Marco," Maggie said, her cheeks blushing to just the right shade of pink. She was going to have him eating out of the palm of her hand. "I hear we're the designated babysitters tonight?"

Tori crinkled her nose. This whole setup situation may have been her idea, but she was in no way prepared to witness two of her closest friends bat their eyelashes at each other while making flirty small talk. "Is my date here yet?" she asked, checking out the possible contenders. Only three looked to be in the right age range. One wore a wedding ring. One hadn't looked up from his beer since she'd walked in. And the third—well, he was a possibility. At least he didn't look like a psychopath, whatever they looked like.

"No. Tony texted and said he'd be here in five minutes," Ramos said, waving the bartender over. "What are you ladies having?"

"Just water. I'm driving," Tori said.

Ramos cast her a doubtful sideways glance.

"And I want to keep my head clear tonight. Don't want to make any decisions in an alcohol-fueled haze."

"No, that's my job tonight," Maggie said with a wink. "I'll have a glass of the Riesling."

"Coming up," Ramos said, leaning forward at the bar to place the order.

Maggie turned to Tori and mouthed, "So cute."

As Tori watched Maggie and Ramos get cozier by the second, she began to second-guess this whole plan of hers. Despite what everyone else said, maybe she wasn't ready to get back into the dating game. What was the point if she didn't have the chemistry with someone the way Maggie and Ramos clearly had with each other? A cool draft wafted into the bar as someone swung the door open. Tori braced herself before turning to face her fate, wishing she had gone for something more bracing than water.

"There they are!"

Tori froze, her eyes widening, and her mouth falling open in a silent gasp. Ramos stood facing her, wearing a similar expression. He mouthed, "I'm sorry," then waved. "What are you guys doing here?"

"We couldn't pass up an opportunity to make sure you did right by Keller with this setup," Beast said, draping a heavy arm over Tori's shoulders.

We? Stretching her neck forward, Tori strained to see around Beast's massive form. Owens, Delaware, and Fitz. It was like the start of shift roll call. All of them present and accounted for. Great. Fantastic.

"Delaware," Tori said, using her best admonishment voice, "don't you have a kid's game tonight, or something?"

Delaware smiled and puffed his chest. "Nope. It's a by-week, and the wife took the kids to the in-laws for dinner."

"Shouldn't you be with them?" Ramos asked.

"And miss this? No way," Delaware said, taking the empty seat next to Tori, which she had previously assumed would be for Tony, the poor guy, whenever he showed up. "It's a special night."

"Not that special," Tori said, relieving herself of Beast's heavy arm.

"Are you kidding? It's not every day we convince the lieutenant to come out and play," Fitz said, motioning for a round of beers for them all.

All the heat drained from Tori's face and hands. Blind dates were miserable enough—like getting a root canal during a job interview. Blind dates with her crew there to witness it, worse. Blind dates with her crew and *Jon Nichols* standing next to her the whole time? Her head could quite possibly implode in a matter of minutes. That would be better than having to endure a date that wasn't with Jon Nichols—*with* Jon Nichols.

"Ramos, Mags, can I speak to you a moment, please?" Tori said loud enough for only them to hear. "Excuse me, guys. Time to go powder something."

Ramos and Maggie followed a step behind her as she marched through the nearly empty bar toward the bathrooms. There weren't even enough people in the place to get lost in. Her hands began to tingle, and a trickle of sweat formed on the back of her neck.

"Are you kidding me with this?" Tori hissed as she whipped around to face them. "They're all here. All of them! And Nichols is on his way. The only thing that would make this worse is if Davies strolled in—oh, God—you didn't tell Davies about tonight, did you, Ramos?"

Ramos shrugged. "He was in the room when we were all talking about it. But, listen, I didn't invite these guys. I didn't know they would show up here."

Tori held her head in her hands. "What am I going to do? I can't go through with this. Not with them all hanging over us."

"Safety in numbers, you said, right?" Maggie said. Why was she on their side? Why wasn't she punching Ramos in the arm yet?

Tori groaned. "Is it too late to cancel?"

"On Tony?"

Tori nodded. If they pretended Tony stood her up, they could salvage the night with an all-crew plus Mags night on the town.

Ramos motioned to the door. "Yeah, I think it is."

Tori's eyes followed Ramos's head tilt and watched in silent horror as Lieutenant Nichols walked in, followed by another man dressed as though he were going on a first date.

"Please tell me that's not—"

"Yep, that's Tony."

If Tori had ever wondered what it felt like to be pulled under by quicksand, she didn't need to wonder anymore. Everything and everyone moved in slow motion. From her shadowed corner, she watched as all the heads from Truck 19 turned in Jon's direction. Delaware rose from his seat and clapped Jon on the back, while Fitz raised his hand to order another drink. Beast threw his head back and roared with laughter. And through it all, poor Tony stood there like a lost puppy.

Tori rubbed her temples. "You should go talk to him, Ramos. He looks worried."

Ramos studied her for a moment. "What's going on? I know you don't mind the guys giving you a hard time." He followed her gaze, which was stuck on Jon settling into her seat at the bar. Ramos shook his head and looked at Maggie for help. "No. No. Tell me it's nothing. Tell me Davies was wrong."

"Davies was wrong," Tori mumbled.

"Was he?"

"Mostly." Tori covered her face with her hands and let out a soft moan. "Nothing's going on." Ramos arched an eyebrow and waited for her to continue. But she didn't.

"The other day at his building? Did I walk in on something?" Ramos asked.

Tori shook her head. "Just talking." Ramos crossed his arms and said nothing. "But I forgot my phone inside, and when I went back to get it, we ended up grabbing something to eat. That's all. I mean, we grab dinner all the time, right?"

"Right," Ramos said. "But you don't get all stressed out and weird after *we* eat together."

Tori glanced at the crew again, all laughing and joking, and generally having a good time. She would never want to mess any of that up. "I may have the teeniest of crushes on the lieutenant," she whispered through her hands.

"I knew it," Maggie said with a victorious smirk. "It's about time you admitted it."

"But it's never going to be more than that," Tori added quickly. "And I'll get over it soon. I just haven't dated in a while, that's all."

"That explains your sudden willingness to meet Tony," Ramos said.

Tori lifted a shoulder. "See? At least I'm willing to give it a shot." She put her hands on his shoulders and shook him slightly to make sure she had his attention. "Please don't say anything. I swear nothing will happen. I'll be normal. I'll be better than normal. You'll see."

Ramos let out a heavy sigh and lowered his head to his chest. "Fine," he said, lifting his head again and squaring his shoulders as though Tori had asked him to heft a heavy load. "But you'd better get over it fast."

"I will. I promise."

She would definitely give it her best effort. That was better than nothing. Better than letting useless feelings fester into an unhealthy attachment at the very least. The first step to getting over it was to put herself out there and open herself to new possibilities. And that night's possibility was Ramos's friend, Tony, who still looked as confused as a penguin in the desert.

"Should we get this over with?" Maggie asked, motioning to their empty seats at the bar. "I'll meet you over there."

Tori nodded and followed Ramos's lead, making her way across the bar to greet her date for the evening.

"Tony, this is Tori," Ramos said, making the introductions. "Tori, Tony."

Tori bit the inside of her cheek. It sounded even worse when someone else said it.

Tony's eyes roamed the length of her in a curious but non-threatening way. In fact, everything about Tony was non-threatening. Only an inch taller than her, and barely any wider, Tony was as mild and unassuming as they came. His confusion gave way to a peaceful expression, and even his handshake, though warm, was nothing more than a languid rise and fall of their hands.

"It's a pleasure to meet you," Tony said, the corner of his eyes creasing as he smiled. "Marco has told me a lot about you."

Tori returned his smile. "It's nice to meet you, too, Tony. Should we get our seats? I have to apologize. It looks like we have more company than we originally thought."

Tony's smile wobbled like off-balance scales as he took in the sight of the five not-so-subtle men gathered at the bar, giving him the once over.

They weren't even trying to hide the fact they were talking about him. It did look like they were having fun, though. All except Jon, who leaned stiffly against the bar, his face a stern mask like he was about to discipline someone for going against orders. Had Tori been alone, she would have wasted no time in joining them, and maybe seeing if she could loosen up the lieutenant a bit. See if she could find the Jon Nichols from dinner the other night. But she was on a date, and that meant having to consider Tony's feelings. Ramos, the traitor, had already retreated to reclaim his place at Maggie's side, leaving her to fend for herself.

"It's okay. I don't mind," Tony said. To his credit, he kept the smile on his face, though the apprehension in his eyes gave him away. But they'd just met, so what did she know?

"Great. Come on," Tori said, guiding Tony to the bar, past Owens and Fitz, stopping when Beast blocked her path.

"Aren't you going to introduce us, Keller?" Beast asked, somehow raising himself another inch or two. Not that he needed to. He already towered over poor Tony.

"Tony, this is Beast. He's on the truck with Ramos and me. They all are," Tori said. Then pointing to each one, she finished the introductions. "Delaware. Fitz. Owens." She swallowed the lump stuck in her throat. "Lieutenant Nichols."

They all took turns shaking his hand, Jon going last. "Tony," Jon said. "You're a friend of Ramos's?"

Tony nodded. "Yeah, from college. We lived in the same dorm."

"And what is it you do now?" Delaware asked.

Tori's breath hitched in her chest, hearing her father's voice in his question. She felt a little bad for the guy, but not enough to step in. It was a good question, one she would also like to know the answer to, and it saved her from having to ask it herself. Not that she wouldn't have gotten around to it, but at the moment, she found it challenging to put together a decent sentence while Nichols sized up her date with that intensity she always found so appealing.

"I'm an accountant at Pricewaterhouse."

Impressive. And just the sort of job she imagined for someone as docile as Tony seemed to be.

"Is there a lot of travel involved?" Fitz asked, handing Tony a beer.

Tony took a swig before answering. "Some. I go to London about every six weeks. New York. Madrid once. Australia last year."

"Wow," Tori said. Maybe Tony wasn't as vanilla as she'd previously thought. "What's been your favorite trip so far?"

"New York," Tony said. Tori was surprised he didn't pick something a little more exotic. "I didn't have to worry about exchange rates or anything."

Never mind. Tony was as exciting as a piece of toast. And not cinnamon toast. Rye toast. Without butter.

Tori made the mistake of catching Jon's eye as Tony continued listing the ways traveling inside the country was superior to seeing the rest of the world. She easily recognized the amusement written in his eyes, and the mockery aching to get out. If they'd been at the firehouse, there would have been no holding back, and judging by the look on the rest of the guys' faces, Tori was in for a healthy dose of torment on their next shift.

"So, you like the accounting gig, then?" Jon asked.

"It could be exciting," Tony said, and Tori knew he meant it. "We're dealing with millions of dollars at a time. You have no idea what an adrenaline rush that is."

Tori turned her back to Tony and braced herself on the bar before he could catch her laughing. She had no doubt he enjoyed his job, as everyone should, but did he really tell a bunch of firefighters about an adrenaline rush at work?

"You okay there, Keller?" Jon whispered in her ear. His breath on her skin sending a trail of shivers down her spine.

Covering her laughter with a cough, she leaned closer to Jon. "Yep. All good, Lieutenant."

"Good to hear. This should be a fun night."

Jon's interpretation of fun was nowhere close to Tony's, and what worried Tori was knowing that her definition aligned more with Jon's. Still, she vowed to give Tony a chance. He deserved that much. Ramos thought they'd be a good fit, and she had to trust him.

"So, Tori, how much do firefighters make, anyway?" Tony asked.

Tori hailed the bartender. "Moscow mule, please." She could always take a cab home. It was going to be an interesting night, at the very least, and in the morning, she was going to have a long talk with Ramos.

CHAPTER FOURTEEN

Jon couldn't believe he'd wasted the last two days being envious of this guy. What had Ramos been thinking? This Tony was a monstrously wrong fit for Tori, not that any guy would be a good one, but this bland piece of stale bread was an absolute joke. Jon should thank Ramos. As long as Tony was the type of guy he continued to set her up with, Jon could coast through the remainder of her probation hearing about her dating life without any further anxiety attacks.

"What do you think?" Delaware asked, tilting his head in Tori's direction where she'd taken a seat further down the bar, presumably so she could continue her date without the five of them hanging over her.

"It ends tonight," Beast said. "No way there's a second date."

Tori's laughter spilled over and floated down the bar until it reached Jon, lapping at his feet like the lake on a summer day. He wished he could dive in and swim in her presence. But he was stuck on shore, his feet firmly planted in the sand.

"I don't know," Fitz said. "She seems to be having a good time. Hey, Ramos, Jennis, get over here."

Ramos and Jennis were supposed to be acting as Tori's wing-people, but they'd abandoned her to tend to their own date. Maggie slid into the seat next to Jon at the bar, nudging him with her elbow.

"How's it going over here, Lieutenant?" Maggie asked, casting one brief but sharp look in Tori's direction. "Are you enjoying yourself?"

"What were you thinking, setting up Keller with this guy?" Delaware asked, dropping his fisted hand on the bar with a thud for emphasis.

"I was thinking that he's a nice guy," Ramos said. "A nice guy who doesn't know anything about the fire department, and she can be herself with."

"What does that mean?" Fitz asked.

Ramos sighed. "It means, all day every day, she has to be Chief Keller's daughter. She was raised by a firefighter, grew up in a firefighter neighborhood, went to school with firefighter kids, and now she is one. After what happened with the chief, it's only gotten worse—the talk and stuff. I thought she could use a break from that. Meet a nice guy. Have some fun."

Jon's chest tightened. He hadn't thought about it like that before— that she would need a break from her life. Maybe Ramos was right. Maybe Tori needed a break from being Chief Keller's daughter. But this guy?

"People talk behind her back, you know?" Ramos continued. "About how the chief must have pulled strings for her. She denies it, but that doesn't stop the talk. Just a bunch of jerks like Davies who can't handle the idea of a woman being better than them at something. She has to prove herself constantly. But with a guy like Tony—"

"Yeah, yeah, we get it," Beast said, raising his hand to order another round. "What do you think, Lieutenant? Did Chief Keller pull any strings?"

Jon shrugged. "Come on. You know Keller. She would have gotten into the academy on her own. She certainly works harder than most of you," he said with a smirk. "But it doesn't matter, anyway. She's here now, and she pulls her weight. Strings or not, she makes one fine firefighter."

He tried not to look at either Ramos or Jennis while he spoke. Ramos's gaze drilled into him, and Jennis leaned closer with every word. While the rest of the crew remained oblivious to his growing feelings for Keller, these two had dialed into them as easy as finding a station on the radio.

"Hey, let me in," Tori appeared outside their little circle, squeezing herself between Delaware and Beast until she was nestled safely in the middle of their huddle. "What's going on over here?"

"Where's Tony?" Ramos asked, glancing at their vacated seats.

Tori waved her hand. "Bathroom."

"Having a good time?" Beast asked. His tone sounded more concerned than teasing, and Jon wasn't the only one who noticed.

Tori furrowed her brow. "What's going on? Why are you being weird?"

The evening wasn't going to end well if someone didn't steer this conversation in a new direction. As much as Jon didn't want to hear how great Tori's date was going, his desire for her discovering they'd been talking about her was even less.

"I think some people may have reached their limit," Jon said, punching Beast in his gigantic shoulder. "Maybe it's time you switched to water for a bit, buddy."

Thankfully, Beast caught on without any more prompting and backed away. Tori watched him leave, checked to see if her date had returned—he hadn't—then settled herself on the barstool next to Jon. The one Maggie had suddenly vacated without Jon noticing. Tori's eyes were shining, the kind of brightness that came with a buzz, which might explain how she found the accountant so amusing. Jon would need a couple of drinks in him to be entertained by Tony, as well.

"How'd they convince you to come out?" Tori asked, moving closer. "Rumor has it: you're too busy running an escort service on your nights off to hang with the guys."

Jon lifted an eyebrow. She was baiting him, trying to get him to spill his secret before she did, giving him one last out. "Last minute client cancellation."

She smirked; one side of her red lips pulled into a wicked grin. "Is that right?" she asked, glancing over her shoulder to make sure she had her audience. "And what kind of clients are these exactly?"

Jon leaned an elbow on the bar and bent his head closer to hers. He liked this playful side of her, maybe a little too much, but he was curious to see how far she would go. "You would know."

Fitz, who sat listening to the whole exchange, blew up in laughter. "Owens, Delaware, did you hear this?"

Tori scanned their audience with no trace of embarrassment; instead, their presence emboldened her. "What are you implying? That I require the service you provide?"

"Not in the least. You're not my usual type of client, anyway." He could play this game of hers, too. "You're a little old, honestly."

Both Beast and Fitz roared with laughter. Jon knew that last line would get them going. They were laying it on thick, and these guys were eating it up.

"What exactly are we talking about here?" Owens asked, looking from Jon to Tori.

"Keller was just asking how I was available to be out and about this fine evening," Jon said, holding Tori's playful gaze. She was daring him to keep talking and to tell them everything. It would be so easy, too. They were all there, waiting to be filled in on the joke. But he wasn't ready to give in yet. Not with Tori sitting next to him, staring into him the way she was. He could sit there all night with her looking at him like that. He had nowhere better to be.

"I think it's a fair question," Delaware said. "It didn't take much to convince you to quit your hermit ways for the evening."

Tori tilted her head to the side, waiting for his answer. He'd been sitting at home reviewing the catering menus Sara had given him to choose from for the party when Delaware had texted him that they were all going out—to spy on Tori's date. That was all it took for him to toss out his plans of staying in and working again.

"Is that right?" Tori asked, without looking away from Jon. His pulse quickened. They were dancing dangerously close to the truth, and not about his therapy practice.

"Tori," Jennis said over her shoulder.

"What could possibly entice you to slum it with the crew? Since I joined Truck 19, I can remember at least three times the we all got together, and you've declined. Why now?" Tori pressed.

"Keller," Ramos said, more forcefully. Jon shot him a warning glance and returned to the more intriguing conversation.

"Maybe it was time," Jon said, swallowing down the words that were getting harder to hold back by the minute—*I came for you.*

"Timing is a little suspect."

"Tori," Jennis said again, shaking her shoulder to get her attention.

"How is it suspect?" Jon asked, pleased when Tori showed no signs of paying either Ramos or Jennis any mind.

Tori shrugged. "Oh, I don't know. You hear I can divulge your deep, dark secret, and all of a sudden, you find time to honor us with your presence? I think, maybe, you want to stop me."

"Tori!" Ramos shouted, stepping between them, forcing Tori to look at him and not Jon.

Jon tightened his fist in his lap. Had Ramos been anyone else, he wouldn't have remained in his seat as calmly as he was struggling to at the moment.

"What is it?" Tori asked, blinking as though waking from a daze.

"Tony left," Jennis said, pointing to the door.

Tori swiveled in her seat, but it was too late. He was already gone. "Why did he do that?" she asked, though her expression didn't match how upset she tried to sound.

"I don't know," Ramos said, shooting a glare at Jon. "Maybe because he thought you would rather be somewhere else."

Tori's eyes widened, and her cheeks colored as her gaze roamed over the faces of the men standing around her, settling at last on Jon. He couldn't look her in the eye. Had he ruined it for her? Had he, they, taken away the thing she needed the most? A relationship with someone not connected to the fire department? Her lifeline out of the shadows? They'd sabotaged her, him more than anyone with his games, and need to be close to her. He looked away.

"I messed it up, didn't I?" she asked Ramos, who nodded his response.

It all went downhill from there. Maggie and Ramos swept Tori away and brought her home, at Tori's request, leaving Jon stranded at the bar with the guys. All Jon could think about was how long he would have to stay before he could duck out as well. About an hour later, people flowed through the door, taking up all the space Jon had been enjoying in the nearly empty bar. And while the new crowd bothered him as they clamored over him to get their drinks, they provided the perfect cover for him to slip out before any of the guys noticed.

The next morning, Jon stood in the middle of the gymnasium-sized room where the obstacle course waited to be constructed. The new floors had been installed, including tumbling mats in the space to prevent any trips or falls from doing any more damage to his clients. If only life came equipped with built-in tumbling mats to break the inevitable falls.

Jon's brother-in-law, Mitch, was due to arrive soon to help Jon install the first of the fifteen stations on the course. Jon wanted to use these last few minutes to review the course plan one last time to ensure he'd set everything in the proper place, but he couldn't get his mind to focus on the paper in his hands.

"Uncle Jon!" AJ yelled, running through the empty building, his shouts echoing off the high walls.

Jon turned around just in time to catch the boy as he launched himself into Jon's arms. "Whoa, buddy. What are you doing here? Are you here to help your dad and me?"

"Can I?" AJ asked, jumping to the ground. "Mom's with Nicki. This floor is cool." AJ hopped on his toes, testing the new padding.

"You don't mind, do you?" Mitch said, following his son into the course area. "Sara wanted me to tell you the painters will be finishing a few things up today, too."

"No, I don't mind," Jon said, his heart picking up speed as he wondered if Tori would be one of those painters, or had Ramos let her go. But he couldn't worry about that now. He had a wall climbing unit to build. "AJ, there's a box of footholds in the front. You wanna grab that for me?"

AJ hopped out of the room as Mitch, Jon's assumed big brother, turned to him. "So, Sara tells me you know the painter?"

"A candidate and his father," Jon said, nodding.

"Thought there was a woman, too." Mitch was fishing.

Jon sucked in a breath. Did Sara have to tell him everything? "Another candidate picking up some extra cash."

"That's all?"

Unfortunately. "That's all."

Mitch didn't believe him. Jon knew by the way he lowered his head and peered at him under hooded eyes. He'd given Jon that look since he'd been a teenager caught sneaking out of his sister's house. Mitch hadn't squealed on him then, and he wouldn't now.

"Let's get to work, then." Mitch clapped him on the back and took the plans from him. "We should probably start with the stations in the back and work our way forward."

Jon was a handy guy. He could put together a piece of prefabricated furniture like nobody's business. Fix a leaky faucet? No problem. Change his car's oil? On it. But even so, Jon was grateful to have a construction expert like Mitch on hand as they labored through the next few hours, putting together the first two obstacle stations. It would have taken twice as long if Jon had to stop and explain what to do, or why certain things had to be at certain angles.

He was also grateful to have AJ bouncing around, keeping his mind from wandering where it shouldn't. He'd finally fallen into a good rhythm when Jon felt the air shift around him, like there was a storm on the horizon, a moment before AJ's laughter rolled through the building. She was there. It had to be her.

"Painters must be here," Mitch said without looking up from his drill. "I can finish this if you need to check on them."

Jon cast Mitch a sideways glance. Mitch thought he was so smooth, but a master of deception he was not. This wasn't the first time Jon was grateful Mitch hadn't tried his hand at being a spy. This also wasn't the first time he and Sara had tried to push a relationship on him. And with the grand opening party coming up, and Sara's determination for him to bring a date, she must have roped Mitch in as her accomplice. If Jon didn't love her as much as he did, he would have told her to butt out a long time ago.

Leaving Mitch to grapple with the climbing wall footholds by himself, Jon did as was asked and checked on his nephew. Voices flowed in from the reception area, light and carefree, and he stopped short of the doorway, careful not to be seen. He didn't want to interrupt them, but more than that, he didn't want Tori to know he enjoyed listening in on her conversation with his nephew.

"No way. Iron Man is way cooler than Captain America," Tori said.

There was some rustling, then AJ said, "But Cap is like their leader."

"Bu-ut, Iron Man has all the cool toys."

AJ giggled, warming Jon's heart. In the few years he'd been with Jackie, she'd never been able to make AJ laugh like that. Neither of the kids ever really warmed up to her, something that had always irked Jon. But two minutes after meeting, and AJ was laughing at Tori's jokes like they were old friends.

Suddenly, listening wasn't good enough anymore. He had to get a peek, just see her for a second. Leaning forward, he peered around the doorway and spied both of them on the new floor, spreading out a large tarp.

"Uncle Jon?" AJ asked, startling Jon from his hiding spot.

Busted. "Hey, buddy. Your dad asked me to check on you. Everything okay?" Jon asked, stepping into the reception area. Tori's eyes flickered in his direction before returning to the tarp. "Keller. Good to see you again."

She smiled and bit the corner of her lip but didn't look up. "You too, Lieutenant."

"I'm fine," AJ said with a clenched jaw. Apparently, the little man felt he was too big to be checked on. Then an idea hit him, and he brightened. Kids. It was just that easy to flip a switch from one thing to another. "Can I show Tori the obstacle course we're making?"

"If it's okay with Tori," Jon said, watching her pretend to straighten the drop cloth.

"I guess I have a minute before my boss gets here," Tori said, finally lifting her gaze to meet his.

AJ jumped from the floor and ran past Jon into the gymnasium. Jon held Tori's gaze until the padded floor muffled the sound of AJ's footsteps. "Come on, Tori," he yelled behind him.

"We should finish today," Tori said, motioning to the empty room with stiff arms. "Sara was waiting for some stencils she ordered. They came in yesterday, Ramos said."

"Well," Jon said, "since it's your last day, would you like an official tour?"

She smiled and relaxed her shoulders. "I've already seen it, remember?"

"But not with my commentary."

"Does it make a difference?"

Jon nodded with exaggerated head bobs. "Like night and day. Black and white. Truck and engine."

Tori tilted her head back as a laugh trickled from her lips. "Since you put it that way . . ."

CHAPTER FIFTEEN

Yes, Tori knew when Ramos had called to tell they would be finishing the waiting area, there was a good chance she would see Jon. And, yes, she also knew she was a hired professional there to do a job. It shouldn't matter that she'd almost made a fool of herself the night before. Or that if Ramos and Maggie hadn't dragged her out of there when they had, she would have crossed that line she'd promised to stay behind. She blamed the Moscow mules. And Tony. Had Tony been the tiniest bit more interesting—like an ant's size, a baby ant even—she wouldn't have been tempted to spend her time with the crew ignoring him.

"This building is huge," Tori said as Jon walked her through the office space. "All this just for you?"

"Sara is talking to potential renters. Other therapists who need office space," Jon said.

Tori noticed how his shoulders straightened, and he stood taller as he showed her his dream. He was proud of himself, as he should have been. His new practice was amazing. And though she'd already seen every room, he'd been right. It was different seeing it through his eyes.

"How late did you and the guys stay out last night?" Tori asked as he closed an exam room door behind him.

"I'm not sure about the other guys, but I was only out about another hour."

Tori's heart skittered in her chest. On the way home the night before, Ramos had mentioned something about Nichols only showing up to ruin her date, but she hadn't believed it, though she'd wanted to.

"I'm glad you came out at all," Tori said, testing the waters. "Why don't you come out more? With the group, I mean."

Jon shrugged and shoved his hands in his pockets. "It's nothing personal. The guys are great. It's just . . . I guess I've been busy building a client base, saving up for this place, now everything that goes into setting up a new practice. There's not enough time for everything, so something had to go."

"A personal life?" She hadn't meant it to sound as critical as it had. "I'm sorry. I didn't mean it like that," she said when she saw him shift uncomfortably.

"It's okay," he said. "Your assessment just brought back some memories I've been trying to forget."

Don't ask. Don't ask. Not her business. "Memories of what?" Never mind.

He took a deep breath, then let it out with a rush of words. "I was engaged once, but she left and took a job in California. She said I didn't have enough time for a relationship. She wanted me to quit the fire department."

Tori gasped. "What? You can't quit the fire department. That's crazy."

"I thought so, too. So, I didn't," he said. "She quit me, instead."

"What a—"

"Tori, are you coming?" AJ yelled from the reception area.

"Coming," Tori yelled back. She searched Jon's eyes while they stood in the dim hall, neither one of them had thought to turn on the lights, and waited. She didn't know what she expected, just *something*. A smile. A touch on the arm. Anything that would lead her to believe that the spark she'd felt the night before, the one Ramos kept warning her about, was real and felt by him, too.

"Sorry your date ran out on you last night," he said, stepping closer.

"It wouldn't have worked with him anyway," she whispered into the space between them.

"Why not?"

Because she had feelings for someone else. Because he wasn't Jon. "I could never date an accountant."

"Tori, where are you?" AJ shouted.

Tori looked toward the reception area expecting to see AJ bounding toward them. "I should go before he starts bouncing off your newly painted walls."

Jon nodded, his lips parted as though he was going to either say something or kiss her. When he did neither, she turned and walked away.

"Tori," he said from behind her. She paused but didn't turn around. She couldn't. She was afraid he would see things written on her face that weren't supposed to be there. "I'm glad I came out last night, too."

Tori sat on her bunk, sipping her Davies-made coffee. It was disgusting. And if she weren't trying to hide from Lieutenant Nichols, she would have made a new pot herself. But dragging herself out to the kitchen—

where he was—wasn't an option. She could have barely lifted her head during roll call, not able to look any of them in the eye, especially Ramos.

Ramos knew. He'd known before she had. He'd warned her, but she'd been in denial.

She wasn't in denial now. After the previous two days, there was only one conclusion: she was falling for Jon Nichols. Or maybe she had fallen already, and she was just coming to realize it. Either way, it wasn't the teeniest of crushes like she'd said, and hiding it was going to be more of a problem than denying it had been. The safest course of action was to avoid Jon, seeing him only when she needed to, preferably with ninety pounds of Kevlar and two protective helmets between them.

"Keller," Ramos said, poking his head in the doorway. "You alive in there?"

"Hey, Ramos, what's up?" She could pretend to be sick. If she told them she didn't feel well, maybe they would leave her alone and let her enjoy her quarantine. It was a tricky line to balance, though, because if she played it too well, Nichols could end up sending her to the department doctor and putting her on sick leave.

"Everything okay? You seem more antisocial than usual."

Tori appreciated his attempt at drawing her out with humor. Normally, she would have taken the bait, but she wasn't in the mood to be coaxed out of hiding just yet. "My head is pounding," she said, rubbing her temple for show. "I wanted to give it a rest for a bit while I wait for the meds to kick in."

"You need anything else?" Ramos asked, concern lacing his tone, making Tori feel guiltier for lying to him twice now. Once, when she'd said she would get over her crush on Jon, and again when she'd said she had a headache. At the rate she was going, she'd rack up an impressive array of lies by lunch.

"No, thanks," she said, offering him a weak smile. "I'll be out in a minute."

Ramos nodded but didn't leave her doorway.

"Is there something else?" Tori asked. She should have known there was more to his wanting to check on her.

Ramos glanced over his shoulder toward the common room. "The guys are all talking . . ."

Her stomach sank. "Yeah, and?"

"They want to know if you're still going to tell them about Nichols."

Tori sighed. In all the commotion with her date, she'd forgotten she'd left without spilling the beans. She'd been trying to get Jon to admit it, but he wouldn't cooperate, instead stringing her flirty banter further than she'd intended. That wasn't entirely true. She had intended to flirt, thanks again Moscow Mule, but she hadn't expected him to flirt back. Lieutenant Strictly Business Nichols was supposed to take the hardline, not aim his magnetic smile at her, drawing her closer until she felt like she floated out of her seat.

"I kind of forgot that part," Tori said.

Jon wanted her to tell, and they were all there—seemed as good a time as any. She might as well get it over with, especially after her little display on Friday night. Maybe this would give them all something to focus on other than her interaction with their boss. At least she could be grateful Davies hadn't been there to witness it.

"Where's Nichols?" Tori asked. She didn't think she could go through with it if he were in the room.

"Holed up in his office," Ramos said, knowingly. "He's avoiding us, too."

"I'm not *avoiding*. I'm . . .resting. Come on. Let's go break the news that our lieutenant is not a drug-dealing pimp."

"Fitz will be disappointed."

"He'll get over it," Tori said. She glanced at Ramos from the corner of her eye. They hadn't spoken much the day before, not with his dad in the same room, and he wouldn't yell at her at the firehouse with everyone twenty feet away. "Speaking of getting over things. . ."

"Tony's fine," Ramos said as they rounded the corner into the common room. "He said he knew there wasn't any spark when you ordered your third drink without finishing your second."

Tori cringed. "I hope I didn't hurt his feelings. But, seriously, Ramos—that guy? I mean, he rambled on for a full twenty minutes about the changes in corporate tax law. What is it about me that makes you think I would find that interesting date conversation?"

Ramos chuckled and hung his head. "You're right. Maybe he wasn't the best idea. I was trying to pick someone not like, well, not like us."

"What's wrong with us, candidate?" Beast bellowed, drawing everyone's attention.

"Nothing's wrong with us," Ramos said. "But Keller doesn't want to date us."

"Speak for yourself," Delaware said, flexing his arms. Beast and Owens erupted into fits of laughter. "But I'm taken, so she's out of luck."

"That's alright, Delaware. I think I'm going to stay out of the blind date game for a while," Tori laughed.

The crew groaned.

"Ah, come on, Keller," Owens said. "What are the rest of us supposed to do for fun?"

"I don't know—spend time with your families. Go on dates of your own."

"Nope. Uh-uh," Delaware said. "I told you, I'm taken."

"Then, take your wife out, but you can stay out of my dates from now on." Her tone was stern, but she couldn't help smiling at their antics. These guys had accepted her, and she didn't want to have to leave them in a few short months when her training was over. But she also didn't see a way she could stay on Truck 19 with the way her heart swelled every time Jon walked in the room.

"Just because you didn't have any fun, doesn't mean you should ruin it for the rest of us," Beast said with a fake pout that looked comical on such a large man.

"I'm so sorry to disappoint you all," Tori said, clutching her hands over her heart. "How can I make it up to you?"

"What are you making up for?" Lieutenant Nichols appeared behind Tori and Ramos, his brow furrowed.

Tori froze under his gaze, her heart squeezing tight, sending a rush of warmth straight to her face. His eyes drilled into her, as though trying to see through to the other side. She opened her mouth to answer, but she couldn't take a big enough breath to push words out, instead emitting a soft squeak. Jon arched an eyebrow in response, clearly enjoying her discomfort.

"Keller's giving up on dating," Delaware said for her. "Seems she's too heartbroken to continue."

"Heartbroken? Over the accountant?" Jon smirked. "I thought you could never date an accountant."

"I'm not heartbroken," Tori said, darting her gaze away from Jon's. "But that's not the point."

The lights flashed, and the alarm sounded. "Truck 19. Apartment building fire. Corner of Harrison and Oakley. Truck 19. Apartment building fire. Corner of Harrison and Oakley," dispatch announced.

Everyone jumped to their feet, abandoning their coffees and breakfast. "Get to work!" Jon shouted, heading for the apparatus floor.

Owens flipped on the lights and blasted the horn three times before pulling out of the house. Everyone else settled into their seats and adjusted their gear, hitting the pause button on all the jokes about her pathetic love life.

It never failed to amaze Tori how quickly they made the change. One second, they were full of laughs and good-natured ribbing. The next, it all halted. Conversations and arguments were placed on hold to be taken up later in the day, or the next shift. Nothing took precedence over those few sentences blaring from the speakers.

Lieutenant Nichols had been conversing with dispatch on the ride to the three-story apartment building. It looked to Tori that there were nine units—three on each floor. She hoped because it was mid-morning, they'd be lucky again, and most, if not all, of the residents would be out for the day. When Owens stopped the truck, they all jumped out, waiting for Nichols's command.

"Dispatch says there's potentially someone on the second floor and the third. Everyone else is accounted for," Nichols said.

"By who?" Beast asked, pulling his mask over his face.

"Building manager called in the fire, then contacted the residents," Nichols said, also adjusting his helmet and mask. "There's an elderly woman on the second floor. Beast and Ramos, she's yours. Up on three, a stay-at-home mom and two littles."

Tori's stomach tightened at the thought of two kids trapped on the third floor. *Kellers don't leave anyone behind.*

"Fitz and Keller, with me on three," Nichols said, heading toward the front door. "Davies and Delaware, do a sweep. Make sure no one else is in there."

Tori adjusted the weight of her air tank on her back, fixed her face mask, and fell in line behind Fitz and Nichols. They huffed up the stairs, taking two at a time. The fire had originated in the first floor's southeast corner but had already spread to lick the outer wall of both the second and third floors. Tori kept her eyes fixed on Fitz's back as they climbed higher, hoping she'd be able to hear the shouts for help over the sound of her blood pumping in her ears. Smoke flowed through the air vents, filling the hallways and stairwells.

The communication units attached to their shoulders beeped once before Owens's voice met their ears. "Engine's here. Flames all up the south end of the building, creeping center."

"Got it," Nichols said, then stopped, stooping low to keep below the smoke line as they reached the third floor. "Building manager said the central unit is where we'll find them. Fitz, check the other two. Keller, you're with me."

"On it," Fitz said, then disappeared down the hall to check the farthest apartment first.

Crouched low to the ground, Tori followed Nichols to the apartment in the middle of the floor. He pounded on the door. "Fire department," he yelled. They paused, listening for a reply.

Tori strained, reaching for a sound, any sign of life behind that door, her Halligan poised and ready to bust the door in if she needed to. When no reply came, Jon raised his hand to pound again, but Tori stopped him. One more second confirmed what she'd thought she'd heard coming from deep within the apartment. A baby crying.

"They're in there," she said, raising her iron bar.

"We're coming in," Jon shouted, then gave her the nod.

One swift motion and Tori busted the lock on the door, sending splinters flying as the door swung open. Smoke had begun pouring into the unit from the outdated, central venting system in the building. Tori's heart squeezed again. Somewhere in there were two babies, scared and possibly sick from the smoke. They had seconds to find them.

"Fire department," Tori shouted into the clouds of ash. "Yell out." She paused and listened. The sounds of a child crying reached her louder without the door between them. "Back room," she said, pointing in the direction of the cries.

Jon nodded. "You lead."

Owens's voice came over the radio again. "Beast and Ramos are out with vic one."

"Delaware and Davies?" Jon asked from behind Tori.

"On their way to you."

"Copy that," Nichols said. "Where are they, Keller?"

Tori checked under tables and behind sofas as they made their way to the back. "Where are you?" she called. As Tori approached a partially closed door in the back corner of the apartment, one little hand shot out from behind it and waved. "There!"

Tori's air tank banged against her back as she hurried through the door, one thought racing through her head: get the kids out. Crouching low to the ground, she peered around the door, finding a young girl cowering in the corner, cradling her baby sister in her lap.

"Hi, honey, my name is Tori, and you're going to come with me, okay?" Tori said, invoking her calming schoolteacher voice. "What's your name?"

"Melissa," the girl said. "This is Katie."

Jon knelt on the floor beside Tori. "Where's your mom, Melissa?"

The girl, who'd been holding it together surprisingly well until then, burst into tears. "I don't know. She said she was getting the laundry and to wait here with Katie."

Tori glanced at Jon, who immediately was on the radio. "Got the kids. Mom went to the laundry room. Anyone got eyes on mom?"

"Is the laundry in the basement?" Tori asked, relieving Melissa of her baby sister. Melissa nodded. "Basement, Lieutenant."

"Copy that," he said, then clicked the radio on again. "Beast, Ramos, did you sweep the basement?"

"Affirmative, Lieutenant," Beast replied. "All clear."

Tori took Melissa's hand and pulled the girl from the floor. "Come on, sweetie. The firemen will find your mom. We're going to take you outside." Melissa froze, her feet rooted to the floor, terror making her eyes three times wider than normal. Her face paled, and her little lip trembled. Katie, who watched everything with curious eyes, studied Tori without making a noise. Thank goodness she was young enough to be oblivious to the danger. Tori handed Katie to Jon. "We're right behind you."

Jon gave Tori one last look, then took the baby, unlatched his coat, and tucked Katie inside. "*Right* behind."

Tori opened her coat as Jon had, then swept Melissa up in her arms. "How old are you?"

"Four."

"Big girl," Tori said, holding the girl on her hip and wrapping her coat around her. "Can you put your arms around my neck and your head down? There's a lot of smoke out there."

Melissa did as Tori asked, wrapping both her arms and legs around her. Tori made her way back through the apartment and out into the smoke-filled hall. Jon and Katie were nowhere in sight. Tori's legs quivered beneath her as she trudged toward the stairwell. The urge to run overwhelmed her, but she had to be smart about it, not just for her sake, but for little Melissa clinging to her like a frightened spider monkey.

"Keller, location," Nichols commanded over the radio.

"Approaching third-floor stairs. You?"

"Second-floor landing. Smoke thicker here. Stick to the outer wall."

"Affirmative, Lieutenant." Tori pressed her left shoulder to the wall and descended the stairs one at a time while her heart beat wildly in her chest. As she hit the second-floor landing and saw Jon and Katie already gone, a sudden panic gripped Tori when she saw the smoke had not only grown thicker like Jon had said but seemed more threatening. None of their drills had had smoke like this. Bits of ash floated in the air and muffled any other noises. It was as though they were cut off from the world, and if Tori weren't careful, she'd get turned around and head toward the fire instead of away.

"Keller," Jon said over the radio. "Location."

"Second landing," she said, willing her voice not to betray her growing panic.

The radio crackled. "It's eight steps down, then straight to the door. You got this."

Pressing her shoulder to the wall and reminding herself to breathe, Tori inched forward where she thought the stairs would be. Ducking her head, she whispered in Melissa's ear, "You're doing so good, big girl. We're almost there."

"One step at a time, Keller. Count them out for me," Jon said over the radio.

"Three. Four. Five."

"A few more, then straight. You can't see it, but the door's there. One foot in front of another."

"Almost there, brave girl. Almost there," Tori whispered over and over again. By the time she reached the open air, and a paramedic lifted Melissa from her arms, she wasn't sure who she'd been reassuring more, Melissa or herself.

Tori looked back at the building and stifled a gasp. The flames shot higher and had spread farther and faster than they should have, putting up a good fight for the engineers.

"Keller," Jon said behind her, low enough for the crew not to hear. "Did you close the apartment door behind you?"

Tori froze. This was her fault. She'd left the door open, feeding more oxygen into the hungry blaze. Because of her carelessness, the fire was worse than it ever should have been.

"Lieutenant, I . . ."

"This is what happens, Keller," he said, his mouth pulled in a tight line. "What if we had to go back in? What if there were more vics? Always close the door."

CHAPTER SIXTEEN

It was a quiet ride back to the firehouse. Jon had a pretty good idea why Tori stared out the window in a pinched silence. She'd made an honest mistake—leaving the apartment door open—but he'd still needed to correct her, even though no one had gotten hurt. This time. And that was the point. Better she learned when no one's life was at risk than on some other scene where that seemingly simple task was the actual line between life and death.

It didn't help that the mother of the two girls had eventually been found—down the street at a "friend's" house. The fire in Tori's eyes matched the flames consuming the building. The paramedics had taken the lead in alerting child services, much to Jon's relief. He was tired of having to make those calls and filing those reports. Each one left him feeling drained, just like Tori looked.

Jon didn't know why it was taking longer than usual for the rest of the crew to bounce back to their usual selves after the run, but a melancholy had settled itself over Truck 19, and Jon knew of only one way to knock them out of it.

Standing in the center of the common room, he clapped his hands once to draw everyone's attention. "Listen up," Jon said, pausing to give them a moment to focus. "I know there's been some talk about what I do on my downtime."

"Pimp," Fitz blurted out.

"Dealer," Beast added.

"Mafia," Delaware said, before returning to his solitaire game.

"Get it all out now while you can," Jon said. "Any last minute guesses? Owens? Ramos? Davies?"

"International man of mystery," Owens said, waggling his eyebrows.

Davies narrowed his eyes and tilted his chin as though regarding Jon for the first time. Jon met his glare, tilted chin for tilted chin. In the firehouse, Jon was the ranking officer, but out in the real world, where there were no ranks and medals on pressed uniforms, Jon knew he and Davies would have had some serious problems.

"Nah," Davies said, still taking Jon in, sizing him up. "If it were anything that cool, he would have copped to it long ago. He's got to be a librarian or something."

The urge to knock the smug look off the candidate's face roared through Jon as the muscle in his clenched jaw pulsed. Lucky for Davies, there were strict codes in place protecting him.

"Librarians could be cool," Tori said. She stood behind the kitchen counter, helping Ramos chop vegetables for dinner. Her features were still, but the glimmer in her eyes returned, having been missing since the fire.

"If you say so, Keller," Davies said, flopping down on one of the battered couches in front of the television.

Jon ignored him and turned to the others. "As much as I like the idea of you thinking of me as an international man of mystery—"

"Pimp," Fitz corrected him.

"Sure, pimp," Jon said, rolling his eyes. "I'm sorry to disappoint you, but—"

"Wait," Delaware interrupted, "are you about to tell us the real story?"

Jon nodded, noticing the way Tori's knife had stilled, and she was staring at him with a grin playing on her lips. "I am. Are you ready?"

The room stilled, the only movement coming from Davies's bouncing leg. Tori dipped her chin with a nod of encouragement, while the rest of the crew waited without blinking.

"I am a pediatric physical therapist. I've been working at a practice on the northwest side for the last seven years, or so, and in two weeks, I'll be opening my own practice. My sister is the office manager, and she's planning this big grand opening party to celebrate, and you're all invited."

Jon held his breath. No one moved or said a thing. After all these years, there wasn't one reaction? No questions? He supposed it was a letdown after the mythical status they'd elevated his personal life to, but it couldn't be that bad.

"Party?" Beast asked. "Why didn't you lead with that?"

The guys burst out laughing as Delaware rose from his seat and clasped Jon's hand in his. "Congratulations, Lieutenant. None of what you said sounded like it was easy to get to."

"Explains a lot of your flaking out on us," Owens said, clapping Jon on the shoulder.

Jon accepted their handshakes and congratulations, answering their questions and teasing them back when warranted. Through it all, Tori remained behind the counter, a safe distance from the fray, and watched with a mischievous smirk. Jon met her gaze, and her lips widened into a broad smile before she mouthed, "Told you." Then, she whispered something to Ramos and turned back to her chopping.

Jon's moment of contentment was short-lived as the crew returned to their solitary tasks and moping. He'd tried, and sometimes there was nothing more to do. Some days were off days. As long as the job got done, he wouldn't spend more time worrying about their moods. They were grown adults, quite capable of handling their own emotions.

The only thing that bothered Jon was the fact that Tori retreated to her bunk whenever there was any downtime like she was hiding from him or the crew. If it was Jon she was worried about, he should be the one to squirrel himself away, not her. It wasn't as though he wasn't used to it. He'd spent a few years doing just that when he'd had to squeeze out any few minutes he could to study. The guys wouldn't blink an eye at him disappearing behind closed doors again.

But Tori—her reputation as a firefighter and a team player was still in the making. Being the antisocial candidate wouldn't do her any favors. While ideally a firefighter's worth was judged on his or her skill and prowess under pressure alone, Jon knew it wasn't the case. She might be avoiding him, but it was still his responsibility to look out for her best interests and provide the best training he could.

Later that night, Ramos handled the communications control room by himself for the first time. Jon liked to check up on the candidates to make sure first, that they were still awake, being that it was in the middle of second watch—two in the morning—and second, that there weren't any issues.

Tapping the door to announce his arrival, so he didn't scare the poor guy, Jon gave Ramos a moment to collect himself before entering.

"How's it going, Ramos?"

"Good, Lieutenant," Ramos said, turning the volume down on his computer where he'd been streaming a movie. "It's quiet tonight. Not too much going on in the city."

Jon checked the log of printed communications that had come over since dinner time. Ramos was right—the action was pretty light. "Everything looks good. Fitz will relieve you for third watch in another two hours or so."

"Sounds good," Ramos said, stretching his arms over his head. "I'll be ready."

Jon chuckled. "I'm sure you will be. Have a good night, Ramos."

Jon had planned on returning to his bunk, but he wasn't as tired as he'd initially thought. He'd grown accustomed to sleeping in spurts, and his body didn't know what to do now that he was up walking around. He strode out to the apparatus floor, something he often did when he couldn't sleep. He liked to open the overhead doors and sit on the front bumper of the truck in the stillness of the night, breathing in the fresh air and gazing out at the city skyline. It soothed his nerves when they were on the brink of fraying. Second watch seemed to be the only time the city was quiet enough for a man to collect his thoughts.

Though on that night, he hadn't been the only one looking to soothe frayed nerves, and his coveted spot on the truck's bumper had already been claimed. With her legs pulled up and her knees tucked under her chin, she looked like she belonged sitting by a campfire, not in the firehouse garage. She looked peaceful with the streetlights filtering in and illuminating her features. She was so still, she could have been asleep, but Jon knew she wasn't. He thought about backing away and leaving her to her moment, but then just before he could sneak away, she let out a slight snicker.

"Something wrong, Lieutenant?" Tori asked, laying her head on her knees and gazing at him, her eyes two deep pools of warmth. "Am I in your spot?"

Jon shoved his hands in his pockets and drew closer. Kicking the truck tires, he shrugged. "You were here first. The spot is rightfully yours."

Without extending her legs, she scooted to the side, then patted the bumper. "There's room for two. I promise I won't disturb you. I couldn't sleep."

"I know the feeling," Jon said, sitting in the newly vacated spot, the metal still warm from her body heat. "I've spent a lot of time out here. It's my favorite spot in the firehouse at night."

"I can see why," she said. "I should leave you alone."

"It's okay," Jon said, cringing at the eagerness in his tone. He might as well be a puppy begging for table scraps. "Like you said—there's room for two."

She sat still with her eyes on him a moment longer. Jon couldn't read her expression as they sat in silence, something that both frustrated and amazed him. He knew when she focused on a task, and he'd gotten to recognize the playful light in her eyes when she was in a good mood. He even knew the look of frustration or annoyance when it flashed across her face. He'd have to be blind to miss it. Her expressions mirrored her father's so much at times, Jon sometimes wondered if she'd practiced them while growing up. But the expression she wore now was a mystery to Jon.

It wasn't that she was just peaceful. It was more than that. She was . . . fulfilled. She radiated with a satisfaction that almost glowed as brightly as the downtown lights in the distance. Drawn to her warmth, Jon steeled himself against wrapping his arms around her and bringing her close.

He must have been staring at her longer than he realized because she shifted in her seat and cleared her throat. "So, how does it feel to come out to the guys?"

Jon pinched his eyebrows together in confusion.

"Telling them about your practice?" Tori said, clarifying when it became apparent he didn't know what she was talking about.

"Oh, that," he said, rubbing the back of his neck. "It was easier than I thought it would be. I don't know why I thought it would be such a big deal. Then again, the idea of a party with free food and booze will soothe any of their wounds."

Tori chuckled along with him. "That's true. Especially Beast."

"Hey," Jon said, nudging her with his elbow—the closest he allowed himself to touch her, "sorry you lost your chance to cash in on the bet. Personally, I think they should honor it. They all knew you knew."

Tori shrugged. "It doesn't matter. Most days, I prefer to be busy anyway." She stretched her arms overhead and blew out a heavy breath. "My mom comes home tomorrow, or today, technically, I guess."

"Yeah? Have you talked to her at all while she was gone?"

Tori shook her head. "She sent a short email a few days ago. Sounds like she's been having a good time. Before she left, she was hounding me about going to the ball next week. Are you going?"

Jon swallowed the lump forming in his throat. He hadn't planned on going, but if Tori were about to tell him she'd be there, he might have to rethink his plans. "I haven't decided yet."

Tori bobbed her head as though she didn't blame him. "I wasn't going to, but my mom is speaking at the dinner, and she wants me there."

She rubbed her hands over her face, then turned soft eyes that nearly killed him in his direction. "Do you think it was a bad idea for me to turn down the offer to speak about my dad?"

He didn't know how he was supposed to answer that one. If Tori didn't want to give a speech, she shouldn't feel pressured into it. On the other hand, Chief Keller wasn't just some Joe Schmoe nobody. There were plenty of guys in the department who revered him like a modern-day Superman, Jon being one, and getting one last glimpse into the chief's world would mean a lot to a lot.

"I think you can't force those things. If you're not comfortable eulogizing in front of a ballroom of people, you shouldn't have to."

"I lied to my mom," Tori said. "I told her they didn't ask me. She's probably going to find out, and then she'll be all upset I didn't jump at the chance to hail the conquering hero." She lowered her head and groaned. "But, come on, you knew my dad. He hated that sort of stuff—being called a hero, praised for doing his job. He never wore fire department T-shirts off duty like some guys do. He didn't even have a sticker on the car."

"That's true," Jon said. "You know why, though, don't you?"

"Because he didn't need praise to have pride in his job?"

"That, and in his mind, he was keeping you and your mom safe." The skeptical lift of her eyebrow was enough to bring a smile to his face. "I'm serious. The chief used to tease Delaware all the time about the sticker on his windshield. 'Why not take an ad out telling people when you won't be home with your wife and kids? Why not post a schedule when you're leaving them vulnerable?'" Jon chuckled at the memory. When he was a candidate, he'd thought the chief had a flair for the dramatics. But Jon hadn't cared for anything as much as the chief had cared for his family.

Not until he sat on the truck's bumper with Tori in the middle of the night. Then he knew exactly what the chief had been saying.

"I didn't know he was so old-school. Mom and I were always fine. We could take care of ourselves."

"I think he knew that," Jon said. "But I also think he loved you both so much, he couldn't stand the idea of there even being a remote possibility you might not be."

"He couldn't stand the idea of not being the one calling the shots, was what it was." She said it with a laugh, but it didn't escape his notice the way she swiped at her cheek, not once, but twice. "Did he pull strings to get me in this house?"

Jon felt his breath whoosh out of him as though it had been sucked out with one of the hoses. Was it out of the realm of possibility? Absolutely not. Did he have any concrete knowledge of it happening? Absolutely not. But he couldn't say that for certain. The best he could do was offer her the truth as he knew it.

"He never said anything to me about you coming here. And no one has ever mentioned to me your assignment being at his request." He hadn't realized she'd been so worried about his reply until he saw the tension roll off her.

Tori shuddered. "I probably shouldn't tell you this, you being my lieutenant and all."

"You can tell me anything," Jon said before he could stop himself. It may not have been the professional answer, the smart answer, but again, it was the truth. And if he couldn't offer her anything else, he could at least give that to her.

Tucking that loose strand of hair behind her ear, she leaned forward and rested her chin on the top of her knee. "There was a point today when I didn't know if I could do it. The smoke had gotten so thick, and Melissa was heavier than she looked." She paused and turned toward him again, her cheek resting where her chin had been. "There's only one reason I made it out of there when I did."

"What's that?" Jon asked. Her stubborn hair fell into her face, and he had to sit on his hand to keep it from reaching out and putting it back in its place.

Her eyes drifted closed, then dragged open again in one drowsy movement. "Your voice on the radio. I couldn't see you, but knowing you were there got me through it."

That was bad. That was unbelievably bad. She wasn't supposed to say things like that, and he wasn't supposed to enjoy hearing it. But there it was. How was he not supposed to pull her into his arms after that? Was he expected to sit numbly and ignore the way her lips lifted at the corners when she'd said it? Or turn a blind eye to the way her cheeks flushed as she gazed at him, waiting for him to respond?

She stretched her legs out and yawned. "I should get to bed. Enjoy your alone time."

Jon watched her hop off the bumper and trudge back to the door. The urge to stop her, to say something, overwhelmed him. If he let her go back to her bunk without saying anything, he would regret it. Moments like the one they'd just shared didn't come around every day.

"Keller," he said, his voice getting caught in his throat.

Her hand stilled on the door. "Yes, Lieutenant?"

"You're welcome to share the bumper any time."

Tori glanced at him over her shoulder, her smile brighter than any of the city lights. "Thanks. Maybe I will."

CHAPTER SEVENTEEN

Tori stared at her reflection. Of course, she hadn't heeded her mother's advice about finding a dress and had waited until the last minute to even think about it. What did procrastinators like her do before the internet made it possible to find almost anything on a whim? Formal dresses being only one of the many things she'd found online with immediate delivery.

The shimmery silver spaghetti-strapped bodice hugged her abdomen, while the metallic-ice blue skirt flowed to her ankles, like a waterfall cascading from her banded waist. Last-minute or not, her mother would approve. She smoothed her hand down her skirt and wondered if anyone else would approve—namely, Jon Nichols.

Her heart fluttered at the thought of him. In the ten days since their first middle of the night talk on the truck, they'd had three more shifts and three more late-night rendezvous. Each one lasted longer than the last, even if interrupted by an alarm. They'd simply picked up where they'd left off as soon as the crew had returned to their bunks.

Her phone rang, breaking into the thoughts she'd let go on for far too long. Scrambling to find it, she dug under a pile of handbags and heels, none of which went with her dress. "Hello? Mom?" she panted. As pretty as the dress was, it didn't leave much room for deep breathing.

"I'm two blocks away, and I brought shoes and a bag," her mother said, eighties hip-hop blaring in the background.

"What are you listening to?" Tori asked, picturing her mother bopping along to the perky beat.

"Oh, I don't know. It's the driver's station." Her mother covered the phone and mumbled something to her driver. "We're here. I'll run up the shoes."

"I can come down, Mom." Her mother hadn't been to her apartment since Tori moved in two years prior and had probably forgotten the number of stairs there were from the street to her door.

"In your bare feet? I don't think so."

The line died before Tori could argue more. It was an effective method her mother used to ensure she got what she wanted. Tori would have to remember that for the future.

Tori opened the door and listened for her mother's heels to click up the stairs of her three-floor walk-up. "Hey, Mom, stay there, I'll come down."

"Don't be silly," her mother called up the stairs, already breathing heavily. "I'm almost there." A moment later, Anna Keller rounded the last landing. "Look at you."

"Me? Mom, you look fantastic!"

Her mother had told Tori she'd found the perfect dress for the ball while on her cruise. Some little shop in Greece had one-of-a-kind hand-made dresses, and Anna couldn't help herself. And when Tori saw the original creation, she could see why. It was as though the designer had

Anna in mind when he or she had sewn together the masterpiece that made her mother look like she'd been wrapped in a rainbow. On almost anyone else Anna's age, the bright colors and bold pattern would be too overwhelming, but Anna made it work.

"Shoes, as requested," her mother said, waving a pair of silver heels in the air while pressing a hand to her chest and dipping in a shallow curtsy.

"Mom to the rescue," Tori said, ushering her mother into her apartment. "I'll be ready in thirty seconds."

Tori slipped on the shoes and threw her evening essentials in the handbag: lip gloss, driver's license, phone, keys, and her wallet. All the while, Anna stood by, gripping her handbag as though her life depended on it.

"Mom? What's going on? Are you nervous about your speech?" Tori asked.

"Yes. A little. Would you come up on stage with me? You don't have to say anything, just stand next to me."

"Mom . . ." Tori hadn't even wanted to go to the ball at all but had decided she would for her mother's sake. Had she wanted to be on stage, she would have accepted the offer from the planning committee to speak. Her father's voice rumbled through her head. *Kellers don't leave anyone behind.* They were all they had now, Tori and her mother. "Sure. I'll go up with you."

Anna squealed like a giddy schoolgirl and squeezed Tori's hand. "Tori, what are all these?"

Tori followed Anna's gaze to the pile of boxes outside her kitchen. She could lie and make something up, but her father's handwriting was graffitied all over the sides and top of the little pyramid.

"Is this all the study material your father brought you? The tops are still taped."

Tori gulped. "The academy gave us all the material we needed."

Anna arched an eyebrow but didn't say anything. Tori should have remembered to hide the boxes, move them into her bedroom. Or at the very least, cut open the tops to make them look used. But after sitting in the same place for months, the boxes had become nothing more than background noise, the television you leave on when while you fall asleep.

"Mom, it's not that I didn't appreciate him—"

"It's fine. You had everything you needed," Anna said, pasting a smile back on her face. "Alright, Cinderella, let's get to our carriage."

The car dropped them off in front of the hotel hosting the ball. As Tori feared, as soon as they stepped foot inside, her father's old friends and other members of the department swarmed them, wanting to wish the widow well and tell war stories about Chief Keller. Tori hung back while Anna smiled graciously, though tightly, and answered their questions with polite but vague answers. When Tori had had enough, she took her mother's elbow and steered her away from her father's adoring fans.

"Dad would have hated that," Tori whispered as they walked toward the ballroom.

"Yes, he would have, but he wouldn't have wanted us to be rude."

Tori could always count on her mother to pick up where her father had left off with the life lessons. "I wasn't rude."

"You weren't friendly, either. And you should be. These are your coworkers now, too." Anna looped her arm through Tori's and pulled her closer. "Come on. Perk up. Maybe that nice lieutenant will be here tonight."

Tori gasped. "Mom. You have got to stop with that."

Anna giggled. "You're blushing. That's so cute."

Tori took a deep breath to compose herself. Her mother had been out of the country, and she still saw through Tori's act of indifference. But it wasn't as though anything had happened between them. They'd talked—a lot and late at night when everyone else had been sleeping—but it was still just talk and nothing else. Unfortunately.

After their first night on the bumper, it had become clear to Tori that avoiding Jon wasn't the answer to her problems. She still had seven months left in her probation period, and that was a long time to stay sequestered in her bunk, pretending she didn't have feelings for the man she fell harder for every time she saw him. His steadiness and strength had drawn her to him, but his wit and compassion were what made it difficult to walk away.

"Let's go find our table," Tori said, guiding her mother past a crowd of whispering onlookers to the reception table. Finding their names, she scooped up the seating cards and frowned. "They put us at different tables."

Anna read the cards over Tori's shoulder and reached for hers. "They must have put you with your crew and me with the other old folk."

One cursory scan of the rest of the cards confirmed her mother's suspicions. Tori spotted Delaware's and Ramos's cards, each bearing the same table number as hers. "You'll be sitting with Chief Mulrone. That's good. You like his wife, right?" Her mother nodded, but when she didn't say anything, Tori took it to mean her nerves had struck again. "Don't worry. I'll still go up with you. Let's get you a drink to help you relax."

"Okay, but just one. I don't want to slur my words up there."

Tori pat her arm. "Yes, Mother, no getting you drunk until after your speech."

Anna swatted her arm, but at least her smile had returned, and the creases around her mouth from pressing her lips in a firm line had melted into soft laugh lines. "You are terrible; you know that?"

"And here I thought she always took more after you," Chief Mulrone said, appearing on the other side of Anna. "I guess the rumors I'm hearing about Tori taking after her father are true?"

"Joe, how are you?" Anna asked, smiling brightly for one of her husband's oldest friends in the department. "Tori, you remember Chief Mulrone, right?"

Her mother was being polite—making her father proud again—but Tori could never in a million years not remember Chief Mulrone. Ever. Not only had the man been one of her father's best friends, but he'd also been the man who'd delivered the news that her father wouldn't be returning home after his shift. The actual words he'd used might fade in her memory—one day. But his voice and his face will forever be etched in Tori's mind. Right or wrong, Chief Mulrone will always be Tori's version of the angel of death.

"Of course," Tori said, extending her hand and forcing a smile. "Nice to see you again, Chief."

"Tori, I've heard good things about you from the academy instructors. Seems the apple doesn't fall far from the tree," Chief Mulrone said. "Anna, I wonder if I could speak to Tori for a moment before we head in if you don't mind? Just department stuff. You know how it is."

Anna rolled her eyes. "Do I ever. Will I find Connie inside?"

"Sure will," Chief Mulrone said. "She's been looking forward to seeing you and hearing about your cruise."

Tori watched her mother whisk away, her colorful Grecian skirt swirling around her legs, and found herself wishing her mother had stayed. The shadow in Chief Mulrone's eyes gave Tori the distinct feeling of being chained to a sinking ship. Funny how she'd looked forward to his visits at one time in her life, and now his presence was like a bad omen. She could use some of her mother's cheerful diplomacy.

Focusing on the happier memories of her youth, Tori braced herself for whatever he wanted to talk about—her father, no doubt. "What can I do for you, Chief?"

Chief Mulrone took her arm and led her in the direction of the bar. Good man. Maybe he wasn't the harbinger of death she'd assumed him to be. "Nothing, nothing. Tori. I just wanted to check in with you and see how things were going. You're on Truck 19, right?"

"That's right," Tori said. "Second shift."

"Nichols is the officer?"

"Yes, sir."

"Your father trained him. What do you think of him? Getting along alright?"

The bodice on Tori's dress shrunk three sizes while he spoke. She wasn't sure what he'd heard or where he was going with this, but it smelled like a set up tinged with scotch. What she did know, however, was that she'd better control her gushing, better than she had with her mother. It would be a lot easier if everyone stopped asking her about Nichols.

"I think so," Tori said. Vague but polite—she could be like her mother when she needed to be.

Mulrone ordered three glasses of champagne and handed one to Tori. "Good. Because between you and me, we could make changes if we needed to. Personnel gets transferred around all the time. Sometimes officers and candidates clash in the wrong way."

That couldn't be right. It wasn't like it was a preschool class where little Billy didn't get along with Sam, and they had to be separated. There was no way this was a professional courtesy they extended to every candidate. Handholding and babysitting. That's not what the Chicago Fire Department was all about.

Taking a sip of champagne, she moved away from the bar to stall for time while coming up with a reply. Her immediate reaction was to tell him to suck a hose, but that might have been a tad inappropriate to say to her father's friend, who also happened to be an officer in the department that currently employed her.

"I don't need a transfer, even if there was a problem, which there isn't," Tori said.

People were arriving at a faster rate now, and the lobby area filled quickly. A small crowd hovered nearby, actively not paying them any attention. Like her father, Chief Mulrone had a bit of a social-bug reputation, gathering friends the way a toddler gathered wildflowers for his mother. It wouldn't be long before they were interrupted by someone who outranked her and demanded his attention. Though, at the moment, she would gladly accept it.

"I didn't mean to imply there was a problem," Chief Mulrone said.

"But you did imply I was the type of person to accept unwarranted favors."

Mulrone's face fell. She'd been too harsh and had taken her unresolved frustrations with her father out on an innocent man. He'd only been trying to be kind to her because of his relationship with her father, and she had to blow up just like she had that last day with . . .

"I figured since you already went along with it once, you'd be open to it. No judgment here. If I had someone willing to pave the way for me and make my life easier, I would have jumped on the chance. Most guys would."

Most guys would what? But she wasn't most guys, and she didn't go along with anything. What was Mulrone saying? That she'd consented to special treatment? She most definitely had not. Any special treatment he was under the impression she had been receiving was non-consensual and news to her. Jon had said no strings had been pulled. He'd told her no favors had been called in—that he'd known of. That was the kicker, wasn't it?

"I don't know what you're talking about," Tori said, her voice scraping against her throat. "I told my father I didn't want any favors."

Chief Mulrone chuckled. "Did you? Well, you know your old man. He always had his own ideas. Anyway," he said, raising his glasses. "I'd better go deliver these to Connie and your mother before I hear about how I've forgotten all about them. Just keep me posted on where you want to go after your probation. Or let Nichols know. He'll know what to do."

The voices in the lobby merged into a low hum, like a persistent fly buzzing around her head, except they weren't so easily swatted away. She hadn't wanted to believe it was true—that her father would go behind her back when she'd been so adamant about her wishes. She'd hoped that being an adult had earned her some credibility in his eyes.

The lobby thinned as people filtered into the grand ballroom, but Tori remained rooted in her spot, replaying the chief's casual remarks. When she hadn't taken her seat by the time the salads were brought out, Anna Keller came looking for her.

"Where have you been?" she asked. "Are you sick? It's almost time for my speech."

"Mom," Tori said, grabbing her mother's forearm in a death grip, "did Dad call in favors for me?"

Her mother brushed a piece of imaginary lint from Tori's shoulder, smoothed the hair on the side of her head, then brushed the skirt of her own dress. Anything except look Tori in the eye. "Who knows what your father did?"

"You, Mom, you know," Tori said, stilling her mother's hands. "What did he do?"

Anna sighed and gave in. "What he always did—whatever he thought was right."

Tori stepped away and leaned against the wall. After everything—the fighting, the yelling, the threats of no longer speaking to him, he'd gone ahead and done it anyway. Or, maybe he'd done it before they'd fought, which had been why he'd been so obstinate about it. It was one thing to call in a favor, but once granted, he wouldn't have been able to snap his fingers and take it back. That wasn't how favors like this worked. And if that was the case, their fight had been pointless. Useless. He'd died in that warehouse after Tori had told him to stay out of her life—for *nothing*.

"Why didn't you tell me?" Tori asked, tears starting to form in the corner of her eyes.

"What would it change? There was no way any of those men were going to go back on a promise they'd made to your father after he died. What was the alternative? You quit? You've been talking about joining the department since you were five. So what if your father made sure you trained under someone he respected? You're still on the job, aren't you? You're still walking into burning buildings and doing whatever it is you have to do, right?"

"I asked you, and you lied to me. You never lie to me." The tears grew heavy on Tori's lashes, but she wouldn't let them fall. Not yet. Not in front of her mother.

"I had to do what *I* thought was right." Her mother glanced back toward the ballroom doors. "Are you coming inside?"

"Not yet," Tori said, backing away. "Sorry. I need a minute."

Tori hurried away, not letting her mother get the last word. Had everyone been lying to her this whole time? Her father. Her mother. Jon? Maggie? How much did Ramos know? He'd heard the rumors—which turned out not to be rumors, but did he know that? Now that she thought about it, he'd never come out and said he didn't believe them. He'd only ever said things like, "You're killing it at the academy on your own," or "No one helped you through that drill. That was all you."

The only person who hadn't been lying to her, ironically enough, was Davies. He'd been accusing her of nepotism since day one. He'd told her, repeatedly, that her father had pulled strings, and she'd ignored him. What would Davies know about what her father had or had not done? Apparently, a lot more than she did.

The further Tori walked from the ballroom, the faster she went until she reached an empty corridor that led to the outdoor patio and pool. There were no outdoor lights on, so she had the patio to herself. Tori kept walking until her toes dangled over the edge of the in-ground pool.

It seemed as good a spot as any. She was alone, far from the crowd of firefighters and department personnel, and anyone who knew she was a fraud. This whole time she'd thought she'd earned that spot on Truck 19 through her own merits, not because she'd been Chief Keller's kid.

She stared at her blurred reflection in the water. An imposter's portrait. A fool. But still, the tears wouldn't fall. *Kellers don't cry.*

CHAPTER EIGHTEEN

Jon tugged at his tie, loosening the knot pressing into his throat. He glanced at the empty seat beside Ramos that had been reserved for Tori and wondered if she'd changed her mind about coming. He'd seen Mrs. Keller when she'd entered the ballroom and had been engulfed by Mrs. Mulrone and the other officers' wives. And not to be all super-creep, but he'd looked for Tori's place card on the table outside the door when he'd grabbed his. She was supposed to be sitting at this table, the Truck 19 table. But she wasn't.

"Hey, Ramos," Jon said, leaning behind Owen and his wife to get the candidate's attention. "Any word from Keller?"

Ramos checked his phone, then shook his head. "I'll give her a try. She said she was going to be here."

Jon nodded to Chief Mulrone as he walked in, carrying two glasses of champagne. "She's going to miss her mother's speech if she's not careful."

Something had to have happened. There was no way Tori would break a promise, especially to someone she cared about, without a good reason. Forget good. She would need the perfect reason. Just last shift, she'd sat on the truck bumper while the crew slept off a late run, telling him how she wasn't looking forward to the ball, but couldn't upset her mother.

"Anyone see Keller tonight?" Jon asked the table in general.

"Yeah, I did," Beast said. "She was talking to Mulrone when I came in. I would have said hello, but it looked like they were in a pretty deep conversation."

Jon glanced at Ramos, who shrugged. A pit settled into the bottom of Jon's stomach, where it took root and began to grow. Tori was there but hadn't come in. After talking with Mulrone.

Chief Mulrone was a stellar firefighter, a demanding officer, and one of Chief Keller's closest friends. But unfortunately, he also lacked an essential part of his DNA that dictated social graces. Mulrone was what could be termed a "man's man." After spending thirty years in a male-dominated field and having no daughters of his own with only his forgiving wife as a steady source of female interaction, the man seemed to have forgotten how to talk to women. Or children. Or anyone else with a more sensitive disposition than a rusty fire hydrant.

If Jon were still a betting man, he would take the odds that Mulrone had opened his mouth and stuck his boot in it, and most likely hadn't even realized it. For as hardened and oblivious as he was, he would never hurt someone intentionally. Jon's knee bounced under the table as the servers carried over-sized trays of salad out from the back. He considered going to look for Tori himself when he saw her mother leave her seat and head out into the lobby. But when she returned alone and with the same pinched expression Tori wore when she was upset, Jon couldn't sit still any longer.

"Anyone need another drink?" Jon asked, rising from his seat. "I'm going to hit the outside bar before they close it for dinner service."

Owen and Fitz raised their half-empty beers, while everyone else shook their heads politely. Great, leave it to those two to make things difficult. He'd only asked to be polite about leaving the table while the food was served. Now they were going to expect him to return with beers in hand.

Jon loosened his tie some more as he ducked into the lobby. The two bars tucked into the far corners already had their "closed for dinner" signs up. Too bad for Owen and Fitz, and one less thing for him to worry about. His priority was to find Tori and see if she was okay. He knew the night would be tough for her. Four hundred people were eating their steaks and talking about the one thing she was trying so hard to put behind her. Talk, chew, swallow. And for them, that was all it took to wash away the memory of the man they claimed to honor. They did their duty, raised their glasses, wiped a misty eye, but once the dinner was cleared, so was their grief.

But not for Tori, and not for Mrs. Keller, who were expected to display their mourning on-demand to soothe everyone else's consciences. The more he thought about it, the more he understood why Tori had wanted to skip the whole event. Her father had given his life to the department. The department had no right to lay claim to anything else. Especially something as personal as their memories and healing.

He hurried his footsteps as he left the ballroom lobby and ventured into the halls of the hotel, determined to find Tori and then sweep her away from this place. He wanted to take her where she would feel safe. Safe from other people talking. Safe from the rumors. Safe from her father's shadow. If she would let him. Knowing Tori as well as he did now, she would rather eat her turnout gear than let him do anything that resembled saving her. That was fine with him. He didn't *need* to save her, wanting and needing being two entirely different things. He *wanted* to save her, but he *needed* to know she was okay.

Walking through the hotel halls, he passed small groups here and there, none of them with Tori. The officer from Engine 95 rushed in the opposite direction with wife number two on his arm. Jon shook his head as they passed. It was only last year that wife number one had been on the man's arm, and if memory served him correctly, they had fought the whole night. He remembered Chief Keller making a joke about being sure to pick the right girl or being stuck in a never-ending fight.

Speaking of the right girl, the need to find Tori bubbled in him to the point of a boil. Maybe she'd left. If she'd changed her mind about going into the ballroom, why would she stay? He was about to give up, head back and make up some lame excuse about what took him so long when he caught a glimpse of the patio through a window. Suddenly, the idea of getting fresh air was far more appealing than returning to the stuffy grand ballroom. He'd already been gone this long. A few more minutes wouldn't hurt anything. It wasn't as though there was someone at the table who would miss him.

Jon knew she was there before he saw her. A million tiny needles pricked his skin as he crossed the threshold onto the patio, and his heart fluttered in his chest. There were no swimmers at this time of night, but that didn't mean the patio was empty.

Skirting around tables and chairs, he moved toward the far end of the pool, where she stood at the edge, her back to the hotel and head bent to her chest. She'd wrapped her arms around herself, and other than her signature loose strands of hair swaying in the evening breeze, she was motionless.

She wasn't going to jump, was she? She couldn't, though, there had been crazier things to happen. Besides, she stood at the four-foot end, so even if she did jump, she would only soak her dress, which would be a shame because it looked stunning on her.

Rubbing the back of his neck, Jon contemplated his next course of action. He came all this way to find her, and there she was, only she didn't quite look as though she wanted to be found. She'd come outside and stood in the shadows for a reason. Whatever that reason was, he should respect it.

"Are you going to say something or stand there all night?" Tori asked without turning around.

"I'll be honest, I didn't know what I was going to do next," Jon said, taking a hesitant step forward. She still hadn't unfolded her arms or lifted her head. "How did you know it was me?"

Tori shrugged. "I smelled your cologne."

A baseball-sized lump in his throat nearly choked him.

"And I can see your reflection in the water," she said, dropping her arms and turning on her heels.

Even though he knew she wouldn't drown if she fell in, the way she stood on the slick edge of the pool in her heels spelled disaster waiting to happen. "People are wondering where you are." Something was off with her. He thought they'd moved past the cool professionalism that had driven a wedge between them since the day she'd walked into the firehouse. Hadn't they? If not, then what had they been doing in the middle of the night the last few shifts?

"Are they?" she asked, finally taking a step away from the water. "Did they send you to look for me? Since it's your job to babysit me?"

What the hell did Mulrone say to her? "I don't know what you're talking about. No one sent me."

She took another step closer, and while Jon was relieved her feet were on solid ground away from the edge, the warning flash in her eyes kept his senses on high alert. She was angry, that much was obvious, but he didn't know why. And what was that business about being her babysitter?

"Your mother is about to give her speech," Jon said, taking a different tact.

"She'll be fine. She's a big girl," Tori said. "Tell me, Lieutenant, when were you going to tell me the truth?"

Jon pinched his brow and tilted his head. He hadn't been expecting that question. "When have I not been truthful with you?" He tugged at his tie again, loosening it enough to unbutton his collar and get a little air. The accusation of dishonesty was not one he took lightly, and to hear it coming from Tori deepened the wound it made.

"I asked you—flat-out—if my father pulled any strings on my behalf. You told me no."

That's what this was about? This had Mulrone's brand of idiocy written all over it. "I didn't lie to you. I said nothing was ever made known to me—which it hadn't. I had no clue you were assigned to Truck 19 until I got your file along with Ramos's and Davies's. I have no reason to lie to you, Tori. I have nothing to gain from that, and I wouldn't do that to you."

Tori squared her shoulders and marched up to stand toe to toe with him. With her heels on, she was another three inches taller, almost eye to eye with him. If it weren't for the furious flash in her eyes and the stubborn clench of her jaw, she would have been downright adorable. But Jon couldn't let himself go there at the moment. Tori was upset, and apparently, at him.

"Mulrone told me I could transfer anywhere I want. Now or after probation. He said I should let you know what I decide, and you would take care of it." She jutted her chin out, and Jon had to keep himself from reaching out for her. "He basically said everyone knew about it but me. That my father went behind my back and ignored my request. You can't tell me you didn't know. My mother knew, and she didn't tell me because she was trying to protect him or me. I didn't quite catch that part." She took a shuddering breath. "Am I the department joke?"

"What?" Jon grazed his hand down her arm until it found hers, then held on. He was afraid if he didn't make her stay and talk this out, she would bolt, taking with her any bond they had formed over the last few weeks. Maybe he was selfish, but Jon couldn't stomach the thought of that happening. When she didn't pull away, he kept talking, hoping he could convince her of his truth.

"First of all, I saw the reports from the instructors," Jon said.

"Subjective reports."

"Not the licensing exams—which supported every one of the claims made in those subjective reports. And what kind of officer do you think I am that I would allow someone less than qualified on an active scene. If I had any doubts about your capabilities, I would have ordered you to stay on the truck. There's no way I'm about to endanger anyone, including you and the rest of the crew, by allowing a sub-par firefighter anywhere near a garbage can fire, let alone go inside a burning building."

Some of the storm brewing inside Tori faded, and her features began to soften. Her fingers curled slightly around his, sending a satisfying ripple through him, warming his chest and neck—all that from a handhold.

"I don't know what to believe anymore," she whispered into the night.

Jon stepped closer and took her other hand, his chest aching as the ripples intensified. "I can't speak for the chief, your mother, Mulrone, or anyone else," he said, his voice sounded rough and forced to his ears. "I can only tell you what I know. And I know you, Tori Keller, are a damn good firefighter. You've earned your candidate spot on the truck. Who cares what everyone else says? You know you belong there. I know you know. I can see it in your eyes every time that alarm goes off. Yes, you're Chief Keller's kid. But that only means greatness is in your blood. You can't help it. And if your assignment to Truck 19 were anything other than my dumb luck, then I would love to know who I should thank for bringing you into my life."

He brought her hands to his lips and pressed them gently with a kiss. He had to. He couldn't stand there saying those things, looking at her, and not do something. He crossed a line, and there was no going back. Even if they dismissed the kiss as nothing more than one friend consoling another, it was impossible to misinterpret his meaning. He loved her, as wrong as it was, and knowing one or both of them could be transferred or fired. He loved her anyway. And he needed her to know that even though he'd chosen the worst place to display his affections—a social event with hundreds of their coworkers and superior-ranking officers.

He lowered her hands, ready, but unwilling, to sever their connection. For both of them to keep their careers in the department together, they would have to hit pause on whatever they were starting. They couldn't go any further than where they stood now and still be in the same firehouse.

But instead of letting go, she raised herself on her toes and pressed her lips to his. He'd been imagining what it would feel like to kiss her for so long, he wasn't sure at first if he was trapped in another daydream or if it was really happening. Her hands slid up to his shoulders, then to the back of his neck. His head spiraled with the contact, and he wrapped his arms around her waist to anchor himself.

This was real, and this was happening. He held her closer as her lips parted with a sigh. Kissing Tori Keller was everything he'd thought it would be. It made him feel whole and completely undone at the same time. It was coming home and being in foreign territory. It was inevitable and a total surprise.

And it seemed to have surprised her as much as it had him because she pulled away as suddenly as she'd kissed him, covering her mouth with her hand and staring at him with wide, unblinking eyes.

"I'm sorry," she gasped, stepping back from him.

Jon blinked away the haze, focusing on those magical lips of hers. "Why, exactly, are you sorry? I sure as hell am not."

"I shouldn't have done that," she said, shaking her head. "You were just being nice, and I—"

"Whoa," Jon said, closing the gap between them and taking her hands in his again. "First, I wasn't *just being nice*. I meant everything I said. And second, don't ever apologize for kissing me."

"We can't be doing this," she said, her eyes glancing over his shoulder. "There are rules."

The thought of her transferring before her probation ended almost brought him to his knees. He'd been promised nine months of her at his firehouse, and he planned to soak in every minute of that allotted time. When her probation ended, and it came time for her permanent assignment, then he'd deal with her absence. But not a minute before.

She shook her head and backed out of his reach. "We can't do this," she repeated. Each word was a crowbar crashing into his chest. "I'm sorry. It's not right."

"Tori—"

"I'm sorry."

Then she was gone.

CHAPTER NINETEEN

"There you are." Maggie, dressed in a floor-length black evening gown, swept Tori into her arms. "I've been looking everywhere for you. It's time for your mom's speech."

"Mags? What are you doing here?" Tori blinked away the fog she'd been moving in since she'd felt Jon's lips against hers. It had been a mistake, for sure, but she couldn't say she surprised herself after she'd been thinking of doing that for weeks. The only surprising thing about it was the timing of it all. But how could she not when he'd said all those things to her, with his hands wrapped around hers and that intense gleam in his eyes she couldn't resist?

"What do you mean?" Maggie asked, looping her arm around Tori's waist and guiding her back to the ballroom. "Paramedics are part of the fire department, too, you know?"

Tori nudged her with her shoulder. "I know that, but I thought you were on shift today?"

"I am. But that doesn't mean I can't ask someone to cover for me for a few hours so I can be here for my best friend and her mother on an important night." Maggie glanced over her shoulder and pulled Tori closer. "Is that Lieutenant Nichols?"

Tori didn't have to turn around to look. She felt him following them at a safe distance. "Yes." Maggie opened her mouth, but Tori squeezed her back. "Don't ask. I'll tell you later."

Maggie nodded and cast one more glance in Jon's direction, while Tori practically pulled a muscle keeping her head facing forward. She'd kissed him. And not a small, chaste-like kiss, either. She had pressed her lips to his and had let him hold her. When she brushed her fingertips along her lower lip, it still tingled from meeting his.

It had been a mistake. A delicious, toe-curling, knee-weakening, still want more of it, mistake.

But maybe it didn't have to be. Maybe they could hit pause for the rest of her training. Then, once she was assigned, assuming it wasn't to Truck 19, they could lift their moratorium, pick up where they'd left it on the patio. If he still wanted to after the way she'd run out on him. She would just have to find a way to convince him. At least a dozen ideas popped into her head, causing her whole body to flush with heat.

Just when Tori started to believe that it wasn't such a bad idea, after all, to fall for another firefighter, especially one who left her wanting more every time, she found her mother pacing outside the ballroom, wringing her hands raw and chewing her bottom lip. Her mother, who had always been the rock of the Keller clan, the stabilizing force caught between the clashing wills of her husband and daughter, looked ready to crumble. And in a flash, Tori remembered exactly why she could never love another firefighter.

"Mom," Tori said, rushing to her side. "Are you okay? You look like you're going to be sick."

"Tori, I'm sorry," her mother said, gripping her arm with her icy hand. "I should have—"

"It doesn't matter, Mom," Tori said. "I'll be fine. What about you, though?"

Anna gulped then took a deep breath. "Hello, Maggie. It's nice to see you. You look lovely."

"Thanks, Mrs. Keller. But do you need to sit down?" Maggie said, jumping into paramedic mode.

"I'm fine, girls. Just nervous." The master of ceremonies welcomed everyone to the ball on the other side of the door, and any remaining color drained from Anna's face. "Tori, I don't know if I can do this. How am I supposed to stand up there and talk about your father? How do I sum up what he meant to me, to all of them, in just a few minutes? What if I didn't pick the right words? What if it comes out wrong? It wasn't supposed to be like this. He was supposed to be here, next to me, asking me to dance, not. . ."

"One foot in front of the other, Mom," Tori said, drawing her mother into a hug. "You put one foot in front of the other. Then you say what's in your heart. Who cares what anyone else thinks? You speak your truth. And I'll be right next to you."

"You'll come up with me?" Anna asked, suddenly seeming so small to Tori, like the little girl Melissa burying her face in Tori's neck.

"Kellers don't leave anyone behind, Mom. Especially not one of our own."

"Ladies," Maggie said, pulling the heavy ballroom door open a crack. "It's time. I'll be here by the door, just in case you need a quick exit," she said with a wink.

Anna patted her cheek as she moved toward the door. "Maggie, always with the escape plan."

Tori was about to follow her mother into the ballroom when a hand on her elbow stopped her. Thinking it was Mags with another quick joke, she turned and almost collided with Jon, who had caught up to them. "Good luck up there, Keller," he whispered. "Your dad would be proud of you."

The next morning, Tori walked into her mother's favorite diner and scanned the packed dining room for an empty table. Her mother had wanted to hash out their issues the night before after the ball, but Tori had been too exhausted, physically and emotionally, to deal with it, so they'd agreed on meeting for breakfast to clear the air. Tori yawned while leaning against the hostess station, waiting to be seated.

"How many?" the hostess asked, materializing at the station.

"Two, please," Tori said.

The hostess reached into her podium for menus, and then stopped and narrowed her eyes. "Are you Tori?"

"Ye-es," Tori said, tilting her head. "Do I know you?"

"Oh, honey, no," the hostess said. "Your mother told me you were coming. Come on. She's over here."

"She's here?" Tori asked, falling in line dutifully and serpentining between the tables.

"Here you are," the hostess said with a warm smile.

Tori gaped at her mother, sitting in a corner booth with two cups of coffee in front of her. Hopefully, one of those had Tori's name on it. "Thank you," she mumbled as the hostess sashayed away. She slid into the booth with her hand pressed to her sternum. "Is the world ending?" she asked, then pulled her phone out and made a dramatic show of checking the time. "When has Anna Keller ever been on time to anything?"

"I've been on time to things before," Anna said, moving one of the coffee cups in front of Tori.

"When?" She reached for the cream and sugar with an arched eyebrow and smiled at her mother.

"My wedding, for one," her mother said. "And today, for two."

"You win," Tori said, wrapping her hands around the coffee mug, hoping to absorb some of the caffeinated goodness through the porcelain. "So, really, why are you so early?"

"Because this is important," Anna said, placing her hands in her lap and pressing her lips together. "We're all we have, and we can't afford for there to be any grudges or resentment between us."

"I don't resent you, Mom," Tori said, staring into the depths of her coffee mug. "I was just . . .in shock, I guess? I was hurt and felt a little betrayed. Okay, a lot betrayed."

Anna nodded and drummed her fingers on the table while waiting for the waitress to come and finish taking their orders. Tori knew she was on borrowed time before Anna's train of thought derailed in another direction, so she made sure to line up her words correctly before speaking again.

"Mom," she said, swirling her coffee around in the mug, getting lost in the spirals. "The last time I spoke to Dad, we fought about his wanting to interfere. I told him not to. I said I would—" she choked back a sob forming in the back of her throat— "I said I would never speak to him again if he did." Tears she'd been holding back for months rushed forward, lining her lids, but not falling. They wouldn't dare. Not in front of Anna. "And he did it anyway."

Her mother leaned forward and placed her hands over Tori's, stilling both her movements and the tiny tidal pool in her cup. "First of all, why were you making empty threats like that? No one in their right mind would believe for one minute you would stop talking to your father. You've been a daddy's girl from the moment you were conceived. Second, and I'm not saying I condone his behavior, but you have to understand, if he was willing to ignore your strong wishes, then it was because he thought it would be the best thing for you. Yes, he liked to be right. Yes, he liked to be in control of things. But more than any of that, he wanted you to be safe and happy."

"Was he really okay with me being in the department?" Being a firefighter was pretty much the opposite of safe in a parent's eyes.

Her mother shrugged. "Most days, he was proud of your decision, despite his objections. But that didn't mean he didn't worry. He knew better than anyone what you would be up against—with the department itself and the job. But I will tell you this: he never once doubted your dedication and your skill. And I think that eased some, but not all, of his worry." Anna sighed. "I don't want you to think he died thinking you couldn't do the job. That wasn't it at all. He wanted to give you the best experience he could."

Unfortunately, that wasn't how the rest of the department saw it. Tori's mother had always been able to read her thoughts and now was no exception.

"No one needs to know," she said quietly, as though afraid of being overheard.

"No," Tori said. "But they all do. You know Chief Mulrone. A few drinks, and he'll tell you everything."

"That's true."

"I just have to prove myself. Time will take care of everything else."

"Including your pride?"

Tori arched an eyebrow and took a large bite of her pancakes. She didn't even want to answer that question. Tori's pride was not something to mess with, another trait she'd inherited from her father.

Tori arrived at Nichols Pediatric Therapy Center promptly at noon, as Ramos had requested. The door was unlocked, so she let herself in and was greeted by Ramos and one shocked-looking lieutenant. Judging by his slack-jawed expression, he hadn't been expecting her either.

She'd thought they'd already finished the job the day she and Ramos had stenciled patterns on the walls, and her first impulse had been to come up with an excuse to get out of meeting Ramos. But she couldn't leave Ramos shorthanded, not after begging him to hire her. So, there she stood, staring at Jon like she'd seen a ghost, and him returning the favor.

"Thank you so much for coming," Sara said, hurrying forward from the office area. "We thought we'd be farther along by now, but the obstacle course is taking longer to build than Jon thought. And then the furniture delivery arrived a week later than we planned. It's just been crazy."

"Sounds like," Tori said, keeping her eyes away from where they wanted to go—to Jon.

"Anyway," Sara said, waving her hands in front of her. "Tori, why don't you come with me. Jon, you can have Marco."

Tori shrugged and followed Sara. She didn't know what was going on, but if it got her paid with minimal confrontation with Jon, she'd do it.

"We have to unwrap the furniture in the offices and exam rooms and make sure it's all placed properly, then hang pictures and add final touches. Same for the waiting room. The guys are finishing up the course.

Unless—" she stopped and pointed toward the gymnasium. "I'm sorry, I don't mean to be rude and imply you can't—"

Tori laughed and waved her off. "I'd much rather hang pictures and stage a room than swing another hammer with that lot. I get enough of them on shift." Sara had no idea how much Tori preferred to be as far away from her brother as possible.

Sara smiled warmly, and Tori wondered what it would have been like to grow up with a sister like her. As an only child, she'd often daydreamed about having siblings, a sister in particular.

"Perfect. I could use another set of eyes out here anyway," Sara said. "Plus, we can gab while we work instead of listening to Jon and Mitch bark orders."

Sara led her to the office at the end of the hall. What looked like a giant cube of bubble wrap sat in the middle of the room. "Desk, chairs, and a bookcase, I think," Sara said, pointing to the mound of plastic bubbles. "I went a little crazy picking out the artwork and informational posters to hang. Jon wants a mix of both in each office and exam room. Our job is to figure out what goes where. The rooms are all kind of themed—"

"I remember," Tori said, perusing through the selection of informational posters leaning against the walls she'd painted and stenciled.

"Right. I almost forgot," Sara said with a chuckle. "You know this building as well as I do by now."

Tori pulled a poster with cartoon zoo animals demonstrating how to stretch before physical activity and showed Sara. "So, this one would work in the room with the animal border?"

"You got it," Sara said, rifling through the artwork. "These would work, too." She held up a pair of elephant prints. "I figure we can sort through these all and put them in the room where they belong, fill in any gaps with what's left, then pull all the rooms together."

Tori got right to work, starting with the posters, separating them by theme, while Sara did the same with the art prints until they had a nice little bundle for each of the rooms. As they sorted, Tori had heard the guys filter into the building, and Jon's unmistakable voice as he greeted each one and put them to work. Casting a side glance to Sara, Tori silently thanked her for being the anchor keeping her from running out to see Jon, too.

"Pizza's here," Ramos said, poking his head into the office.

"You go ahead," Sara said without lifting her head. "I'll finish putting these in the right rooms, so we can start with the furniture and hanging. You'll need your strength."

"I see where the lieutenant gets his bossy ways from," Ramos whispered as they headed toward the break room and the heavenly smell of cheese and sausage.

"Why didn't you tell me what we were doing today?" Tori hissed.

Ramos shrugged. "Does it matter? Nichols asked about general handiwork, and I said yes. We're still getting paid if that's what you're worried about. The other guys volunteered to help last night when they overheard him asking."

It shouldn't matter, but it did, and what made it worse was that she couldn't tell Ramos. She'd made him a promise that she was on the verge of shattering. "It's fine. Just caught me by surprise."

"Like this?" Ramos pinched her side, causing Tori to flinch and erupt into much-needed laughter.

"What's so funny?" Delaware asked, handing Tori an empty plate as they entered the break room. "When did you get here, Keller?"

"Just now," she said with a wink. "I followed the pizza guy."

"Who are you? Fitz?" Delaware asked, eliciting laughs from the rest of the crew, even Fitz, who grinned with a mouthful of crust.

After lunch, everyone went back to their assigned tasks. Over the next few hours, Tori and Sara had managed to put all the offices and exam rooms in order. And because she wasn't ready to go home yet, she cleaned up the break room, which still held the remnants of their lunch. The guys had been returning for quick bites before tackling their next tasks, and now the formerly clean room resembled a school cafeteria after an epic food fight, which probably wasn't the look Sara was going for. Tori threw out the empty boxes and swept up the crumbs before wiping down the counter and tables. She was washing her hands when Jon found her.

"Wow. Did you clean up in here?" Jon asked, running his finger down the length of the crumb-free table.

"I didn't want to leave Sara with the mess," Tori said, drying her hands. "I know what it's like to clean up after all of you. It's not pretty."

"I would have done it," Jon said. "I looked in the offices. You and Sara did a great job. I appreciate your help. I know Sara does, too."

"Well, a job is a job."

"We appreciate it, anyway. Sara said it would've taken at least twice as long to finish without you. Now she gets to go home and have dinner with her family."

"I'm glad. If you need more help this week, I'm available," Tori said, then caught herself and clamped her mouth shut. She was supposed to be avoiding temptation, not creating more of it. They hadn't even talked about what happened at the ball. How could they with everyone around, and her avoiding him all day like he had the plague? Wasn't she the one who said it couldn't happen? Then freaked out and ran away like a big, old coward? And now, here she was, practically throwing herself back into those strong arms of his.

Jon rubbed the back of his neck, and Tori wished she could somehow throw a net over her words and pull them back in so he could stop looking at her like she'd sprouted two extra legs and a tail. "I'd like that, but. . ."

"I know. Sorry," she said quickly. She wished she hadn't cleaned up so well, because now she had nothing to do with her hands. They were just hanging there, flapping in the wind. "I guess I'll see you at the firehouse, then," she said, folding her arms and tucking her hands away.

She had to squeeze past him to leave because he hadn't moved his broad frame from the doorway, forcing her to practically run him over. Stopping her with a finger on her waist, he lowered his head, so his mouth almost brushed the top of her ear. "Sara wants me to bring a date to the party."

Tori's heart twisted in her chest. She'd had her chance, and she'd thrown it away with both hands. And because Jon was an old-school gentleman, he was giving her fair warning so she wouldn't be caught off guard. He was forever doing the noble thing. And she was forever going to regret not taking the chance when she could have.

"I'm not going to bring anyone," he said, his voice a husky whisper. "But you're coming, right? You'll be there when all this opens?"

"I wouldn't miss it. I promise," Tori said, with a smile, as her heart slowly began to unwind.

CHAPTER TWENTY

J on climbed into the truck and wiped his forehead with the back of his hand. "Let's get a move on," he said to Owens.

Owens glanced behind him into the cab of the truck and cleared his throat. "Lieutenant? We're short one."

"I know," Jon said, well aware of the fact that Davies had not taken his seat yet. Davies had been yanking his chain all morning, and it was beginning to piss him off. Jon could take some good-natured ribbing like the rest of them, but what Davies had been doing was downright disrespectful, and Jon had taken enough of his crap. Davies could haul himself back on foot for all he cared. Maybe by the time he got back, he would have adjusted his attitude.

"Shouldn't we wait?" Owens asked, his hand ready to shift gears.

Jon grunted. "He's got sixty seconds. If he's not on the truck in one minute, we're leaving him behind." Setting the timer on his phone, he leaned back and waited, tapping his boot along with the passing seconds, wishing Davies didn't make it.

At fifty-two seconds, Davies pulled himself into the back of the truck and plopped himself in his seat with a grumble.

"So glad you could join us, Davies," Jon said, sarcasm dripping from his tongue. He didn't bother to turn in his seat to face him. Davies hadn't earned that respect from him on this shift. "I hope we didn't put you out any."

"My apologies, Lieutenant," Davies said with equal contempt. "Not all of us can hold the record for the fastest time in."

There was no mistaking he was referring to Tori, but why Davies turned his bitterness on her was lost on Jon. Jon didn't need to see her either to know she understood the full force of Davies's words, as well. Jon felt her seething in the seat behind him. Davies was dangerously close to crossing a line he should be nowhere near.

"Not expecting record-breaking time," Jon said. "But I, and any other officer you report to in the future, do expect you to hustle up when told to. This isn't your time. You're on department time."

Davies fell silent—the first smart thing he'd done all day. The rest of the crew remained quiet the entire ride back to the house. Davies's sour mood infected everyone, which would make for another miserable seventeen hours, and Jon didn't even have a meeting with Tori on the truck bumper to look forward to.

"Fitz, stow your gear and meet me in the office," Jon said, jumping out of the truck on the apparatus floor. He was getting to the bottom of this Davies situation one way or another. Jon tried to catch Tori's eye as he walked past her, he could have used one of her smiles right about then, but she stubbornly kept her head down as she unlatched her turnouts and stepped out of her boots.

Fitz followed two steps behind Jon and closed the office door behind him. "Is this about Davies?"

"What's gotten into him?" Jon asked. He'd assigned Davies to Fitz for the shift, so if anyone had a read on the guy, it would be Fitz. "How was he on that run?"

"Quiet but followed orders okay. Up until the end, that is," Fitz said.

"Quiet, how?"

"Pouty." Fitz sat in Jon's chair and propped his feet up on the desk. Jon let him only because they'd worked together for so long. Had he been Davies, he would have knocked his boots off without a moment's hesitation. "Something's bothering him. He hasn't said, though. Maybe Ramos would know. They were all huddled up this morning before roll."

Jon considered hauling Ramos into his office next, but he didn't want to be that kind of officer, tempting as it was. He had to nip this issue with Davies in the bud before it escalated into something else, but the problem was he didn't want to deal with the man himself. Jon had always prided himself on working things out directly, instead of weaseling around behind people's backs like some of the officers he'd heard about.

"Give him a warning," Jon said. "Let him know he'd better put his attitude in check."

"Got it," Fitz rose from the seat with a mock salute. "Hey, yo, I can bring a date Saturday, right?"

Jon cocked an eyebrow. "You conned some poor woman into spending an evening with you?"

"Not conned. I simply told her there would be free food and drinks. There will be free food and drinks, right?"

"Yes," Jon laughed, slapping Fitz on the back in humor as they walked out of Jon's office. "Anything to help you wine and dine the ladies, Fitz."

"Fitz is wining and dining the ladies?" Tori asked, coming up behind them from the direction of her bunk. "I think I'd like to see that."

Fitz shook his head. "No monkey business from you, young lady."

"Let me get this straight," Tori said, planting her fists on her hips and staring Fitz down. Jon couldn't help but grin. He liked this feisty side of her that didn't take any crap from the guys and knew how to dish it right back to them. Jackie had always been too sensitive, getting upset too easily over something as harmless as a comment from Fitz. "It's fine for all of you to crash one of my dates, but now that you've tricked someone into going out with you, I'm put on notice to behave myself?"

Fitz shrugged. "What can I say? Life isn't fair sometimes, candidate." He winked at them both and strode off to find his mentee for the day, leaving Jon alone with Tori in the hall.

"So . . ." Tori said, turning the smile he'd been craving in his direction. She'd made him wait way too long to be on the receiving end of that sunshine.

"Keller," Ramos said, coming out into the hall, staring at his phone screen. "You still want a ride on Saturday?"

Tori's smile faltered, making Jon wish he could send Ramos back to the academy. "Yes, please. If it doesn't cramp your date."

"Whoa, Ramos has a date?" Jon asked. He needed to jump back into the conversation sooner rather than later. He couldn't stand there glaring at his candidate all day for interrupting him and Tori. "First Fitz, and now you, Ramos? What's her name?"

"It's Maggie Jennis, actually," Ramos said, shifting from one foot to another. Now he was the uncomfortable one.

"Jennis? The paramedic?" Jon asked, looking to Tori for confirmation, who smiled and nodded. "Good for you, man. She's cool. Pretty cute, too."

Tori flashed Jon a side-eye glance he could have sworn held some jealousy. Interesting. He'd been stewing over her rejection for days, unable to sort out if it had been because of work—or him. He knew he was rusty on the dating scene, but there was no way the connection he felt between them was one-sided. She'd had to have felt something, too. It wasn't possible she could kiss him the way she did if she didn't have some feelings behind it. Maybe her little flash of jealousy meant there was hope for him, after all.

"So, there's no problem with me dating a paramedic, right?" Ramos asked.

"Not with me," Jon said. "Different house, different officer. It's all clear."

Ramos nodded. "That's what I thought. I just wanted to confirm before things got out of hand."

Out of hand. It was as though Ramos was sending him coded messages. Or warnings. Had Tori divulged to him what had happened out on that patio at the ball? Or maybe Tori had said something to Maggie, and Maggie had told Ramos, like some crazy game of telephone. Was he the only one who didn't know what was going on?

Or maybe Jon was losing his mind, growing paranoid and insecure.

"Garage fire. Truck 19. 64th and Kostner," dispatch announced over the loudspeaker.

"Gear up," Jon said, leading the way to the apparatus floor, relieved to think about anything else for the time being.

He'd hoped to be able to find another minute when he could talk to Tori alone, but she seemed determined to keep a distance between them after they'd returned to the firehouse. He'd respected her decision, no matter how deep her indifference cut him. He wouldn't force his company on her any more than was necessary to do the job. He'd even had his lunch in his bunk, claiming too much paperwork from the morning call.

Jon had become addicted to their late-night talks after everyone else had turned in, and this was the first shift in weeks he'd have to go without. He'd messed everything up the night of the ball. Why couldn't he have stayed in his seat and mind his own business? It was a system that had been working for him for years until Tori Keller walked into his firehouse, and now there was no going back.

He tried to focus his thoughts on other things while he laid in his bunk, like the Nichols Pediatric Therapy offices opening in a matter of days. Running his hands through his hair, he stared at the ceiling. It would all come together, eventually. It always did. Usually. Checking the time, he groaned and rolled to his side, shutting his eyes. He might as well take advantage of his bumper boycott and get the extra sleep before an alarm interrupted his night.

It wasn't dispatch over the speakers that stirred him minutes later, but the sound of voices in the hall—angry voices. And one of them was Tori. Jon sprung from his bunk and crept to his door. She'd retired earlier than he had, and he wondered if she'd gone to the garage anyway. Had she been upset when he hadn't? His chest squeezed at the thought of disappointing her, something he never wanted to do.

It was definitely Tori in the hall. Even if she weren't the only woman in the firehouse, he would still recognize her voice anywhere. And right now, she sounded agitated. Whoever she was with kept his voice low, too low to distinguish who it was, but Jon's money was on Davies. He'd been trying to push her buttons all day, despite the warning Fitz had given him. Jon had almost stepped in during dinner when Davies had made some rude comment about women in general, but Tori had quickly halted him and jabbed Davies right back. Jon had to admit, he'd been impressed, but it didn't stop him from wanting to lay the guy out.

Tori kept her tone flat, but sharp. Every muscle in Jon's body tensed. Tori could take care of herself; she'd proven that time after time, and as long as this confrontation stuck to words, he'd stay out of it and let her do her thing. But if he was right, and it was Davies she argued with, then he couldn't walk away until he knew she was safely locked in her bunk. He didn't trust Davies as far as he could throw him, especially after his blatant disrespectful attitude all shift.

"Why can't you just leave me alone?" Tori hissed.

Jon's hand rested on his door handle. Just in case. A low murmur answered her. Where was Ramos? Ramos should be on watch in the control room unless it were Ramos she argued with. In that case, Jon had every right to storm out there and put him in his place. Ramos could deal with his problems on his own time. He shouldn't have left his post, and especially not to harass another crew member.

"It's none of your business," Tori said. Another low murmur, then, "Don't touch me."

That was all Jon needed to hear. He tore the door open and stepped into the hall to find Davies with his hand wrapped around Tori's arm. The muscle in Jon's jaw twitched, and his hands fisted at his side.

"Get your hands off her now." Jon took three steps forward until he was within swinging distance of Davies's nose. "What the hell do you think you're doing?"

Davies dropped her arm and squared his shoulders to Jon; defiance etched in his features. "Just having a discussion with another firefighter, Lieutenant."

"Really? Because to me, it looks a lot like you have your hands on someone you shouldn't." Jon flexed his fingers and stared directly into his eyes. If Davies thought he could intimidate him with his slightly larger size and belligerent demeanor, he had another thing coming.

Davies curled one side of his mouth into an ugly snarl. "Playing favorites again?"

"There's nothing playful about it, Davies. I think if you were to take a poll, you'd find anyone here would take Keller over you any day of the week."

Davies took a step toward Jon, a challenge for sure. "I'm not talking about anyone else. I'm talking about you, Lieutenant."

Jon pulled himself up another inch and matched Davies's stance, toe to toe. He didn't know who Davies thought he was talking to, but clearly, he had underestimated him. "And who, exactly, are you to question anything I do, *candidate*? You're not in the academy anymore. Your test scores got you here, but that's where they end. You earn what you get."

Davies's snarl turned to an ugly smirk. "And how did Keller *earn* her special treatment? Been out to the apparatus floor tonight, Lieutenant?"

Jon didn't have time to think twice about it. He simply drew his arm back and let his fist fly, landing his punch, as though Davies had a target painted on his nose. To Davies's credit, he didn't yell out or even fall to the ground, as Jon had hoped. Instead, he grunted, covering his face with his hands. Blood appeared between his fingers and dripped down his chin, which warmed Jon with satisfaction.

Tori gasped and grabbed Jon's arm. "What are you doing? Are you trying to get yourself suspended?"

"What's going on out here?" Delaware said from the doorway of the bunk room. "Geez, Davies, are you bleeding?"

Davies wiped his face with the bottom of his shirt, shooting a wicked glare in Jon's direction. "I'm fine. I'm perfect, actually."

"Back to the bunks," Jon said with a rumble. He couldn't stand the sight of Davies's smug face anymore. Jon had pretty much signed his suspension papers with that punch, but he couldn't help himself, not after the way Davies spoke about Tori, who had been nothing but professional and was ten times the firefighter Davies was. She was smart and competent and could climb the ranks in the department, with or without the Keller name. A person like that didn't deserve the disrespect Davies had spewed.

Delaware took one last look at Jon and Tori, whose hand was still on his arm, but didn't say anything. Then with a withering glance for Davies, he retreated into the bunk room. Davies, however, wasn't so smart about it.

"Have a good night, you two," he said with a smirk, tempting Jon to beat it off his face. If Tori's hand hadn't tightened her hold, he might have.

They waited until the door closed before saying anything. "What were you thinking? You can't punch him on duty," Tori said, a worried expression darkening her eyes.

"Me? I was defending your honor. You're welcome. What was all that arguing about?"

Tori removed her hand from his arm. He could still feel the heat from her touch, tempting him to take back everything he'd just said so she would put her hand where it had been. But he didn't.

"First, I don't need anyone to defend me," Tori said. "Second, Davies was just being stupid."

"He had his hands on you."

"Nothing I haven't dealt with before. My dad taught me to throw a punch when he taught me to ride a bike." She rubbed her temples and groaned. "He's going to report you."

Jon nodded and flexed his fist. He hadn't realized how hard Davies's head was until the adrenaline wore off. "It was worth it."

CHAPTER TWENTY-ONE

Tori sat in her car outside the Nichols Pediatric Therapy Center one full hour before the official start of the party. She'd called Ramos earlier and made up an excuse about having to see her mom before the party to get out of hitching a ride with him and Maggie. Honestly, he sounded relieved. Tori hoped to catch Jon before the hustle and bustle of the party started to talk about what happened the other night between him and Davies.

With one punch, warranted as it had been, Jon had put his entire career on the line—because of her. She couldn't live with that amount of responsibility, not when she had nothing to give him in return. She took a deep breath and tapped the heel of her hand on the steering wheel, psyching herself up for the task ahead. Walk into a burning building? No problem. But this? This was a whole different type of fire to walk into. What was the worst thing that could happen, anyway? He broke up with her? She chuckled.

A knock on Tori's window startled her, and she pressed her hand to her chest as she lowered her window. "Sara, you scared the crap out of me."

"Sorry," Sara laughed. "But what are you doing out here? The party isn't for another hour."

"I know," Tori said, feeling her heart slow back to its normal rhythm. "I was hoping I'd be able to talk to Jon for a minute, though, before he got too busy meeting and greeting."

"He's right inside," Sara said, smiling knowingly the way only a big sister could pull off. "Hey, Jon said you were a teacher before joining the department. Is that right?"

"It is," Tori said, taking one of the bags Sara carried from her hands. "For five years while I sat on the waiting list before I got the call from the academy."

"That's great. Was it awful, though? Is that why you do the painting on the side instead of tutoring or something?" Sara led them through the front door and into the newly decorated waiting area she had set up with cocktail tables and extra seating. Sara had transformed the receptionist desk into a welcome station with business cards and brochures about the center's services for guests to take with them. A bar had been placed in the corner, and tables lined the walls waiting to be filled with appetizers and finger foods. "You can set that stuff over there," Sara said, pointing to one of the tables.

"What? Oh, no, I loved teaching," Tori said, placing the bags on a table. "But tutoring jobs aren't always easy to come by, at least not in the beginning, and I needed the extra money faster than that." She began unloading the bags' contents: plates, napkins, and tiny utensils in silver plastic.

"A lot of Jon's patients end up needing tutoring to keep them on track at school while they go through their therapies," Sara said, again with the signature sister smirk.

"Really?" Tori had never thought of tapping into that market. She'd contacted schools and other programs but had never thought of reaching out to hospitals or other healthcare professionals to ask about the need level of their patients.

"If you ever want to send me your credentials, I could make sure we have your contact information on hand for anyone who asks. We may even have an empty office you could use as your classroom."

Tori shook her head. She couldn't possibly accept that level of generosity. "Jon said you've been finding renters for those offices. I wouldn't be able to pay rent at first. I can always use a library study room."

Sara placed her hands on her hips and surveyed the party preparations. "Well, let's think about it some more after the party, and we'll come up with something. Okay," she said, clapping her hands together, the same way Jon did when he was trying to get everyone to focus. "Mitch sent a text. I've got to let him in through the back. He's got about a hundred bags of ice he's bringing in. Jon should be in the obstacle course," she said with a wink.

Tori paused outside the doors and smoothed down her dress. Jon had said it would be a casual affair, but her mom had always told her it was better to overdress to an occasion than under-dress. Even so, she questioned her choice of a little black dress. She looked like she was trying too hard. People would be bringing their kids to run around, and there she was looking like she was ready to go out to the clubs.

She groaned to herself, seeing her reflection in one of the windows. There was still an hour before the party. She could leave and change into something more appropriate for a family event. But Sara had already seen her, and she would tell her brother his flaky candidate had been there stalking him before running away. At least Sara had been in a dress, too.

Tori stepped into the gymnasium with her breath held, feeling the gravitational force shift around her, trying to pull her closer. He stood with his back to her in gray suit pants and a white fitted T-shirt. He'd shed his dress shirt and sport coat, draping them over a monkey-bar-looking contraption while he fiddled with a screwdriver and the climbing wall. She stood perfectly still not to interrupt him. Mainly so she could continue ogling him without him noticing.

But her plan was foiled when he dropped his hands to his side and slowly turned in her direction. A slow smile crept across his face when he saw her standing in the doorway, and his eyes met hers. It was the type of smile that sparked flutters in her chest and let Tori know she'd made the right choice in dress.

Jon stalked toward her, seemingly forgetting about his project and his shirt, which Tori didn't mind one bit. She slipped her heels off—she didn't want to ruin his new gym floor—and met him half-way.

"You're early," he said, his eyes taking in her outfit. "You look fantastic."

Tori felt her whole body blush. "Thanks." Doubts rushed forward. Doubts about coming early and taking time away from his last-minute party preparations. Doubts about whether he even wanted to see her after she ran from him at the ball. But doubts about why she ran in the first place were taking precedence as he stood there looking at her like that, and God help her, she didn't ever want that look in his eye to go away. "Do you have time to talk a minute? I don't want to get in the way or anything."

He furrowed his brow, but that expression in his eyes remained the same. For now. "Should we sit down?" he asked, motioning to a row of benches running along the wall.

Tori took a seat and closed her eyes, waiting for him to settle next to her, and pretended they were sitting on Truck 19's bumper again. It always seemed more natural to bare her soul in the cover of darkness with a three-ton piece of machinery beneath her.

"See, the thing is," she said, smoothing an imaginary wrinkle in her skirt. "You shouldn't have done what you did."

"You've already lost me. What did I do?" Jon asked, with the beginning of a scowl pulling the corners of his mouth down.

She had to get it together and say what she needed to say, because judging by the look on his face, he didn't have a clue what she was talking about. "The other night between you and Davies. You shouldn't have punched him. You can get suspended for that. Scratch that. You *will* get suspended for that. And that's if you're lucky. They could kick you out of the department."

"They won't kick me out. And that's only *if* Davies says something."

Tori slapped her hands down on her knees and threw her head back with a groan. "Listen to what I'm telling you. There's no *if*. Davies *will* tell. That's the way he is. We called him The Snitch in the academy for good reason. And he will make it sound worse than it was. You could get fired."

Resting his elbows on his knees, Jon leaned forward and balled his hands. "Then, what's done is done. What can I do about it now? Did you come down here, tonight of all nights, just to tell me I screwed up? I know I screwed up. Don't you think every time the phone rings, I'm checking to see if it's HQ calling to tell me not to report next shift?"

Tori ducked her head. The man wasn't stupid, by any means. Of course, he knew the ramifications of his actions. But she knew Davies better than he did, and she wanted to make sure he knew what he was in for. "I'm trying to warn you. So you can be prepared."

Jon snorted. "Prepared. Like anyone is ever prepared to get canned over a moron like Davies."

"I shouldn't have come," Tori said, more to herself than to Jon. Clearly, he thought she shouldn't have either. "I just . . .I don't know. I guess I don't want you to get in more trouble because of me. If you need me to make a statement or anything, I will."

Jon's half-grin almost ripped her apart. "You know it won't mean anything. They won't care about the why when it comes time. I broke regulations. Flagrantly and knowingly. I'm the officer, and he's the candidate. Besides, you don't want your name associated with any of this."

"Why not?"

"Chief Keller's daughter caught up in a firehouse brawl? Are you kidding? If you thought people were talking before, wait until that gets around. And it will."

Tori covered her face with her hands and let out a small scream of frustration. "You're right. I don't, but I will if you need me to."

"Why would you do that? It's only another six months or so. Then you can move on."

Tori's face stung. "That's what you think? That I'm just riding out my time?"

"Aren't you? You made it clear the night of the ball that you wanted nothing to do with anything your father wanted for you. And that's Truck 19. I'm sorry you landed in the one spot you were hoping not to, but that's how it is. You can always transfer out. Take Mulrone up on his offer."

She heard the words, but she couldn't make sense of them coming from him. "You want me to transfer?"

Jon sighed. "I don't know, Keller. I don't know anything anymore. I do know I wouldn't have punched Davies if he hadn't grabbed you like that."

"So, it was my fault?" She should have listened to her gut. She should never have come. This whole conversation had taken a turn into a territory she wasn't prepared for.

"No," he said, hanging his head. "Yes. Maybe. You've got me so turned upside down, I don't know which way I'm going anymore. You kiss me and run away. You flirt with me but push me away."

He lifted his head and pinned her to her seat with his stare. She sucked in a breath, unsure of what to do, and unable to move even if she was sure. The intensity of his gaze didn't just render her speechless; it knocked the entire English language right out of her head.

"Tell me what to do, Keller. What do you want from me? You want me to be your lieutenant? I can do that. You want me to be more than that? I can do that, too." He gulped, his eyes flickering away then back. "You want me to sign the transfer papers? I will. For you. Just tell me one way or the other."

Everyone had a moment in their life they could point to in the end and say, "There. That was it. That was the moment my life changed." This wasn't that moment for Tori.

"I can't." The words nearly choked her as she forced them out. She couldn't lose what she never had. If she never said the words, never put a name to what it was she felt for him, then she never had to feel the searing pain when it was ripped away from her.

"You can't or you won't?"

"Both." She rose from the bench and wrapped her arms around her chest, holding herself together. "I'm sorry. I should never have come here tonight to talk about this. Not before your big night. It was stupid and selfish of me. I'm going to go."

Tori couldn't look at him as she rushed by. Twice now, he put himself out there, and she rejected him. Twice. What was wrong with her? Any woman would give almost anything to be in her position. Who wouldn't want a man like Jon Nichols saying those things to her? Tori Keller, apparently.

Except that she did want those things. She wanted him, but she couldn't allow herself to have him. If he was hers, it meant he was hers to lose. She barely held it together on a daily basis as it was. If anything were to happen to Jon—

She couldn't think about that. He wasn't hers. She'd made sure of that.

"Whoa, Keller, where's the fire?" Davies asked, laughing at his own joke.

She hadn't even seen him as she hurried through the waiting area and out the front door. It was later than she'd thought, and people were going to begin arriving for the party. But what was Davies doing there? Even though Jon had invited the whole crew, any man with sense would understand his presence was no longer welcome. Did it have to be spelled out for him? The only reason Davies would have to walk through Jon's doors after their last confrontation was to cause trouble.

"What are you doing here?" Tori asked, filling her voice with all the venom she could shove in those five little words. "There will be kids here. You better not have come just to start something with Nichols."

"What? Are you his guard dog now?" he sneered.

"Cut the crap, Davies," Tori said. "What are you up to? You're not here to support the lieutenant, so why'd you come? You that hard up for food and liquor?"

"I'm not hard up for anything," he said, taking a step closer than Tori was comfortable with given their last confrontation. She could smell beer on his breath and seeping from his pores. He was definitely at the clinic to cause trouble. "I came to talk to the lieutenant, that's all, before shift tomorrow."

"You provoked him the other night, and you know it. You were practically begging to get hit."

"Maybe, but it doesn't really matter, does it?" Davies said with a drunken smirk. Sure, the guy couldn't walk a straight line, but he could remember every fire department code and regulation ever written. "Besides, there's nothing to worry your pretty little head over. This is between him and me."

"What do you have against Nichols, anyway?"

"Nothing." He said it so genuinely, Tori almost believed him. "Nichols just got caught in the middle, but it works to my advantage."

A cold sweat broke out on Tori's back, and the hair on the back of her neck prickled. This wasn't a case of alpha dogs battling it out for dominance. This was calculated.

"You haven't figured it out yet, honey?" he asked. "It's you. I have a problem with you. The only reason you're on Truck 19, to begin with, is because of your daddy. You're a menace. You don't take orders, and I know you're the reason that apartment building flared up. A truck like 19 is no place for someone like you. You want to play firefighter? Do it at a quiet house, where you're out of the way. I thought I could get Ramos to talk some sense into you, but you've got him wrapped around your finger. But then I saw the way Nichols responds to you, and well, why not?"

"What do you want from Nichols?" Tori said through a clenched jaw. From the corner of her eye, she saw Delaware and his wife escorting their youngest two children in their direction. "Make it quick."

"You transfer out of Truck 19, or I report him."

Delaware raised his hand in greeting as he approached with his family. Tori's heart thundered in her chest, and her limbs felt as though bound to cement blocks, yet, somehow, she managed to lift her hand in a wave and force her mouth to curve into a smile. A weak smile, but it was there.

"Leave him out of it," Tori said out of the corner of her mouth.

"Can't now," Davies said. "I can't believe I made it here before Delaware."

"Keller. Davies," Delaware said, his gaze bouncing between them. "You remember my wife, don't you?"

"Of course," Tori said, accepting the woman's embrace and cursing herself for never finding out her first name. "Nice to see you again."

"You okay, Keller?" Delaware asked. "You're looking a little pale."

"Actually," Tori said, taking a step away, "I'm not feeling too well. I think I'm going to head home, so I don't make anyone else sick."

"Are you sure?" Delaware's youngest daughter hung off his arm and swung like a monkey in a tree, but he didn't budge. He kept his eyes fixed on Tori.

Tori attempted another smile and fell short again. "Yeah, I'm sure. I'll see you guys tomorrow."

Struggling to keep her head held high, she walked back toward her car, with Davies's glare heavy on her back. She'd always known he wasn't her biggest fan, but resorting to blackmail? It was just the probation period. They would be separated in six months anyway. But Davies was thinking long term. As much of a buffoon as he was, Davies was no dummy.

The candidates who'd trained at the choicest houses got the choicest assignments—the houses with a higher volume of calls. Transferring out to a fringe house with low volume meant a career most likely in the same five fringe houses. Davies asked her to commit what amounted to career suicide for any firefighter in it for the love of the job.

Which she was.

So, it came down to one essential question. What did she love more: her career or Jon Nichols?

CHAPTER TWENTY-TWO

Tori had taken her shoes off without being asked before walking on the new gym floor. Jon shook his head and picked up the screwdriver. He still had to remind Sara to watch it with her heels on the new floor. Not Tori. She hadn't even hesitated. And that dress she was wearing—Jon paused and let the image burn into his brain. That was a keeper. He would remember the way she looked walking toward him, barefoot in his gymnasium, for the rest of his life.

Jon finished securing the footholds on the climbing wall to his liking. He should have known not to leave Mitch in charge of that task. The only thing his brother-in-law had ever climbed was a ladder, which explained why when Jon had checked on the result, he'd found all the holds in one vertical line. He slipped his dress shirt over his shoulders and dropped the screwdriver in the toolbox in the closet. Jon had thought rearranging the climbing wall was going to be the worst part of his evening. He'd never been more wrong.

He wished he could hit pause on the evening when Tori walked toward him. If he could somehow figure out how to delete everything that had come after, he could go on with his life as a happy man. Maybe happy was pushing it, but he'd be fine. Okay, even. The problem was, he couldn't hit pause or delete, and the night that was supposed to be the start of something incredible wound up being the night he'd discovered something truly incredible would never happen.

Buttoning and straightening his shirt, he checked his reflection in the waiting room mirror. Presentable, but not overly stuffy. Sara had suggested a tie, but he'd put his foot down. He'd agreed on the sport coat, but that was as far as he was willing to go. The next time he wore a tie, he'd be walking down the aisle.

His throat clenched as another image of Tori Keller flashed in his mind. The "what if" questions crept forward, overtaking the pretty picture he'd rather think about.

What if he hadn't been so stupid and punched Davies? What if Tori hadn't come to the center early? What if he hadn't let his stress and worry boil over? What if he'd been able to control himself better and he'd never taken it out on her? What if he hadn't pushed her to decide about him? What if she'd come for a different reason? What if she'd given him the answer he'd been praying for?

There was no use dwelling on it. Tori had made up her mind. She couldn't, or wouldn't, ask for anything more from him than what he was—her lieutenant, her officer, her teacher. He had one job, and that was to prepare her to move on. If only someone could teach him the same.

"You ready?" Sara asked, AJ and Nicki hot on her heels. "One minute until party time." She fixed Nicki's braid and smoothed down a piece of AJ's wild hair, then looked up with a startled expression. "Where's Tori?"

Jon focused on adjusting his cuffs in his sport coat so he wouldn't have to look at his sister. "She had to leave."

"Had to?" Sara asked with a raised eyebrow. It was that exact expression Jon was trying to avoid.

"Yes," Jon said. "She dropped by to say congratulations and has somewhere else to be." Anywhere not near him. Part of him had hoped she'd stick around for the party and give them both a chance to calm down before trying to speak again. But the other part of him knew he wouldn't have been able to calm down knowing she was in the same room with him, and he was unable to talk to her the way he wanted to.

"Hmm." Sara gave him the look she'd always given him when she didn't quite believe him, but with the doors about to open to the public for the first time, it was no time to start dissecting hidden meanings. "Well, you better put a smile on that face. You don't want people thinking you're a miserable person."

"Sounds about right to me," Delaware said, bursting through the front door with his wife, Marie, and two of their children.

"Funny," Jon said, reaching out to shake Delaware's hand. "Thanks for coming. You're the first to arrive. Couldn't resist the free food, huh?"

"First?" Delaware asked, pointing to Davies behind him, then Tori retreating down the street. "Number three, at best."

Jon watched Tori walk away from him. Again. He would have to revert to his hermit ways around the firehouse. Hiding in his office during downtimes. Declining social invitations. And just when he was remembering how to have fun again. Granted, a lot of that fun was because Tori had been involved, with her quick humor and natural smile. It was only for six months. Once training ended, and she moved on, he could come out of hiding though it wouldn't ever be the same.

"It's nice to see you again, Jon," Marie said. "Don't let him fool you.

He couldn't wait to get here and see the finished product."

"Don't embarrass him," Delaware said. "I've still got to report to the kid tomorrow, you know."

Davies snorted and rolled his eyes behind Delaware. Though Jon knew he was going to have to pay for it somehow, the purpling half-moon under Davies's eye did lift his mood.

"AJ. Nicki," Jon said, ushering his niece and nephew forward. "You remember Lizzie and Joey, right? Delaware's kids? Why don't you take them to the gymnasium and show them the obstacle course?" All four kids bounced on their toes, waiting for Marie's nod of permission. Once given, they tore through the double doors and disappeared into the gym. "That should keep them busy for a while," Jon said, steering them toward the bar. "Drink?"

People continued to stream through the front doors for the next hour. How many people had Sara invited? It looked as though the whole west side of the city had come out for the party. Jon recognized maybe one out of every three. Maybe. Sara, on the other hand, worked the room like a seasoned politician, shaking hands, giving tours, everything short of kissing babies' heads. Mitch, the less social half of the couple, occupied himself monitoring the caterers in the back, and if the party weren't in honor of his own business, Jon would have been back there, as well.

"Jon," Sara said next to him. "Have you met Alderwoman Kinney yet?"

Jon pulled his focus from where he wanted to be to where he needed to be. "No, I haven't," he said, extending his hand. "Thank you for coming, Alderwoman Kinney. It's nice to meet you."

"You too, Mr. Nichols. This is quite the practice you have here. It will be a nice addition to the community," Kinney said.

"I certainly hope so," Jon said, glancing over her shoulder to Davies leaning against the back wall, his eyes trained on Jon. He strained to keep a smile on his face but could feel it fading fast. "Have you seen our custom obstacle course yet?"

"No, I haven't," Kinney said. "But I've heard good things about it."

"Can I have my niece, Nicki, show you around? She loves giving tours of the gymnasium and can explain the different stations better than anyone," Jon said, waving his twelve-year-old niece to his side. "Nicki, can you please show Alderwoman Kinney around the gymnasium?"

"Sure, I'd love to," Nicki chirped. "Right this way." Jon squeezed her shoulder. She was going to grow up and be just like her mom—not a bad person to take after, in his book.

"You know," Sara said, turning on him once Nicki led the alderwoman away. "It wouldn't kill you to walk around a bit and mingle. The other therapists are doing that. They're showing people their offices and exam rooms. They're giving gym tours themselves. Are you glued to this spot or something?"

Jon's eyes flickered back to Davies, so brief it shouldn't even have registered. But nothing got past Sara.

"What's going on with you and him?" she asked, keeping her voice low. "You two have been trading death glares since he walked in."

"That's my candidate, Davies," he said with a clenched jaw.

"Davies? The one you—"

"Yep, that's the one."

"Why is he *here*?"

Jon had been wondering the same thing. "I suppose I'll go find out."

"Be careful, okay? You're already a breath away from suspension as it is. Do you really want to push the envelope?"

The short answer was no, but he wasn't about to allow Davies to come into his building on his night and try to intimidate him, or whatever he was trying to do, with that scowl of his. "I'll be fine," he said, letting his annoyance seep into his tone. "I am an adult now, you know. You don't have to look after me anymore. I can handle my own life."

"Can you?" she asked with a raised eyebrow. "Like it or not, little brother, you're stuck with me."

Jon stared at her from the corner of his eye. She was right, of course. She usually was. He watched as Davies prowled around the edge of the room and stopped outside the hall leading to the offices. He wanted to talk. And if listening to his moronic ramblings would get him to leave sooner, Jon was willing to sacrifice those few minutes. On the bright side, it would get him out of the crowd.

"Where are you going?" Sara asked as Jon walked away, but he wasn't about to waste time answering her.

Jon didn't say a word, just nodded at Davies as he walked past, knowing the candidate would follow. He led Davies to the end of the hall and the largest office—his. Squaring his shoulders, he pulled himself up to his full height, which was still a shade shorter than the other man.

"Davies," Jon said, lowering his voice to a threatening octave. "I didn't expect to see you here tonight."

"You said the whole crew was invited, didn't you?" Davies asked with a smirk. "Well, I'm part of the crew."

There was no way this guy was as dense as he seemed. Davies hadn't gone through the bother of a shower and shave to be supportive of Jon, not after what happened. "I did say that. And, yes, *for the time being,* you are part of the crew." Jon trained his eyes on Davies and lowered his voice further. "There's not going to be any trouble here."

"No trouble," Davies said, that sneer still on his face. "Just here for the food," he said, holding up a plate of half-eaten appetizers. "And a little conversation."

"I'm busy here, Davies. What do you want?" Jon may have to put up with this guy's attitude at the firehouse, but nowhere in any regulation or code, did it say he had to deal with him outside the house. And his patience had come to an end.

"Alright," Davies said, dumping his plate into Jon's wastebasket. "Let's cut to the point."

"Chase."

"Whatever. I want to stay on Truck 19. It's an active house with decent call volume. After probation, with your high marks on my evaluation, I can be assigned there permanently."

"Seriously," Jon said, crossing his arms over his chest, "that's what this is about? An assignment?" Davies might get assigned to Truck 19, but Jon would make sure it wasn't on his shift.

"It's more than that," Davies said. "We've got three candidates on one shift. The most any shift should have at a time is two. So, I asked myself, why three? Is it because one of the three happens to be the kid of a respected chief who just died?"

Jon felt his blood pressure rise with every word Davies uttered. "You're going too far, Davies."

"I don't think I am," Davies said. "Look, here's the bottom line. Keller has no business in the department, let alone a truck like 19. As long as she's there, she'll keep siphoning the attention and training that rightfully belongs to Ramos and me. So, it comes down to this—you or her. One of you is leaving. I'll leave that up to you. I'm pretty sure you'll make the right decision."

Davies stomped out of Jon's office and out of the building, which had been the smart thing because Jon barely held his composure together. He counted to five, forcing himself to take a breath, hoping it would ease the increasing amount of pain in his chest. When that didn't work, he quietly closed his office door, slid his jacket off, and wound it around his fist.

Sara had done a stellar job selecting the furniture, especially in his office. All the hours she'd spent poring over catalogs and scouring websites had paid off. She'd managed to find pieces that made the space sleek and warm at the same time—for example, the filing cabinet. The cabinet itself had a soft nickel finish, but the drawer fronts were some sort of wood. Bamboo, maybe? It really was a slick piece of work.

Until Jon rammed his fist into the smooth nickel side of the cabinet, causing the panel to buckle so that the drawer would never be able to fulfill its destiny and slide open on the now damaged track. But he'd been right. The pain in his chest had eased, replaced with the pain in his hand.

It wasn't until a few hours later, as the party wound down and the crowds thinned that Jon finally had a moment to breathe and even sit down. Mitch had already left with the kids, so Jon happily took up the job of giving tours of the gymnasium to anyone who hadn't seen it yet. At least that was what he'd told Sara when she'd caught him sneaking off through the double doors.

He needed a moment of quiet. He'd spent the last few hours talking to dozens of people whose names he would never remember. The only ones he made sure to commit to memory were the few therapists he would be working with who had signed their leases for the empty offices. Sara had assured him everyone else had been necessary guests: pediatricians, orthopedics, and other business owners in the neighborhood. His head hurt. His hand hurt.

Standing in the middle of the obstacle course, Jon rubbed his bruised knuckles and flexed his hand. He was sure he hadn't broken anything, but he had to keep an eye on it in case. He looked around at what he'd spent the last few years on. In another fifty years, when he reflected on his life, this should have been a highlight, a moment of pride and satisfaction.

How had everything gone so wrong?

It had started with his argument with Tori and had snowballed from there. The night that was supposed to be the launch of a new phase of life might, instead, be the night another one ended.

Jon was living the longest bad day in the history of bad days. He couldn't see how anything could get worse than they were. To save his career in the department, he had to effectively end Tori's. Not really end hers, she'd still be a firefighter, but it wouldn't be on her terms any longer. She would have to take what she could get. A transfer at this point in her training meant taking whatever spot was open unless she appealed to Chief Mulrone to pull strings on her behalf—which she would never do. It could take her years to make up the training she'd lose by leaving Truck 19.

After what had happened earlier that night, she probably wanted a transfer anyway. Why else would she have walked out? Kellers didn't leave anyone behind. If she cared for him at all, even as just a friend, wouldn't she have stayed? She'd been hurt and angry the night of the ball, but she'd stayed and stood by her mother's side and made small talk with all her father's old friends, the very people she'd been upset with. But she couldn't stay for him.

Maybe he was worrying over nothing. Maybe signing Tori's transfer papers wouldn't be as selfish as he'd thought.

CHAPTER TWENTY-THREE

Tori arrived at the firehouse earlier than usual. She'd had a difficult time falling asleep after the party the night before, which would have been fine with her if she'd been up all night thinking about Jon, something that had happened once, maybe three times, before. But she hadn't been that lucky. Instead of drifting off to sleep with images of Jon in his tight T-shirt, thoughts of Davies and his demands plagued her.

Her stomach churned, thinking about it.

She'd hoped to avoid seeing Jon at this hour of the morning. He'd be able to tell something was wrong as soon as he laid eyes on her, and then he'd do that thing where he'd try to be all noble and stop her from doing what she had to do. That was if he were still talking to her after she'd rejected him—again—and then ran out of the party like she'd been on fire.

She didn't bother wasting time depositing her gear in her bunk. Instead, Tori headed toward the officer's bunk and met Lieutenant Connors, the officer on the first shift, on his way out.

"Keller," he said, slinging a duffel bag over his shoulder. "You're early."

"I have a meeting down at headquarters this morning. I was hoping you could let Nichols know when he relieves you?" Tori asked, ignoring the fact that there was a cell phone in her hand, and she could have done the task herself. But Lieutenant Connors didn't ask, so she didn't offer any more of an explanation.

She'd called Mulrone's office on the way into the firehouse and had made sure his assistant put her on the schedule for the first thing that morning. She knew she'd be able to—that was the magic of the Keller name at headquarters.

Connors nodded and stifled a yawn. "I'll make sure Nichols knows."

"Thanks, Lieutenant."

Tori's hands shook as she scribbled a note for Ramos and shoved it in his locker. She turned off her phone in case anyone wanted to play hero and talk her out of her decision, and shoved it in her pocket, promising herself she wouldn't touch it again until after dinner. To be safe.

She immediately replayed the last shift in her mind, picturing her confrontation with Davies. She'd been returning to her bunk after grabbing water from the kitchen when Davies had appeared out of nowhere. He'd been argumentative and insulting—shifty—questioning her about what she'd been doing and where she'd been going. And then he'd grabbed her, and Jon had been there.

Clenching her jaw, she headed to the parking lot and ran head-first into none other than Mr. Ryan Davies. She moved to step around him without saying a word but let her eyes flicker to his face, still black and blue three days later. She wished she'd had the chance to punch him herself. Was that wrong of her? Who cared?

"Where you headed, Keller? Firehouse is that way," he said. His smug expression made her sick.

She should hold her tongue and not rise to the bait he dangled in front of her. But she couldn't help herself. "You know where I'm going, or were you too drunk last night to remember?"

"I've told you before," Davies said, squaring off his shoulders and the muscle in his jaw ticking. "I'm only interested in the integrity of the firehouse."

"Which must mean it's okay to blackmail people," Tori said, matching his stance. There was no way she was going to let him think he scared her. "And you talk about integrity?"

He tilted his head and laughed at her expense, as though she were some silly little girl with no idea how the world worked. "Must be easy to be so righteous when you're a legacy. Have a good day, Keller. Hope to see you soon." He walked away, laughing and shaking his stupid shoulders.

Despite her best efforts to keep calm and collected, Tori's knee bounced like a jackhammer while waiting for Chief Mulrone to join her. This was the last place she'd expected to find herself, and it was more humiliating and nerve-wracking than she'd imagined. How did people do this willingly?

"Candidate Keller, what a nice surprise," Chief Mulrone said, stomping into his office, out of breath from the walk from the elevator down the hall, the result of desk duty for twenty years. She'd heard the stories from her father. Mulrone had been in her father's academy class. They'd climbed the ranks together, much like she and Ramos planned on doing, until Mulrone hurt his hip in a roof collapse. He'd been on desk duty ever since. "Social call or business?"

"Business," Tori said, pressing her fist into her thigh to keep it from jumping. She hoped he was teasing her with his question. Or did he think she would be late for her shift because she felt the sudden need to drop by and say hello?

"How are things going at Truck 19, Tori?" Mulrone asked as though they hadn't had a conversation just a week ago at the ball.

But she noted his switch from using her last name to her first. It was a subtle difference, but one that signaled he'd made the mental shift from seeing her as another candidate to seeing her as his dead best friend's daughter. He knew what was coming, and like any good firefighter, knew how to prepare for the situation.

"Good, sir." She emphasized the title to remind him of their respective ranks. She was going to make her request, but she wanted him to turn her down. He had that right as a chief. He didn't have to cave in to her whims because of her last name, and she silently cheered him on to stand his ground.

"No problems? No one giving you a hard time?" he asked, rubbing his chin with one hand and playing with the corner of a paper on his desk with the other.

Yeah, Davies. "Do you think someone there would give me a hard time? Sir?" This was a new line of questioning since the ball. Maybe she could lead this conversation in a different direction. Davies didn't want to work with *her*, but why did she have to leave? Why not transfer Davies?

Mulrone shrugged. "Sometimes, our female candidates have a harder time transitioning into the field. Some of the guys, we've heard, have trouble adjusting, too. We try to nip it where we can."

This was it. This was her out. She could turn the tables on Davies and report him for harassment. He'd be detailed out, maybe even booted out of the department. Was that so bad? Not for her, by any means. Except for two things: she'd be found out as the snitch and have to carry that label around—Chief Keller's kid, the snitch. And second, he would still file a complaint against Jon. Worse, he'd file actual charges.

Tori leaned forward and narrowed her eyes. "Chief Mulrone. We're both adults here. Can I speak honestly with you?"

"Of course, Tori. You know that," he said. "Your father would have wanted it that way."

Tori's gut clenched. She knew, deep in her bones, without a doubt, her father had never wanted *this*.

"Chief, if it's all right with you, I would like to spend the remainder of my probation period at a different house. I was wondering, sir, if you could please detail my assignment elsewhere." There. She'd said it, in one long breath of rushed words. But it was out there, just as she'd practiced, and there was no going back now.

With a sigh, he ran his hand down the side of his face, then leaned forward. "Did something happen? Did Nichols—"

"Nothing happened," she said before he could finish that question. "Nichols is a great officer and instructor. This isn't about Nichols." Not the way he had implied, anyway.

"Then, what is it? At the ball, you said—"

"I know. But I was thinking—we have three candidates on Truck 19, and maybe it would be best for all of us if we spread out a little." She gulped, but the lump in her throat wouldn't budge. Why hadn't she thought of bringing a bottle of water? "I know my father asked for a favor, but he couldn't have known at the time how crowded it would be. He would've wanted the best training for all of us. Wouldn't you agree?"

Mulrone nodded thoughtfully. "He would."

Bile rose in the back of Tori's throat, burning away the lump and the taste of using her father's memory like that. She'd sworn to herself never to invoke his name that way, and yet, there she was, tossing it around like an old hat. Jon Nichols had better be worth it. The thing was, she already knew he was.

"Wait here a minute." Mulrone stepped out of his office, taking that paper from his desk with him, and mumbled something to his assistant. A few minutes later, he returned and set the same document in front of her. He'd been expecting her request and had a detail order sitting on his desk the whole time. The wheels in Tori's head spun at full speed. Firefighters were detailed out to other rigs all the time. Sometimes a crew was left short-handed when firefighters went on furlough or decided to take a training class that pulled them off duty.

"Can we keep it between us that the request came from me?"

"Of course. That's between you and me."

And his assistant, who Tori didn't trust not to run her mouth. Bits of information always leaked out of HQ offices. The crack in the system had to be somewhere, why not the assistants?

Chief Mulrone wiped the back of his hand across his blotchy forehead and heaved a sigh while Tori stared at the order in her hands. There it was in black and white. Everything she'd worked to avoid, gone with a signature.

"Well, that's everything. Consider yourself detailed to Truck 32 unless you hear from us. We'll inform Nichols that Domenico is expecting you," Mulrone said.

Tori second-guessed herself straight through the morning and most of the afternoon. It wasn't only that she missed Jon; she missed the entire crew. Almost the entire crew, anyway. Davies she could live a long, happy life never laying eyes on again. And it wasn't that the crew on Truck 32 were terrible—they were just different. The guys on Truck 19 had spoiled her with their pranks and their teasing. They'd made her feel welcomed and part of the team. The guys on Truck 32 were standoffish by comparison. Not rude, by any means. Distant. Everyone kept to themselves.

There was a lull between calls late that afternoon, and Tori found herself with nothing to do and no one to hang out with. Typically, at a time like that, she'd be chatting with Ramos or playing cards with the guys. Maybe she'd watch some television with Owens and Delaware. The crew on 32 all seemed to be doing their own thing. Some were plugged into their tablets. A few were in the workout room. Tom Leone, the designated cook for the day, was peeling the first of a mound of potatoes.

"Hey, Tom," Tori said, picking up one of the spuds. "Need a hand? I can peel a mean potato."

He quirked an eyebrow. She wasn't sure if he was more surprised by her talking to him or her offer of help, both being something out of the ordinary in this house, by the looks of it. "You sure?"

"Absolutely. I'll take over the potatoes." She surveyed the rest of the dinner's ingredients spread over the counter. "It looks like you've got plenty of other things to do here."

"Yeah, thanks," he said, happily handing over the peeler.

Tori started peeling while Tom moved on to chopping onions next to her. After a minute of working in silence, it was Tori's turn to be surprised when Tom struck up a conversation. "You're making quick work of those potatoes, Keller," he said with a touch of admiration in his voice.

"I worked in a restaurant in college. The staff was mostly students, so sometimes schedules would be a little hard to manage, and they'd need extra help in the kitchen to prep. Do those carrots need peeling, too?"

"If you don't mind," Tom said with a pleading grin. "You peel, I chop?"

"Deal," Tori said, pleased to have found a place in this firehouse, even if it was temporary. "So, Tom, how long have you been on Truck 32?"

"About five years now," he said. "Started on first shift for two years, then switched to second."

"Any reason?"

"Yeah, we're prettier," a large man rivaling Beast said. "Leone couldn't stand looking at their ugly faces anymore."

Tom laughed. "First shift is rough, man. Have you met any of those guys yet?" Tori shook her head. "Good. You'd be scarred."

"I doubt any of them own a mirror," Duncan, Beast's rival, added. "They got sick of them breaking all the time."

Tori joined their laughter, then slid a pile of corn cobs in front of Duncan. As they continued talking and laughing at first shift's expense, Duncan picked up an ear of corn and started shucking. Soon, the other guys in the room put their devices down and joined the conversation. Tori finished with the potatoes and moved on to the carrots with a smile on her face. Maybe Truck 32 wouldn't be so bad, after all.

Ramos called her later that evening to check on her. She'd just turned her phone back on when the ringing began. "Fitz says everyone on 32 is a recluse, that you could hear a pin drop on the apparatus floor from the kitchen."

"What?" Tori asked, slightly offended for her new friends. "No. You

- 243 -

just got to get used to them, that's all. They're good guys. So . . .what's the scuttle around the house?"

"I don't know," Ramos said, lowering his voice. "Mostly that manpower screwed up staffing or something. Owens is certain 32 is full up, though, and doesn't need a candidate. Even one as stellar as you."

"You didn't tell anyone, did you?"

"Of course not. Davies has been sketchy all day, though. He said something earlier about things finally being the way they were supposed to be and being man enough to take care of business."

"I bet that went over well in that crowd," Tori said with a snort.

"Not so much," Ramos said. "Are you going to tell me the real reason you asked for a transfer? Because I know you—and I know there's no way Tori Keller would take advantage of her father's name and reputation on a whim."

Ramos was right about one thing. This wasn't a whim. She'd spent the whole night before thinking this through. Davies had left her without options. Jon had been defending her. She couldn't leave him to fight for his career against Davies on his own. Not when she could do something about it.

"It's like I wrote. The house was too full of candidates, and I didn't want that to affect our training. And I needed a change in scenery. For several reasons. I am sorry I had to break my promise."

"It's okay," Ramos said, and she knew he meant it by the lightness in his tone. "Because I also know Tori Keller would never break a promise without an excellent reason. But I have to ask—did Nichols really punch Davies?"

"Is that what Davies is saying?"

"He's not saying much. It's more what he's not saying. A lot of alluding to without pointing a finger outright."

"Things got out of hand, all the way around," Tori said, still not giving Ramos the answer he was fishing for. She hated all this cloak and dagger nonsense she had to go through with Ramos. One day, she'd tell him everything. But right now, the less he knew, the better. She didn't know what sort of blackmail Davies pull next. The farther she could keep Ramos from the fallout, the better.

"Drinks tomorrow night?" Ramos asked.

Tori almost said no, remembering the last time Ramos had convinced her to go out for drinks, and he'd blindsided her with Davies. But that had been before all this craziness. There was no way Ramos would even think of attempting that stunt again.

"Sure," she said. Why not? It wasn't as though she had other plans, like a date or anything. "I'll text you tomorrow."

CHAPTER TWENTY-FOUR

"So, exactly what am I in for here?" Captain Domenico asked. He'd called the firehouse directly to speak to Jon after dinner, annoyed over being given less information than Jon had been.

"I'm not sure what you mean," Jon said, staring at Tori's detail order.

"You know. Is she one of those eggshell people? Gotta watch what we say? Up to her waist in entitlements? What's the story on this one?"

A low heat simmered inside Jon. Domenico had been working with Tori all day. Anyone who knew her for five minutes knew none of those things were remotely close to being true about her. Jon sat at his desk in his bunk, drumming his fingers on the wood surface, collecting his thoughts.

"There's nothing wrong with her," Jon said. "I don't even know why she was detailed out." Though he had a few theories. "If I were looking to unload a candidate, it wouldn't have been Keller."

"The request didn't come from you?"

"No. HQ told me you were down a man."

"We're full up here, even without Keller," Domenico said. "Ah, well, manpower screwing things up again. Good to know we're not in for a hurricane."

After hanging up, Jon joined the others in the common room. Delaware glanced up from his solitaire game with a raised eyebrow, and Owens paused his pot-scrubbing long enough to determine Jon wasn't about to make some announcement before returning to his chore. Jon found Ramos scrolling through listings for used motorcycles at the table. He remembered watching Maggie Jennis climb on an older Kawasaki and chuckled to himself. Ramos had it bad. Grabbing a piece of pie the crew had eaten for dessert while he'd been on the phone, he sat down next to Ramos.

"You talk to her at all?" Jon asked. He didn't need to specify who. They'd all been wondering the same thing. Maybe Jon a little more than the others.

"I did," Ramos said. Fitz and Beast perked up and lowered the volume on the television. Davies, however, sat still as a rock. "She's fine. Not thrilled to be detailed, but she said they're decent to her. They had a few good runs today, which helped."

Jon nodded. A good run could turnaround almost any bad day. Any real firefighter knew that.

"How long they plan on keeping our girl?" Delaware asked, his cards slapping against the table.

Jon leaned back and laced his fingers behind his head. He wanted a nice, clear view of Davies while he answered the question. "Not too long, I would think. Domenico says they're full up. They don't need another body in 32. Manpower must have screwed up."

Davies squirmed, confirming Jon's suspicions about him having a hand in the situation, but didn't say anything. In fact, by the way Davies pressed his lips together, it looked as though he was doing everything he could to keep from outing himself with some response. But it was all Jon needed to know that Davies must have issued Tori the same ultimatum.

"Good," Beast said. "32 shouldn't be poaching our candidates, anyway."

Later that night, Jon lay in his bunk, staring at his phone. If this had been two weeks prior, he would be sitting on the truck bumper, having one of the best nights of his life just talking to a girl. He'd even be content knowing she was in the bunk down the hall. But thanks to Davies, Jon was at Truck 19, and Tori was in 32, too much of the city between them.

The worst part was he wasn't even one hundred percent certain anything would be better if Tori were still at 19 after the way they'd left things. When, or if, Tori came back, nothing guaranteed that she would even look in his direction, let alone talk to him.

"Lieutenant," Owens said, coming into the kitchen from the communications room. "Manpower is on the line for you."

It was a good thing they caught him. Another five minutes and Jon would have been off duty. He'd already stowed his gear and cleaned his bunk and had been enjoying a cup of coffee while he waited for the next officer to clock in.

"Thanks," Jon said. "See you next shift."

Owens bumped his fist, then threw his bag over his shoulder and exited through the open overhead garage doors. Jon set his coffee on the console and picked up the phone, ready to hear HQ tell him to expect his candidate back next shift.

"Lieutenant Nichols? This is Chief Mulrone."

"Good morning, Chief. What can I do for you?"

"I know you're getting off duty, but do you have time to swing by headquarters this morning? It's pretty serious."

Jon's stomach tightened, as well as every muscle in his back. "Sure, I've got some time." No, he didn't, but how could he say no when the man on the other end of the phone held the power to bring Tori back to 19?

"Good. Good. I'll see you soon." Mulrone hung up, leaving Jon to stare at the receiver in his hand.

This impromptu meeting couldn't be about Tori coming back to Truck 19. Jon wouldn't be called into headquarters, off duty, for something that required nothing more than a signature on a form.

"See you next shift, Lieutenant," Davies said behind him.

Jon's fist clenched as he turned to face Davies. "You've got something you want to tell me?" Jon asked, his temple throbbing.

Davies shook his head and shrugged as though to say he didn't know what Jon was referring to, but his eyes said differently.

"What kind of game are you playing?" Jon asked, taking one threatening step forward.

"I assure you this is no game."

He'd punched Davies once and wasn't against doing it again, but they were drawing a crowd. This was neither the time nor the place for Jon to let his anger take control of him. He'd deal with Davies eventually.

"Do you get some sort of sick joy messing with people's careers?" Jon lowered his voice to keep the incoming shift from overhearing too much as they pretended not to notice the tension between Jon and Davies while setting up their gear and clocking in.

Davies narrowed his eyes, his hand tightening around his bag's strap.

"I'm just protecting my own. Lieutenant." Davies jutted his chin and strode away.

Jon regretted not knowing more about the man, like where he hung out, or what he did to occupy his time off duty. Knowledge like that would come in handy at times like this. A time where "accidentally" running into him somewhere far from the firehouse suited Jon's needs. It wouldn't do his fist any good, but his soul would be dancing.

Jon arrived at headquarters thirty minutes later and stomped straight to Chief Mulrone's office, pausing long enough to rap his knuckles on the door to announce his arrival, before pushing his way in. He wasn't usually so abrupt, and never minded adhering to the formalities of the ranks, but his conversation with Davies, if that was what it could be called, had left a pit in his stomach that had tripled in size by the time he'd stepped foot in the administrative offices.

Chief Mulrone looked up from his stack of papers when Jon entered his office. "Nichols," he said, paying no mind to the way Jon had barreled in. "I'm not going to waste your time standing on any formalities here. You know how things go."

Jon took a seat without waiting to be asked. The man did say he wasn't big on formalities, after all. "I do. What is it this time?"

Mulrone inhaled a deep breath and puffed his cheeks. "There's a charge leveled against you that you've got a romantic relationship going on with a subordinate."

Jon forced his features into a blank slate. "Who made the accusation?"

"An anonymous tip," Mulrone chuckled. "A bunch of garbage if you ask me. If you're going to make a charge like that, a charge that could take a man's job, then you should put your name on it. Anyway, this new commissioner we've got has a zero-tolerance policy on anything that could lead to potential harassment charges."

"Are you telling me I'm going to lose my job over an anonymous tip?" Jon asked, his blood racing through his veins, making his head spin.

Mulrone waved his hand in front of his face. "No. I can't in good conscious let an officer with your record go over a ghosted accusation. I do need you to sign this paper acknowledging you've been made aware of the situation. Right now, it's your word against whoever this other person is. And since you're in front of me, you've got the stronger case."

Jon failed to point out that he had neither confirmed nor denied the anonymous accusation, but his presence in Mulrone's office seemed to be enough for the chief to put his faith in Jon's innocence. Jon signed the paper, which was nothing more than a two-sentence statement confirming that yes, Mulrone had informed Jon there had been an anonymous accusation against him, then rose to leave before the chief dug deeper into the mess.

"Nichols, listen," Mulrone said just as Jon was one step away from freedom. "You're a grown man. Who am I to tell you who you can have a relationship with?"

Jon cringed. Was he about to have a conversation about relationships with Chief Mulrone? All he needed was for the man to start talking about the birds and the bees to make his discomfort complete. He'd barely gotten through the talk with his own father without crawling out of his skin.

"But the point is this: we have a no fraternizing rule in place for a reason. We can't have people distracted in this line of work. *If* something is going on, especially with a subordinate, it's best to come forward and get it on record. We'll get it sorted out and change assignments if we need to. It's safer for everyone all the way around. If you don't, and things end up going sideways, well, we'll be having a very different kind of talk. Kapeesh?"

Yeah, Jon understood. Either he confessed to not having, but wanting a relationship with Tori Keller, his candidate, and have her temporary detail become a permanent assignment. Or he denied the whole thing, and finally laid to rest any shred of hope, however small and withering it may have been, that one day Tori would open her eyes and see that they could be good together.

"I understand," Jon said, bracing himself for the next part. "There's nothing going on with anyone." It was the bitter truth. One kiss, okay two, didn't make a relationship. Nor did a handful of conversations—albeit the best conversations he'd ever had—commit either of them to anything. Tori's priority was her training and her career in the department. She'd made that clear.

Setting his ego aside, he had to do what was best for her. He owed her that much. He owed her father that much. Nothing but strict professionalism when, or rather if, they worked together. Eyes would be on him going forward until the day she no longer reported to him. Any whiff of a relationship, or any romantic feelings on his part, would be trouble for them both.

He arrived at the pediatric center five minutes before his first appointment of the day in a worse mood, if possible. Sara looked up from the reception desk when he walked in, but said nothing, recognizing the storm clouds he felt brewing behind his eyes. In the time it took him to drive from headquarters to his office, he'd let the anger sink in and take root.

It started directed squarely at Davies, but then eventually, it spread.

He was angry at Chief Mulrone for giving any weight to Davies's anonymous complaints. He was angry at Tori for getting under his skin and into his heart. He was angry at himself for letting his guard down and letting Tori win him over. He was even angry at Chief Keller for putting his nose in his daughter's business when she'd asked him not to.

Stomping into his office, he slammed his door, then sunk into his desk chair. It creaked and groaned against his weight, giving sound to the pain in his chest.

"Jon," Sara said through the closed office door. "Your first appointment is here."

Jon gritted his teeth and glared at the dent in the side of his file cabinet, wondering if Sara had seen it yet. "I'll be right there," he said. He always kept spare clothes in his office for the days he didn't have time to go home and change before meeting his first patient. He tore his department shirt off and replaced it with a clean T-shirt with the practice's new logo on the chest. He washed his hands and face in his private bathroom and ran a hand through his hair. It would have to be good enough for now. If he hadn't had to meet with Chief Mulrone, he'd been able to squeeze in a shower and manage a smile on his first full day at his very own practice. Davies had managed to ruin both the party and the first day. Bravo, Davies.

Jon paused before entering the exam room, not wanting fourteen-year-old Madison to see the expression on his face. Madison was how he imagined the cast of Mean Girls like when they'd been freshmen in high school. She had a way of targeting someone's biggest insecurities and worries, then exploiting the crap out of them. She'd almost had him in tears the day he'd told her he was striking out on his own. What would she do if she got a whiff of his heartache?

If he left Madison waiting any longer, it would throw off his whole day. On top of everything else, he didn't want his first day at the new practice to go down in history as one that got derailed from the start. He took a steadying breath and made sure to wipe the scowl from his face. Then he knocked on the door and swung it open.

"Geez, Dr. Nichols, it's about time," Madison said, hardly looking up from her phone. She was going to get carpal tunnel with the amount of texting and swiping or whatever it was that kids did these days. She finally looked up at him then, and Jon instantly wished she hadn't. "Who killed your puppy? Or is this what heartbroken Dr. Nichols looks like?"

Best first day. Ever.

CHAPTER TWENTY-FIVE

Ten shifts. One month. At least, it would be ten shifts once the day ended, but Tori might as well count it now. The guys on her detailed assignment had warmed up to her, and those periods of silence in the house were no longer awkward. Tom Leone and Duncan, in particular, made sure to include Tori in as many house activities as possible. She'd even attended Duncan's son's first birthday party the week before.

But even with her new friends, she missed Truck 19. She missed watching Delaware slap his playing cards on the table in frustration over a game of solitaire, and the hum of the blender as Beast mixed up one of his post-workout protein shakes. She missed listening to Owens and Fitz exchange verbal jabs, and she especially missed working with Ramos.

She'd expected the yearning ache to bury itself in her chest when she thought about her old firehouse. What Tori hadn't expected was the sudden feeling of being adrift. She hadn't realized the strength of the bond with her father she'd felt at Truck 19 until she'd been removed from it, cut-off from his memory and legacy. She'd been fighting against the Keller name for as long as she remembered, she'd never dreamed she would miss it when it was gone, stolen from her too soon. She'd always thought she'd be able to step out from his shadow, instead of it being ripped from her when she wasn't ready.

She always loved teaching Peter Pan to her high school students, seeing them relate to the boy who didn't ever want to grow up. The irony of how she ended up being the lost boy, searching for her shadow, and her very own Wendy Darling to sew it back on for her.

The bond with her father wasn't the only thing that had been severed. Her relationship, or whatever there had been between her and Jon Nichols, had been shredded to pieces, as well. She'd seen to that rather nicely, if she said so herself, by protecting his career and salvaging her own.

Twice in the past month, her mother had tried to talk to her about Jon, and twice Tori had shot her down, rather coldly. And when her mother had gotten nowhere with her, Maggie had stepped in with her loving but pointed questions. But Tori had held firm and had kept her lips sealed. She'd made up her mind and had done what she'd needed. As well-intentioned as they were, their prying would only twist her head around more than it already was.

How she'd managed to screw everything up to this extent, she couldn't figure out. The plan had been so simple. Graduate from the fire academy. Bust her butt during her probation period. Earn a decent house assignment. Spend the next thirty-five years doing what she'd always believed she was meant to do. Somewhere along the way, the thought of falling in love, getting married, and starting a family wove around her one-in-three-day shifts. But never had it been an option to fall in love with another firefighter.

So what if her mother didn't understand or if Maggie thought she was a giant, baby coward? Fear could be healthy. It was what kept people from jumping off buildings all willy-nilly, wasn't it? Or from diving into a pit of poisonous snakes? Or from walking into burning buildings, some people might argue.

But those people were wrong. She would never be allowed anywhere near a fire without months of extensive training, a partner to watch her back, and layers of protective gear. Falling in love with Jon Nichols was nothing like that. It was reckless and dizzying, and most days, it left her feeling ripped in half with nothing to hold her pieces together. Alone with nothing to protect her.

She'd been so naive, happy to pretend nothing threatened to tear down the wall she'd built around her heart. As long as they were in the same house, and forced to spend time together, Tori could hide in her fears, and comfort herself with his presence at the same time. Now that she was away from him, she was scared of what not loving him meant, and she realized there was more than one way to mourn the loss of someone.

Whatever. Back to her original plan of not dating anyone at all. It was easier that way. Besides, she had enough of men, working with them all day. She didn't need them off shift, too.

"Keller." Tom knocked on her bunk door. "You want to help out in the kitchen?"

Tori propped herself up on her elbows in her bunk. "Depends," she said. "What are we having?"

"Are you kidding me?" he asked, leaning against the door frame. None of the guys ever set foot in her bunk, which she appreciated, but still found amusing as Tom pressed against the invisible force field, keeping him at bay. Once, Duncan's insatiable sweet tooth had brought him to her door, hoping to raid her candy stash. She'd invited him to check out her inventory and almost doubled over in laughter, watching all the color drain from his face. "It's Taco Tuesday. Mexican food, baby."

Tori smiled. Tacos were just what the doctor ordered. If they didn't help ease her heartache, she wasn't sure anything would. "Making tacos sounds perfect right about now."

Tom nudged her with his elbow as they walked down the hall to the kitchen. "Can I ask you something? Something personal?"

Tori shrugged. "Sure, you can ask anything. But I can't guarantee I'll answer it."

"Fair enough," he said, pausing just outside the kitchen doorway. "Are you seeing anyone?" A horrified expression must have flashed across her face because he immediately stepped away and shook his head as though he'd inadvertently accused her of committing a crime. "Sorry. I was only asking because a couple of guys were talking and said they'd seen you with Ramos from 19 out a few times—"

"Oh," Tori laughed. "No. I'm not dating Ramos. We're friends from the academy. He's seeing my best friend, Maggie Jennis, the paramedic. You know her?"

"Mags?" Tom asked, his demeanor relaxing. "Yeah, she's cool. I didn't know they were seeing each other."

"It's still new. I think they're still trying to figure things out." More like Maggie had her own set of issues, and Ramos had an insane amount of patience. And Tori wasn't about to get in the middle of that mess when she'd so adeptly created one of her own to wade through.

Tom nodded, but Tori had the feeling he'd stopped listening before her explanation had ended. "Okay, Good. I mean, well, I was wondering if maybe sometime you would want to hang out? With me?"

Didn't she swear off dating? What was the universe doing to her? Maybe she should try swearing off a million dollars. Then what, universe? She waited, and so did Tom.

He looked so hopeful. And why wouldn't he? They got along great. He was cute in a boyish sort of way. Sweet. And not her officer. They would have to tell the captain they were dating, though. But, since Tori wasn't officially assigned to the same truck, there wasn't too much he could do about it unless he sent her back to Truck 19. Wouldn't that be interesting?

Did she even want to date Tom? She'd never thought about it since she'd been so hung up on Jon. But here Tom was, willing to give it a try. And there was no good reason not to.

The lights flashed, and the alarm bells pealed. "Truck 32. Apartment building fire. California Avenue. Truck 32. Apartment building fire. California Avenue."

Saved by the fire. "Talk later?" Tori asked, already turning to head toward the apparatus floor.

"Right behind you," Tom said, matching her hurried stride.

"Truck 32," Captain Domenico shouted from the front seat. "We are first truck. Truck 19 is en route."

Tori's stomach tightened. In the past month, they had yet to cross paths with Truck 19 on any of their runs. The thought of seeing Jon for the first time since the night of the party on an emergency call made focusing a monumental task. She buckled her turnout coat and strapped her helmet on, hoping it prevented the rest of the crew from noticing her minor heart attack.

"Dispatch says its four stories. Eight units on each floor. No estimation on how many people are inside," Domenico continued. "Candidate Keller." He always referred to her as a candidate when they were on a scene like she needed a reminder. "You're with Leone today."

"Yes, Captain," Tori called back to him. Tom nodded to her from his seat across from her. Of course, it had to be Tom she was partnered with for her first run-in with Jon. Not that it was important. Focus, Keller.

They pulled the truck up to the scene, and already Tori knew it would be a bad one. Black pillars of smoke rose from several spots on the roof and poured out the second-floor open windows where people hung halfway out, shouting and waving their arms. Residents of the third and fourth floors began to do the same, as more heads appeared in open windows and their shouts joined the chorus.

Tori stepped down from the rig and surveyed the scene closer while waiting for Tom to issue her orders. Thoughts of Jon and Truck 19 turned to ash along with the crumbling walls of the apartment building. She shook out her hands, which prickled with anticipation. There were so many people stranded in that building, and the flames burned too hot and too fast. Jon's words haunted her. *"We save who we can, Keller, and we get out alive."*

The captain barked out orders as Truck 19 arrived at the scene. Lieutenant Nichols jumped out of the front passenger seat and met Captain Domenico, sparing Tori the briefest of glances as he moved past her.

"Captain," Jon said, nodding toward the inferno. "Where do you want us?"

"The engine is setting up on the west side of the building. My guys are gearing up to head in. We've got quite a few residents in there still. Truck 12 is on its way. They can handle the structure and venting. I need your crew inside getting people out."

Jon nodded and motioned Delaware to his side.

"You guys take the upper two floors. Mine will take the first two," Domenico said. Then turning to Truck 32's crew, "Move!"

Tom nudged Tori forward as Jon gave his directions to the crew of Truck 19. Ramos nodded at her, as did Owens and Fitz, their mouths pulled into a tight line. Only Davies had the nerve to smirk at a time like that as she passed him.

Duncan led the way into the building. From what they saw outside, the blaze had originated somewhere in the middle of the second floor. But thanks to the flimsy building material, the flames had roared its way up the building's side to the top two stories and sank its way down below.

"Stairs are over here," Tom said. "You ready?"

Tori nodded. "Let's do it." Dropping into a low crouch, she followed Tom up the stairs to the second floor. Duncan and Keith Wells, another 32 crew member, were behind them.

"We'll take north. Duncan, you guys hit south," Tom said, moving to the first apartment door. "Keller, get the next one."

Tori crawled down the hall, checking for any damaged or weakened spots before one wrong step sent her crashing to the floor below. She banged the next door with the butt of her ax. "Fire department," she yelled. The fire was too aggressive in its destruction for her to wait for an answer. Wedging the blade of her ax in the door frame, she busted the lock and swung the door open. "Anyone here?"

Black smoke hung in the air, making it difficult to see. Even with her gear on, she could feel the heat wrap around her, choking the air from her lungs. Shouts reached her from the corner by the window. These were some of the people she'd seen from outside crying for help. She rushed over to them, a grandmother and a boy of about eight years.

"Is there anyone else here?" she asked.

The grandmother coughed and shook her head. Tori removed her oxygen mask and placed it over the grandmother's face.

"Breathe," Tori said. "We're going to get you out of here." She took the boy's face in her hands. "You okay?" He nodded, his eyes wide with raw fear. "See this belt?" The boy nodded again. "You hold on to this. Stay with me, okay? I'm going to help your grandma."

The grandmother tried to give Tori back her mask, but Tori put it back over the woman's head. "The fire hasn't come this far yet, but the smoke is worse out there. Just breathe." She turned back to the boy. "When we get out into the hall, I want you to hold your breath as long as you can. Tug on my belt when you need to let it out, okay?"

Tori led them out into the hall. The boy puffed his cheeks and stuck close to Tori's side. Tori wrapped an arm around the grandmother, half-carrying and half-dragging her down the hall toward the stairs, where Tom escorted a family of five to safety. The boy tugged on her belt, and Tori pulled him lower to the floor where the air was not as dense with smoke and ash.

"Take a breath." The boy did and gave Tori a thumbs up. Tori squeezed his hand and continued their trek out of the building. This kid was made of steel.

Ambulances waited on the curb, and they were met with paramedics as soon as they exited the building. Tori nodded to Maggie as she swept away the family Tom had brought out. Another paramedic appeared at Tori's side and relieved the grandmother of the oxygen mask, handing it back to Tori. "Don't let the captain see you," the paramedic remarked, then whisked the boy and old woman away.

"Round two, Keller," Tom said, already heading back toward the burning building.

Tori pounded on three more apartment doors and brought out seven more residents. She returned from her fourth trip inside empty-handed, after searching the final apartment and taking another look inside the ones she'd already evacuated, being sure to close every door behind her. The engine's crew battled the blaze from both the outside and the inside, carrying miles of hose into the building, snaking it up the stairs and down halls. The flames rose higher than it had even thirty seconds before. The monster had no intention of going down quietly. She could see the entire west side of the building crumbling as the fire fed, gathering strength.

The rest of Truck 32's crew gathered near the rig after completing their searches, removing helmets and masks to take a breath of fresh air. Tori joined them, leaning against the truck next to Duncan. He offered her his fist, which she thumped with her own.

"Good job, Keller," he said. "Glad to have you here."

Tori ducked her head to hide her smile. After what she'd seen inside, the destruction of these poor people's homes and property, smiling with pride seemed out of place and insensitive. And even though her chest ached from the strain of breathing through the smoke while carrying people twice her size out of a building, it swelled with Duncan's praise. She *had* done a good job. She'd done a job worthy of the Keller name.

Tori's moment of satisfaction didn't last long. The air around her hissed with electricity, and hair on the back of her neck stood on end. Truck 19's crew shifted uncomfortably huddled by their rig, and Delaware was speaking into Captain Domenico's ear. The guys on 32 nudged each other and straightened their backs. Tori knew it was coming a second before it started. She smelled it on the wind mixed with smoke.

The high-pitched alarm bleated in her ear.

Mayday.

Tori's eyes flew around the two crews, mentally taking a roll call. Her blood froze in her veins.

Jon was missing.

CHAPTER TWENTY-SIX

Jon clamped his jaw tight against the pain shooting up his leg and spearing his chest. Three inches. If he'd moved three inches forward or backward, the beam would have missed him, and he'd already be out of the building, slapping his crew on their backs for another successful search and rescue. At the very least, he should never have sent Delaware out ahead of him, and then he would have had an extra pair of hands to help him out of this mess.

Jon had been distracted by movement in the corner, which had only been a stray cat hiding from the fire and smoke. By the time he'd turned back to the door, the flames had done a number on the beams above him. He'd registered the splintering of old wood a second too late, and one of those beams had come crashing down on top of him, knocking him to the ground and pinning him under its weight.

He'd tried to drag himself out from under it, but each strain produced black spots in his vision and caused a cold sweat to break out and shortness of breath. He had two choices: grit his teeth and stubbornly try to free his shattered leg from under the beam, risking the chance of passing out, or pull the ripcord on the alarm attached to his shoulder and call a mayday.

Jon shut his eyes, whispered a prayer, and sounded the alarm. Domenico had warned him he was about to call an evacuation, ordering the search crews out of the building to let the engineers do their thing. Jon had assured him he wouldn't be long, and now he'd gotten himself trapped.

The ceiling creaked and groaned as the fire continued its rampage. It wouldn't be long before another one of those beams gave way. Maybe the next one would land on his head.

Domenico wouldn't send anyone in for him. He couldn't risk someone else's life, and Jon didn't want him to. If it were him on the outside calling the shots, he'd hold them back and hope whoever was stuck would be able to wait out the flames.

Jon thought of Sara, grateful he'd had the foresight to leave her the building if anything happened to him. She could sell it or rent it out. She'd always been the brains behind the business of the practice. She'd know what to do with it.

He thanked God for the life he'd been given and wondered if he would see his parents again.

But all of that distracted him from the one memory pushing its way forward: the image of Tori Keller in her ball gown, her lips pressed to his.

Tears stung his eyes as pictures of a life he'd never wanted flashed in his mind. A life filled with laughter, friends, and love, instead of living like a hermit, keeping to himself for the rest of his days. He pressed a hand into his chest to keep his heart from leaping out. It was better this way—not leaving anyone behind. No wife and beautiful, strong-willed daughter to mourn him.

The mayday alarm pierced through the haze hovering above him, strangely comforting in the dark. It reminded him he wasn't alone, after all. Just outside those walls, his crew stood watch. He knew they would be there until the end, no matter what that ending was. He would never truly been alone, as hard as he'd tried.

*****

Ramos was the one who voiced Tori's nightmare. He stood in front of her, his hand on her arm, holding her up or holding her back, she couldn't tell.

"It's Nichols," Ramos said. "He's trapped in the basement."

Tori's breath dragged out of her in a painful gasp. Her knees buckled, and she fell against the side of the truck. *How?* This couldn't be happening. Jon knew better than that. He knew how to get out, but more importantly, he knew *when.* He wouldn't get himself caught behind the wall of fire. And why was he alone, anyway? Didn't he learn anything from her father?

"Where was his partner?" Tori asked, steadying herself, and adjusting the air tank on her back.

Ramos's eyes grazed past Delaware as he shrugged. "Nichols sent him out ahead of him."

"Who's going in to get him?" Tori frantically looked from Ramos to Tom to Captain Domenico, who was still talking to Delaware and the rest of Truck 19. "Ramos. Who. Is. Going. In. To. Get. Him?"

"Captain called an evac, Keller," Tom said, putting a hand on her shoulder. "No one's going in."

"We can't just leave him in there." Tori's voice rose, drawing the captain's attention. "Captain, you *can't* leave him in there."

"Keller," Domenico said, shaking his head. "We don't have a choice.

I can't take a gamble with any more lives. We have to let the engineers do their job and bring the fire under control first."

"It will be too late then." Tori's hands fisted at her sides, and her legs tensed, gathering their strength back. She'd lost her father to a mayday, an evacuation gone wrong. Domenico expected her to what, wait, while one of their own was trapped? Oh, God, was Jon scared? Was he hurt or fighting to get out? Did he know no one was coming for him?

Tori bit the inside of her cheek to hold back the flood of tears, desperately looking for a release as her heartbeat thundered in her ears. *Kellers don't cry. Kellers don't cry.*

The radio on Ramos's shoulder crackled. He started to move away, but Tori gripped his arm, holding him in place. She would rip that speaker right off his shoulder if she had to, but she wasn't going to miss hearing Jon's voice.

"Truck 19," Jon's strained voice came over the speaker. He was hurt. She knew it. She could hear the pain he struggled to hold back from them. Even at a time like this, he was still trying to do the noble thing. "I'm turning command over to Captain Domenico. The evac stands." He coughed. "It's been an honor." The radio crackled again, then went dead.

*****

Jon wished he could have said more, but he wouldn't have been able to hold it together, so he clicked off the radio and let it fall to his side. They didn't need to hear him break down. The crew didn't deserve that guilt saddled to their backs for the rest of their lives. Besides, they weren't the ones he wanted to talk to.

He wanted Tori.

He adjusted his oxygen mask and considered removing it altogether. Maybe if he passed out from smoke inhalation before the flames reached him, he wouldn't feel it in the end. He could escape the pain in his leg, at least, though even that had seemed to subside—nerve damage.

It would be so easy. Just slip off the mask. Close his eyes. Let everything he'd trained for slip away.

Truck 19 doesn't give up. Truck 19 doesn't quit.

Jon squeezed his eyes tighter. *Okay, Chief. I hear you.* He stilled his hand over his mask and left it in place. Just a few more minutes. Not like he had any longer than that, anyway.

Something snapped above him. Wires, most likely. Orange flames ate away at the ceiling, raining ash down on his face as half the lights went out.

*****

The crews of both Truck 32 and Truck 19 gathered around Captain Domenico. Some hung their heads low. Others avoided looking at anyone else. Everyone was deathly silent. Even Davies showed the proper amount of respectful sullenness. The captain had received a report from the engineers as they worked to beat back the blaze. Structurally unsound. That was what they'd deemed the building. They weren't sending anyone inside with a hose, deciding to fight it from the outside only.

Tori backed away from the group. She couldn't hear any more of this insanity without giving in to the nausea rolling over her. Raising her eyes to the sky, she whispered a prayer, wishing someone, anyone, heard the words from her heart. But there was only one person she needed to hear her, and she hoped her pleas reached him.

"Dad," she whispered so softly, she hardly heard herself over the alarms and commotion. "What do I do? I can't lose him, Dad. I can't. This can't be it. Not like this."

Tori stared at the flames erupting from the apartment building. Windows shattered from the heat, releasing more ominous smoke and burning orange tentacles in the air, looking as though they wanted to wrap the whole building in its fiery embrace and carry it off, along with the only man she'd ever loved.

Then through the smoke and fire, something glinted in the corner of her eye. She turned to find the source and spotted the basement door. Blinking, she cleared her eyes and looked closer. She didn't imagine it. The building's east side hadn't been engulfed in flames yet. Hidden by overgrown shrubbery, a door led to the basement where Jon was trapped.

Did anyone know? Who was in charge of searching the basement? Delaware? Duncan?

There was still time. There had to be.

Her eyes flew to the sky one more time as if the clouds revealed the answers she wanted.

A breeze brushed past her and seemed to carry words meant only for her to hear. *Kellers don't leave anyone behind. Kellers don't give up.*

Tori slid her oxygen mask in place and strapped her helmet on.

*****

Jon tried to remember the last conversation he'd had with Tori. A real conversation. Not one in passing when she'd been on Truck 19, and he'd been pretending to not be completely in love with her, hurting from her rejection. He should have known when he hadn't been able to keep his eyes off her whenever they'd been in the same room that his life would never be the same. And when she smiled—oh, that smile—his chest tightened. He'd do just about anything to see that smile again.

To kiss her again. Even if it had to be another fleeting moment stolen in the shadows, he'd settle for anything he could get.

Tears mixed with sweat and dirt, stinging his eyes. He should have told her when he'd had the chance. He'd been stupid and scared, then stupid again. He should have held her close and told her every day how he felt. He should have told her he'd wait for her to feel the same.

So many things he would have done differently if given a chance. A chance he knew he would never get. This wasn't a movie. There was no fairy godmother, no magic genie. The only thing he could do now was to send his heart out into the universe and hope it reached her somehow.

"I love you, Tori Keller. I always will."

*****

"Keller," Tom shouted. "Where do you think you're going?" He ran to catch up to her, but she'd already reached the tangle of branches covering the stairs leading to the basement door and had begun hacking away at them with her ax.

"The fire isn't bad here," she said without stopping. "We can get to Nichols through here."

"Domenico called an evac."

"I heard," she said, taking another swing at the shrubs. She didn't care how many evacuations the captain called if Jon Nichols wasn't standing outside with the rest of the crew. They could get the mayor, the president even, no chain of command was strong enough to stop her from trying.

"You're gonna get yourself killed," Tom argued, placing a hand on her shoulder.

"Maybe," she said, caring even less about that. "But Kellers don't give up." She shrugged his hand off and swung again and again until she cleared a path to reach the door. "Are you going to help me?" she asked, plunging down the stairs and jamming a crowbar into the space between the door and the frame.

Tom hesitated as Tori put her whole body into popping open the door. When it didn't budge, she picked up her ax and wailed against the doorknob until it and its lock fell straight off.

"Well?" She asked, prying the metal door open.

Tom shook his head. "At the very least, they'll take your job. You'll be off the department. Is that what your father would have wanted?"

She'd never been surer of anything her father had ever wanted. She cast one last glance over her shoulder at Tom, then stepped inside and closed the basement door behind her.

*****

Despite his best efforts not to, Jon couldn't resist turning his radio back on to hear something other than the fire and his impending death. He wasn't disappointed. As soon as he clicked it on, the static on the other end heralded a transmission.

"Keller, get out of there now," Captain Domenico shouted into the radio.

Jon gasped for air, clutching at his chest. *Get out of where? No. She wouldn't be that stupid.*

He remembered that drill and the way she'd asked him how they were supposed to walk away. He'd seen it in her eyes then but hadn't known what it was—that fierce determination and protectiveness for a future someone she hadn't even known. If she'd felt that way about a stranger, what lengths wouldn't she go to for someone she knew?

But this was too dangerous. This wasn't a drill. This was a real fire with real consequences, one that would take her life as easily as it burned through the twenty-year-old shag carpet blanketing the floors. She'd learned her lesson. She'd said so.

The radio crackled again. "With respect, Captain—no." She sounded out of breath, and he knew she was fighting like hell to get to him.

Stubborn, rebellious Tori.

God, he loved her.

A beam of light cut through the darkness, slicing through the soot hanging in the air. His breath caught in his chest as an angel, his angel, followed.

"Jon," Tori called. "Jon, where are you?"

*****

He was here. Tori felt it in her bones. A beam had fallen and was perched in the type of position that could trap someone underneath. Frayed wires hung from the ceiling, their ends sparking, like tiny flares in the fog. She climbed around boxes and junk residents had deposited in the basement pit over the years, stomping on the ones in her way, not caring about the crunch of glass she heard as her foot came down on them. The only thing she cared about saving was somewhere under that beam.

"Jon," she shouted again, hoping he hadn't passed out. Or worse. She pushed those thoughts behind her and moved forward. A thin, shaky light waved back and forth. Throwing chairs and old bicycles out of the way, she followed the light like there was a pot of gold at the end.

She dropped to her hands and knees when she reached the beam, out of breath and shaking from the amount of adrenaline coursing through her veins. But her smile stretched across her face despite their circumstances. She'd found him. He was alive—and pissed off.

"What do you think you're doing?" he yelled at her. "You're going to get yourself killed!"

"Me? Why would you get yourself trapped under a beam?" She shone her light on the piece of wood, following the length of it, assessing the damage to Jon's legs. "Can you feel your legs at all?"

"Tori, you gotta get out of here. This whole ceiling is going to come down any minute. Just go."

Tori ignored him and pushed against the beam, testing its weight. "Can you feel your legs or not?" Rummaging around, she found a pipe near the wall. Grabbing that and a paint can, she returned to Jon, and wedged one end of the pipe under the beam and rested it on the side of the can.

"I can't," Jon said, growing more agitated. "Get out of here."

Tori's radio crackled. "Tori." Maggie's voice was sharp but compassionate. "What are you thinking?"

Tori shook her head once, then pressed the radio call button. "Just be ready for us, Mags." She tore the radio unit from her shoulder and launched it across the room. Moving to the other side of Jon, she wedged the blade of her ax under the beam. "I'm going to need your help. I can't do this alone."

"Tori."

"Jon." Tori took his face in her hands and looked directly into his eyes. "I'm not leaving you. Not now. Not ever. Either you help me, or I can lie down and wait for the end with you. You choose."

*****

Jon couldn't let her die in there. Not because of him.

"You never did learn the meaning of evacuation, did you? Help me sit up," he said, biting the inside of his cheek.

"Blame my training officer," she said, grabbing an arm and pulling him to a sitting position. He leaned over to reach the pipe, grimacing against the pain shooting up his chest and into his neck. Bones could tear through his flesh, but there was no way he would cry out. Not when Tori put it all on the line for him.

- 274 -

"On the count of three," she said.

He nodded and braced himself on the metal pipe, waiting for her signal, already searching for the right words to use to get her to leave him if this plan didn't work. Tori readied herself on her ax, her lips pressed tight, and her brow furrowed in strained concentration.

"One. Two. Three."

In unison, they each leaned on their levers. The beam groaned and raised barely half an inch. Jon draped himself across the pipe, putting his whole body weight into it. He didn't even have time to think of the next step, before Tori grabbed his turnout pants and yanked his legs free from under the beam, nearly taking his feet off with his boots.

She fell on top of him with a breathless laugh. "Let's get out of here."

*****

Tori couldn't believe that had worked. They'd practiced lever drills at the academy, but never when the victim had to help free himself. Adrenaline rocked.

Tori inspected Jon's legs enough to know there was no way he would walk out on his own. One knee bent at an unnatural angle, and thick blood stained the other pant leg. Even sitting was too much exertion for him, draining his face of all its color.

Creaking overhead drew Tori's attention to the ceiling. Jon was right—it was going to come down on them, and soon.

"Leave me," he said, staring at the same spot above them, his pallor turning the color as the ash around them. "You can't drag me out of here in time."

Anger boiled inside her, burning as hot as the fire threatening to engulf them. "Stop saying that," she snapped. "Stop telling me to leave you." She fixed his mask over his face. "We're getting out of here. And it's going to hurt."

Hooking her arms under Jon's armpits, she started to drag him back the way she'd come, every inch causing him excruciating pain. Tori's heart squeezed each time he grimaced or clamped his jaw to keep from howling. She wished she could stop to comfort him and wipe the sweat from his brow, but he was right, there was no time for that. Comfort will come later—after they both made it out.

"Sorry," she muttered and continued to drag his limp body through the basement as the flames above followed them. Pieces of the ceiling fell around them. Wires crackled and melted in the heat, then whatever was left of the lights went out, pitching them in complete darkness, with only the fire to see by. It had crept down the west wall, catching hold of boxes and rolled-up carpets. Tori's eyes flitted around the large room as she yanked Jon back another foot. They were surrounded by kindling. Tightly packed cardboard and synthetic fibers would bring about their death.

"Tori," Jon said, his voice strained and raw.

"Don't—" Another pull, another foot closer to the door—another pain-filled groan from Jon.

"I'm going to pass out," he said.

That was it. The pain and blood loss had been too much for him. It was better this way. He wouldn't feel the pain now, and she didn't have to feel bad every time they moved. And move they had to.

Dropping to her knees, Tori ditched her air tank and oxygen mask, then pulled Jon's body across her back. Crawling on all fours, she headed straight toward the basement door. The fire had already caught up to them, lighting the boxes and piles on either side of her ablaze. Tori gritted her teeth and heaved their bodies forward.

Kellers don't give up. Kellers don't leave anyone behind.

CHAPTER TWENTY-SEVEN

Jon blinked open his eyes to beeping machines and tubes in his arm and nose. A plaster cast encased his right leg, lying in its own little hammock six inches off the bed. The left one was bound in miles of bandages, but no cast. He took a mental catalog of his body and realized there wasn't one inch that wasn't in pain. But he'd take it. Pain meant he was alive.

He turned his head and found Sara sitting in the corner of the hospital room, her head resting on her hand, her eyes closed. "Sara," he tried to say, but his throat was so raw from the smoke, he didn't recognize his own voice.

She stirred and woke with a little jolt. When she saw him staring at her, she leaped from her seat and rushed to the side of the bed. "Jon, you're awake." Reaching over his head, she pressed the call button to alert the nurse on duty. "I can't believe you're awake. I'm gonna kill you when you're better, just so you know."

If he didn't think it would hurt too much, he would have laughed. He couldn't wait to be well enough to let Sara try.

A nurse rushed in, then paused at the foot of the bed. "Well, hello,

Mr. Nichols. I'm happy to see you're awake. My name is Carly, and I'm your nurse." Carly played with the machine at the side of his bed, pinching her eyebrows together the way Tori did when she concentrated. "You are one fortunate man, Mr. Nichols. Do you know that?"

"I have some idea," he croaked.

"Your right leg is broken in three places. Your left suffered severe lacerations. Less than a centimeter deeper, and you would have severed your femoral artery, and you could have bled out. You inhaled a lot of smoke, so we'd like to monitor your breathing for a while," Carly said, writing things in Jon's chart and looking at him as though it was his fault. Maybe it was. "Your guardian angel was working overtime with you."

A guardian angel named Tori.

Carly left with promises of bringing the doctor to talk to him, but there was only one person he wanted to see. "Where is she?" he asked Sara.

Sara pressed her lips together and shook her head. "She was released last night. Her mother picked her up, but she hasn't been back."

Jon closed his eyes, and memories from the fire raged back at him. He'd never been so relieved and terrified to see anyone in his entire life as he'd been when Tori appeared in that basement. She'd risked everything to go after him when the captain called the evacuation: her job, her reputation, her life. Even when he'd told her, begged her, to leave and save herself, she'd refused. Kellers really didn't give up.

What was it she'd said? That she wasn't going to leave him. Not then. Not ever.

But here he was. Where was she?

*****

"Victory Celeste Keller, where do you think you're going?" Tori's mother stood in front of her, her hands planted square on her hips, determined to stop her from leaving her apartment ever again. Maggie leaned against the kitchen doorway, rolling a water bottle between her hands, watching the standoff. "You just got home after spending the night in the hospital."

"I'm fine, Mom," Tori said, sending a pleading glance to Maggie to jump in and take her side. "They wouldn't have let you take me home if I wasn't."

"You're going back, aren't you?" Her mother narrowed her eyes and pursed her lips in the same suck a lemon way she did when she spoke about her ex.

"To the hospital?"

Anna turned her head away and took a long shuddering breath. "Not the hospital."

Tori bit her lip and turned to Maggie, looking for some clarification.

"Tor," Maggie said, sounding exasperated.

"Mags."

Maggie widened her eyes and huffed, throwing her hands down at her side. "Are you serious?"

"What?" It didn't feel like they were having the same conversation. Maggie and her mother were on the same page, but they'd lost Tori somewhere. Maybe her head was still stuck in that smoke-filled basement under a beam.

"Tori, just stop a minute," Maggie said, softening her tone. "Your mom just got her second call from the department in less than a year. Think about that."

"Tori," her mother said, the break in her voice the only outward show of any emotion other than annoyance. "Tori, I just got you back."

Covering her face with her hands, Tori shook her head then wrapped her arms around her mother, pulling her into a tight embrace. Her mother hadn't meant she'd just gotten her back from the hospital. She'd meant she'd just gotten her back from the fire. She'd gotten her back from the same fate her husband had suffered less than a year ago. She'd meant she'd just gotten Tori back *alive*. Anna Keller, the woman who didn't cry, the strongest woman Tori had ever known, sobbed into her daughter's shoulder.

"I'm sorry, Mom. I'm sorry," Tori said, stroking her mother's hair, one lone tear escaping down her cheek. "I'm okay. I promise. I'm going to take care of everything, and you'll never have to worry about me like that again. I'm going to fix everything. I swear, I will. Just don't cry, okay? Kellers don't cry, remember?"

Anna sniffed and pulled away. "Well, I was a Roginski before I was a Keller, and Roginskis cry." She smoothed a piece of Tori's hair away from her face. "I want you to be happy and do what you love. I'm just a silly old woman. Don't mind my blubbering."

"I will be happy," Tori assured her. "And you're not silly. It's okay to cry when you need to, Mom. You're still one tough cookie. You had to be. You were stuck raising me."

The only way Anna allowed Tori to leave was if she promised to text her mother every hour and then spend the night in her old bedroom in the house she'd grown up in. Tori had agreed and packed a bag before leaving. She could use a night of being babied.

Maggie drove her to headquarters, where Tori knew she'd find Chief Mulrone in his office, just like she'd known he would see her without an appointment. Those few minutes she'd spent in that fiery basement had felt like an eternity, and a lot of thinking could take place in an eternity.

Somewhere between dragging Jon's legs out from under a fallen beam, to crawling out of the basement on her hands and knees with her lieutenant passed out across her back, she'd realized something.

Yes, her father had pulled strings to put her on Truck 19 against her will. But it hadn't been to train her. If that had been the case, Jon would have known. Her father had been much cleverer than that. Jon Nichols wasn't the only officer in the city her father had trusted and respected, but he was the only one her father had thought of as a son. He'd sent her to Truck 19, to that shift, not to train—but to fall in love with Jon.

Tori knocked twice, then stepped inside and took a seat opposite Mulrone as he finished with his phone call. She knew the call had been about her by the way he lowered his voice and reverted to using all pronouns. Every adult did that when they thought they were hiding something from the kids. And to some of these guys, she would always be one of the kids.

"You could have taken some time before coming in," Mulrone said. His mouth twitched as though he couldn't decide if he was happy to see her or not. "Technically, you're off shift now."

"Technically, I'm laid up and off active duty."

Mulrone nodded. "True. So, what brings you in so soon?"

"Well, Chief Mulrone, I think it's time you and I had a serious talk about my role in this department. And I thought, why wait?"

Mulrone nodded again and folded his arms across his chest. She knew what she'd done. She'd ignored a direct order. Again. In a real fire, not a drill. She'd violated several fire department codes: disobeyed an evacuation order, gone on scene without a partner, abandoned fire department equipment—namely her air tank, mask, and radio. The Keller name offered some leniency, but she'd gone well past the limit. Yet, even after all that, it didn't look as though Chief Mulrone relished the idea of canning one of his buddies' kids, especially a woman who had just been on the news for saving the life of a fellow firefighter. The press would have a field day with that, and they both knew it.

"You never were one to wait, were you?" His face finally relaxed into that smile he'd been holding back. "Well, I suppose you're right. Why don't you start?"

*****

The entire crew turned up at Jon's bedside the next day. The entire crew minus one. Even Davies walked in with his head bent and shoulders slumped. But still no Tori. The nurse had said she'd gone home, so she must have been okay. Jon couldn't figure out why she stayed away when he couldn't force her out when her life had literally depended on it.

He wanted to thank her, yell at her, make her promise never to do anything that stupid and reckless again. But most of all, he wanted to tell her he loved her. He wanted to tell her all the things that he'd regretted not saying before while he'd lain in a burning building waiting for his death.

But she hadn't come, and Sara refused to let him have his phone back, claiming his only job was to get better. People knew where he was, she argued, they would come to him if they needed to. He didn't need the added stress. And when she wasn't there policing him, Nicki was her enforcer.

Why was he surrounded by stubborn women?

"How are you feeling, Lieutenant?" Delaware asked with his hands shoved in his pocket, shifting from one foot to the other.

Jon studied all the hang-dog faces around his bed. Dark circles rimmed all their eyes. Eyes that refused to meet his. Though there was no reason for them to feel guilty, it was evident that each of them carried the burden of Jon's current condition on their shoulders, like he hoped they wouldn't.

"Like my legs were crushed, and I was left alone in a basement to die," Jon said. He couldn't resist playing with them. It was the most fun he'd had in a few days, and he needed something to divert his attention away from thinking about Tori's absence and what it meant. The whole crew went pale—except for Davies—and Jon let out a peal of laughter, followed by a violent round of coughing. "I'm joking, you jerks. I'm gonna be fine. They've got me pumped up on so many pain meds right now; I barely feel my legs."

"Look, Jon," Owens started, but Jon cut him off.

"You guys did your jobs. Captain called an evac, and you got yourselves out of there. That's what you were trained to do—what I wanted you to do. I don't want anyone feeling bad or guilty. You followed the orders an officer gave you. End of story."

"Fair enough." Owens nodded, some color returning to his cheeks. "So, what are the doctors saying?"

Jon drew in a heavy breath, causing him to erupt in coughs again. "Cast should come off in eight weeks," he said, regaining his composure. "Stitches in the other one come out next week. Then it's physical therapy for another eight weeks. So, I'll be laid up for at least four months."

Delaware let out a low whistle. "On the bright side, I know a killer physical therapy joint that just opened up."

Jon chuckled, then groaned, rubbing a hand over his face. He needed a shave. "Can you believe it? Just opened, and now I can't even be there. What a mess."

"Could be worse," Fitz said. He was right. Jon shouldn't even think of complaining. "Beast is cooking the next four shifts."

Beast punched Fitz in the shoulder while the others laughed, and Jon grinned. He was going to miss seeing these guys every third day. He'd tried not to get attached, but all the hiding away in his bunk and turning down social invitations couldn't break the bond they'd formed over years of close quarters and watching each other's backs.

"What am I going to do with myself for the next few months?" Jon asked no one in particular.

"I can think of a few things."

The room stilled. Jon's heart thundered in his chest. That was what the sound of her voice did to him. He strained to see over the crew's heads, but his leg was still hanging in that stupid hammock thing, and he couldn't wrestle himself free from it. His eagerness to see her must have shown through, because the guys parted like the Red Sea, revealing Tori framed by his hospital room doorway, a playful grin on her gorgeous face, the fluorescent lights in the hall glowing behind her like a halo.

"There you are," Jon said, his mouth spread in a wide smile until his face ached as much as the rest of him. He held one arm out to her, and without hesitation, she flew into his embrace.

*****

Tori pressed her lips to his, not giving a flying flip who was there or what they thought. No more hiding in the shadows or lying to herself and everyone else about who she was.

Her name was Victory Celeste Keller, also known as Chief Keller's kid, and she was unapologetically and irrevocably in love with Lieutenant Jonathon Nichols.

Tori breathed him in and gripped his shoulders, careful not to pull any wires or plugs. Jon was alive and well, sort of. He would heal and be fine, and that was what mattered. It had physically hurt her to stay away for so long, but she had things to take care of before she could come here and tell him everything. And now that she was here, there was nothing she could do but kiss him.

One of his arms tightened around her waist, holding her close, his other hand found its way to the back of her neck, his fingers tangling in her hair. She sank deeper into the kiss, never wanting to come up for air again.

"Get a room," Fitz called out behind her.

Jon pulled back from her lips far enough to answer him. "I have one. You're standing in it." Then he pressed his mouth to hers again before releasing her to the wolves.

"Hello, boys," Tori said, facing her former crew and perching on the edge of the bed. Jon's arm, holding firm around her waist, hadn't left her with any other option, and she was perfectly fine with that. She brushed her fingertips against her lips, feeling them swell from the kiss. "I'm glad you're all here. There's something I have to tell you."

"They canned you, didn't they?" Beast asked, his jaw clenching.

"Filthy bureaucrats," Delaware said. "You pull a man out, save his life, one of our own, and this is how they thank you?"

Davies straightened his shoulders. She had hoped he would be there and would react in his typical smug Davies way. It was much more satisfying to see his expression when he found out his big plans of getting her kicked out had failed. "She flagrantly ignored a command. Again."

"Shut up, Davies," Ramos said. "You've been trying to get her to leave since the first day at the academy."

"She's dangerous," Davies said.

Jon's arm tightened, and Tori knew he was doing everything he could to keep from getting out of bed. Tori squeezed his hand and stepped in before things got ugly, and someone ended up in the room next door.

"Okay, guys, cool it," Tori said. She waited until the grumbling died down before continuing. "Yes, I'm done at Truck 19, or 32, or any other truck. It was my decision, and I'm fine with it. I didn't think I would be, but I am. The truth is: I do not regret one second of going into that building, and I would have done it for any one of you. Even Davies." She got a few chuckles. "It's just who I am. Who my father raised me to be. But I'm not leaving the department completely. Fellas—meet the newest Chicago Fire Department Bureau of Operations instructor."

"You're gonna teach now?" Owens asked.

"Yep. New candidates and the junior training academy high school program. It's the best of both my worlds. I get to stay in the department while putting my teaching experience to good use." She turned to Jon with a smile. "And I was hoping since you have nothing better to do, that you would help me put together my junior class curriculum. I have a whole pile of boxes full of department information to go through."

Jon gazed into her eyes, and Tori felt herself getting lost in their depths, the room and the people in it fading into the distant background. She steadied herself by placing a hand on his chest and felt his heart beating under her palm, its increasing pace matching her own. His eyes dipped to her mouth briefly before holding her gaze again.

Someone cleared their throat behind her, but she barely registered the sound or the implication. "We'll come back later, Lieutenant," Delaware said. "Looks like you two have some catching up to do."

The crew shuffled out, leaving Tori alone with Jon, finally. She hadn't been lying when she'd said she was happy to see them all, but after the initial greetings, she was ready for them to leave.

"I think he was right. We do have some catching up to do," Jon said, playing with a lock of her hair. "I hated not talking to you. I never want to go through that again. If I have to wait for you to come around, I'll wait. I'll do whatever you want me to do, but I love you, and I'm not letting something stupid like department red tape come between us."

A slow grin spread across Tori's face. "You said you love me. Was that the pain meds talking?"

"It was definitely not the pain meds, Keller. And I think you know it."

"Good," Tori said, with an air of authority. "Because I did something I wasn't sure you'd be okay with."

Jon narrowed his eyes but didn't loosen his grip on her. "What did you do now?"

"I was hoping you would feel that way, seeing as how I saved your life and all, so I already filled out a consensual relationship agreement. You just have to sign it to make it official."

"Show me the dotted line, Keller."

Tori pulled a paper from her bag and a pen. "You're sure this isn't the pain meds talking?"

Jon snatched the paper from her hand and signed his name with a flourish. "Listen, if Chief Keller, in all his wisdom, brought us together, who am I to disagree? Besides, you're the one who likes to disobey orders. Not me."

"In that case, Lieutenant Nichols, I order you to kiss me again."

"Yes, ma'am." Dropping the pen, he cradled her head in his hand and brought her lips to his for a lingering kiss full of warmth and promises. "I love you, Tori Keller. I swear I will always fight for us. No matter what comes our way."

"I love you, too. You're stuck with me now. The paperwork says so." She laid her head on his shoulder with a small laugh. "My dad would be so happy. The first relationship he would approve of, and he's not here."

Jon's fingers danced along her scalp as he played with her hair. "I think he knows."

Kellers don't leave anyone behind. Even in death.

"I think so, too." Tori sighed. "He always did love being right."

Acknowledgements

Fun fact: I never wanted to write a story about firefighters. It's true. It was never on my radar. After being married to one for over a dozen years, I guess you could say, the veneer on that particular trope had lost some of its luster. But, one day, as I struggled to write my then work-in-progress, my husband playfully asked, "Hey, where's my firefighter romance story?" And there it was—the seed had been planted.

Because of that fateful day, my first and biggest thank you must go to my husband, who not only sparked the whole idea, but served as my technical consultant, answering the oddest questions, including ones like, "What *do* you guys call the bathroom, anyway?"

I also need to send a big thank you to my pal and beta reader, Anne Barker. Your support and feedback were invaluable. Thank you for always answering my oddball texts and helping me rate book boyfriends in order of preference.

My editor, Nicole Frail, as always, worked her magic and none of my stories would ever see the light of day without her. She deserves all the ice cream. All of it. Thank you, Nicole, for your insight and wisdom, and for bringing the next gal into my life: Kerri Odell. A big, huge, shoutout of gratitude goes to Kerri for the gorgeous cover design, and literally taking the characters out of my head and putting them on paper.

And lastly, thank you to my readers, who make this whole journey so much more fun. I love hearing from you and talking all things life, love, and anything else that comes to mind!

You can find me on Facebook or Instagram any time you want to chat about books, love interests, coffee, cake, kids, marriage, DIY projects—you get the idea.

About the Author

B ex Jalise is an author of contemporary stories about finding love, friendship, and yourself along the way. Her other interests include seeing how tall she can stack her pile of to-be-read books and finding new ways to trick her children into eating vegetables. Bex lives with her husband and three children in Chicago. Her work can be found on Amazon.

www.bexjalise.com

Other works:

Unlikely Events

The Practicality of Dreaming

Rerouting